THE CAVE OF DEATH

ABOUT THE AUTHOR

The Cave of Death is the fourth novel of Phil Hall, and the third in his Surrey Hills series featuring his daring duo of dysfunctional detectives. A further story is in development.

He has previously contributed film reviews to a University magazine and a chapter to an anthology. He attended K.E.G.S. in Chelmsford and studied Economics at UEA, Norwich before embarking on a career in marketing – the perfect grounding for writing. Phil lives in Surrey with his wife and daughter.

His first book was a stand-alone domestic thriller called Dream House.

The second was Game, Set and Death the first of the Inspector Scott Bee series. This was followed by Murder o'clock. You can find more details on the website www.philhallauthor.com or dive straight in and buy it from Amazon.

THE CAVE OF DEATH

Someone is digging for trouble in the Surrey Hills

by
Phil Hall

DISCLAIMER

All characters and events in this publication, other than those clearly in the public domain, are fictitious and any resemblance to real persons, living or dead is purely coincidental.

All rights reserved. No part of this publication may be reproduced, stored in a retrieval system, or transmitted in any form or by any means, without the prior written permission of the publisher.

Published details: Amazon.

Published June 2024.

Copyright © PE Hall 2024
Print Edition

For
All my English teachers
I'm as surprised as you!

THE CAVE OF DEATH

ONE

A GIANT EARTH-MOVING truck overloaded with brown clods of earth stopped with a sudden hiss of air brakes at the zebra crossing in the centre of Reigate town centre. It was early spring, but winter hadn't yet given up the fight and was looking to crash the party. The heavy traffic edged forward another yard and DS Fran Itzkowitz looked up at the huge truck and wondered if the load was secure. She turned to DS Ron McTierney who was walking alongside her about to mention her concern when out of the corner of her eye, she spotted a man grab a handbag from a middle-aged lady fifty yards further down the High Street, outside the M&S store.

A figure in a grey hoodie looked up as McTierney shouted "Stop!" He thought the figure smiled and then dashed down the alleyway that led from the High Street towards Priory Park.

"Shit!" McTierney turned to Itzkowitz. "Where's uniform when you need them? Call it in, get some help down here."

"Surely you can catch him on your own can't you?"

McTierney set off in pursuit, sprinting the first stretch. Ron McTierney was not as fit as perhaps he should have been, he visited the pub more often than he visited the gym, but he was only 39. He didn't consider himself old, a lunchtime chase shouldn't be a problem.

He reached the corner and began panting.

The lady who had been robbed, looked at him with disappointment in her eyes, "He went that way," she said pointing down the slope.

McTierney nodded, unable to speak. The bag snatcher had reached the bottom of the slope and was probably further ahead now. McTierney took a deep breath and began running again. *Why couldn't this be Bee?* he thought.

The wind buffeted his face as he reached the end of alleyway, on one side the air vents at the back of M&S thundered in his ears, on his left the brick buildings gave way and opened out to reveal concrete wasteland stretching two hundred yards across to the entrance of Morrisons' supermarket. He stood with his hands on his hips surveying the scene. No sign of the snatcher. *He couldn't have gone left. No one's that fast.*

He gulped down some air and looked across at the Methodist Church community centre. "Inspiration please," he mumbled as he trotted twenty yards across broken tarmac to the next corner and looked left. A few feet ahead of him a worker at the back of Morrisons was operating a waste compactor. McTierney jogged over to him, "Did you see anyone running through here in the last couple of minutes?"

The youth pulled a white air-pod from his left ear, "What?"

McTierney glared at him but didn't have time to pick a fight. "Police. I'm chasing a bag snatcher, did he come through here?"

"Oh yeah he went into the park," the youth pointed over his shoulder.

McTierney had gone before he finished his sentence. A narrow road led away from the back entrances to both Morrisons and M&S and quickly split into two; one leading back around the Morrisons' supermarket, the other skirted along the edge of Priory Park and provided a short cut through to the western side of the town. Beyond the road was the huge expanse of the park; 65 acres of open parkland with thousands of trees and probably thousands of hiding places too. It was picturesque, busy, and a lost cause.

McTierney scanned the park horizon, no sign of the snatcher. He turned 90 degrees back towards the car park of Morrisons. Nothing, and then suddenly a dark shape dashed across the road 150 yards ahead of him. McTierney began to run, *there better be something valuable in this bag* he thought. *Don't want to bust a gut for a bus pass and a hairbrush.* He reached the corner, stopped and his eyes swept across the horizon; he wasn't even sure what gender the snatcher was; black hair, shortish, probably male, probably a bloody middle-distance runner.

McTierney wiped the sweat from his eyes; he really must go to the gym more often. He arrived at the front of the supermarket, Itzkowitz had walked down the thirty brick steps from the High Street and met him.

"Where'd he go?" gasped McTierney.

"He headed across the car park," Itzkowitz pointed to her left. "He's fast."

"Tell me," panted McTierney.

Itzkowitz and McTierney had been colleagues for 18 months since he'd poached her from Guildford station. McTierney had been the acting DI at the time and was in a fix; Itzkowitz had been one of only two candidates and the only one with the initials FBI. McTierney never tired of saying, "Action FBI!" even though Itzkowitz had quickly tired of hearing it. As he stood outside the supermarket gulping down air, he had never wanted to use that phrase more than he did right now.

Itzkowitz looked at him disapprovingly. "He's getting away."

McTierney took a deep breath and set off again dodging between the rows of cars in the main town centre car park. The figure was heading south and was almost out of the car park. *Where's he going?* thought McTierney, *I'll never catch him, perhaps I can cut him off.* He sidestepped through two rows of cars, then caught his hip on the wing mirror of a Ford S-Max. "Ow!" he screamed. "Always a bloody Ford where you don't want one."

The snatcher had turned the corner and was heading south up Cockshot Hill. McTierney scampered across the car park entrance and swung across the traffic lights on the junction. "Where is he, where is he?" McTierney gasped, his pulse thundering around his body. He stopped and ran his hand through his short blonde hair. A sudden movement on the left suggested the snatcher had turned left just after Richer Sounds. *I'm closing*, thought McTierney. *He must be a fat bastard. And I'm going to nail him.*

With renewed belief McTierney ran diagonally across the main road; a white van blasted him with its horn, McTierney waved at him and mouthed 'Police', he didn't have the energy to speak. He charged past the music shop, pumping his fists, *I've got him* and stopped. The snatcher had vanished. McTierney's eyes zipped left and right. He tried to listen, but the noise of the traffic on the main road swamped his brain.

He spotted a narrow alleyway and ran towards it, turning left at the end. McTierney raced to the corner and burst out on to the other side. Then, whack! Something knocked him flying. The snatcher had been waiting at the other end. McTierney sprawled across the ground and looked up as the snatcher slammed a metal pipe into his ribs. "Aargh." McTierney rolled over holding his side.

The attacker dropped the pipe and jogged away.

It was a good ten minutes before Itzkowitz found him and another thirty before the ambulance arrived.

TWO

REIGATE NESTLES IN the heart of Surrey and is one of those attractive market towns which gets London estate agents excited. Steeped in rich history the town boasts elegant Georgian architecture with narrow cobbled streets winding past quaint cottages and centuries old buildings. But Tuesday April 18th was trying its hardest to change that image. Firstly, there had been a robbery in the town centre and now the police were about to be called to investigate the caves that run under much of the town.

In Norman Times, Reigate boasted a castle, but history and the weather had been unkind to the stronghold and now only a small arch remained. This stood in the park in the centre of the town around which traffic thundered by on the one-way system. But it was a different story below ground.

The entrance to the Barons' Cave sits on the western side of the castle grounds. It's the smaller of the two Reigate caves that are still open to the public, it gets less attention and is closed down for six months of the year when the caving tourist season ends in late August. But arguably it has the most interesting history, and another chapter of that history was about to be written as Phil Burgess and John Ball approached the entrance and readied themselves to make their first inspection of the year. The two men were part of the voluntary group who managed the caves for the local council. Together they ambled down a handful of steps and arrived at a steel gate which secured the entrance to the cave.

"These don't look like the padlocks we left on here when we closed this place up last September," said Burgess.

"It must be. Your memory's fading faster that you are."

Burgess shook his head, "I'm sure the three locks we left here were bronze; this one's silver." He stuffed his hand into his coat pocket and pulled out a bunch of keys, then reached for the silver padlock, but as he pulled the body of the lock towards him the shackle fell open. The two men exchanged anxious glances. Burgess took a sharp intake of breath, "This could be interesting."

The second lock swung open in the same way. There was no avoiding it, someone had been in the cave over the winter. The two men rocked the large metal gate back and stood for a moment in front of the old wooden door. The cave is believed to date back to the time of William the Conqueror when William de Warrenne had built the original castle in the town. The cave had been constructed as an escape route from the castle, should it come under threat from a siege.

In more recent times the Wealden Cave and Mine Society ran short tourist visits on selected Saturdays over the summer. Pulse rates were normally kept in check. But not on this Tuesday. Together they slowly pushed open the main door. A blast of cold air rushed by them.

"Hello?" called Ball, and Burgess dug him in the ribs.

The Barons' Cave is formed in an elongated Y-shape with the main pathway running straight from the entrance for 200 yards before it begins to climb to a small tunnel which emerges into the castle grounds garden, although that is no longer accessible to humans, only bats. The cave is 10 feet wide and roughly 8 feet high. The two men shuffled down half a dozen steps with their torch beams bouncing around the walls. On the left-hand side a control panel had been fitted and they turned the switch to engage the few lights fitted along the roof of the tunnels. As the lights whirred into action, both men felt a sense of relief. They stepped along the passageway to the end looking left and right as they went but saw nothing out of place. They began to retrace their steps and stopped at a small cavern on one side of the main tunnel – the sand mine gallery. The gallery is neither tall nor deep and they could immediately see that there was nothing untoward in it. That left the main gallery; a long curving tunnel where the end was out of sight from the junction with the main tunnel.

Burgess and Ball stood at the junction.

"We don't need to walk down here. We should get the police to investigate."

"How stupid are we going to look when they turn up and find nothing."

Ball didn't reply, he knew Burgess was right, but he still didn't want to be first to move.

"Come on. Together."

They took one bold stride and paused. Nothing happened. Another stride. The same result.

"This is ridiculous, let's get on with it."

The two men began walking across the damp sand floor. Both men knew the layout well; an initial thirty yard straight which then began to curve and culminated in a stone bench which was often the highlight of the many tours which took place in the cave.

As the curve straightened, Burgess saw it first and stopped. Ball looked at his partner and then peered to the end of the tunnel. He saw it too. On a regular Saturday afternoon, a tourist group would congregate at the end and hear fanciful stories about the barons who held King John to ransom in the Middle Ages. But today there was already somebody there waiting for the men. But this person wouldn't be participating in any discussion. This was a dead body. The two cave guides stopped a few yards short of the body.

"Now we need the police," said Burgess.

FIRST ON THE scene was Inspector Scott Bee, he was tall, pale with wiry, short black hair, and he sipped carbonated water from a small bottle. He was accompanied by DS Fran Itzkowitz. She didn't look like your typical southern-England police officer. She had black hair pulled into a ponytail on top of a short and sturdy body; even her doting father couldn't describe her as thin. As Bee shook hands with the pair of caving enthusiasts he could see that they were shaking. "How are you doing? Seeing your first dead body can be traumatic, especially if it's on your patch."

"We're a bit shaken, but I think we'll be okay."

"Good. My advice would be to get yourselves home and if you have wives or partners there, talk with them about this. You need to normalise what you've seen as soon as you can."

"Okay."

"But please don't say anything to the press. We'll take care of the site from here and we'll be back in touch with you shortly."

Bee left Itzkowitz to collect the details from the two guides and wandered into the tunnel, he wanted to get a sense of the place before too many trampled all over the scene. The area was still and silent with only sporadic spotlights in the roof to guide him, but Bee appreciated the chilled atmosphere at a murder scene, it helped him to think. The scene in the Barons' Cave offered an extra dimension of eerie underground twilight, it was as if the body was already in a tomb. Bee stooped over the body; he had seen dozens of dead bodies in his time but never one that had been left to deteriorate like this one. He knew it must be a head, but it didn't look like any head he'd ever seen before; even a head that had been smashed in with a hammer or had suffered a bullet wound still looked like a head, but this one had shrivelled away. There was barely any skin and virtually no hair. If someone had told him it was the head of an alien, he would have believed them. He peered at the ear, it looked like something had bitten a lump out of it, probably a rat. He felt a rush of nausea and stepped back from the body grateful that he was still alone. This case was going to be unpleasant. Bee believed that there was always something of the killer at the crime scene, sometimes something big, sometimes something small, but always something, nonetheless. But standing there quietly in the semi-darkness he was struggling to get a sense of what it could be.

A few minutes later Itzkowitz joined him kneeling in front of the body.

"All okay outside?"

"Yes, one of our officers has just arrived and I've left him securing the site."

Bee nodded his approval and thought that McTierney had made a good choice recruiting this one. "Excellent, we need to keep everyone out of here until SOCO have had a chance to examine this area. I get the impression that the body has been here a while, so apart from the four of us, I suspect the last person in here was the murderer himself. Make sure you walk close to the wall on your exit, if there's any trace of the murderer here, it'll be in the centre of the walkway."

"Sure. I'll stay here until the forensics team arrives."

Bee kept his eyes on the corpse as he spoke. "It's likely that no one else has been in here since the murder and therefore the scene is fresh, so let's not contaminate it. Nor allow anyone else to contaminate it. Get the area cordoned off and set up a crime scene log, station an officer up there to keep these society people out and the scene clean. This is ours now."

"Yep, I'm on it. I've already left a message with Dr Kelly the pathologist."

"Excellent. Keep on top of him, he has been known to plod along at his own pace. Tell him he'll need all the fancy lights in the caves. The initial focus will be here, but there's not much blood, so I think the victim was killed elsewhere, which means someone carried a dead body down into the cave. There could be scraps of skin or clothing on any of the walls. Kelly's halogen lights should help to find traces of blood and he can help us search for fingerprints or even footprints in the damp sand."

Bee stepped away from the body and took a sip from his water bottle.

"You know modern forensics talk about the golden hour

for gathering evidence immediately after the death."

Itzkowitz nodded towards the inspector.

"I think this case will test Dr Kelly. It looks like this crime occurred weeks ago, maybe months even, but I'm sure he'll argue that the same rules apply."

Bee clapped his hands and began to fidget.

"What are you going to do?"

"I'm off to check on McTierney at the hospital. I hate to say it, but we might actually need him on this case."

THREE

BEE STEPPED NERVOUSLY towards the sliding entrance doors of the East Surrey hospital; it was not one of his favourite buildings, but he appreciated the work that was done inside the 1980's building. He crossed the threshold, and his senses were assailed by a cacophony of noise, bright lights, and nauseous smells. The coffee area, the shop and the main medical corridor collided in the space of twenty feet bringing all sorts of people together with different agendas. Bee dodged between out-patients, visitors and medical staff all moving like ants with their own specific instructions. A mother bent down to whisper something to the child in her pushchair, Bee stepped around her and brushed against an extravagant floral display catching a nose full of fruit scents in the process. He smiled at the thought of arriving at McTierney's bedside with a handful of peonies and mused that McTierney would probably expect a four-pack.

He checked the note that Beck's secretary, Maria had given him with the ward name, found it on the ward directory and started off along the corridor. Within a matter of yards, a junior doctor with a crash cart came running along behind him. Bee pulled himself into the wall to allow the medic to pass. The sooner he could deliver his message and escape this place, the better. He rounded the corner and entered Capel ward, three beds along on the left-hand side he found his quarry, asleep.

Bee wasn't sure whether he should wake McTierney and while he pondered the question another doctor approached him.

"Are you with Mr McTierney?"

"Yes, he lives with me."

The doctor raised his eyebrows but carried on, "Good, there's something you ought to know."

Bee wet his lips as the medic reached for a chart from the bottom of McTierney's bed and ran his finger down to the data he wanted.

"Your friend has an unusual metabolism; even though he hasn't had a drink in the last 24 hours, maybe more, his alcohol content is almost off the scale."

A quizzical expression played across Bee's face although it wasn't a huge surprise to him.

"We always say that no matter what colour your skin, all of us are the same on the inside, but it turns out we're not, he's like a walking brewery. All his organs function normally but slowly they are fermenting. One day he'll explode but no need to worry it won't happen for years. I did tell McTierney, but he just brushed the idea aside. Just thought you should know."

"Thanks doctor, I'll talk it through with him when we get home."

On a frame held above the bed a TV screen played quietly, Bee glanced up to see Rachel Riley giggle at some joke made by her co-host. On the bed lay a half-finished sudoku puzzle, Bee glimpsed at it, immediately spotted a number he could add, but fought the desire to pick up the paper. At the next bed an elderly lady who was visiting her husband began to cough. Bee shuddered and decided to keep this visit as short as he could. But the coughing caused McTierney to stir and on seeing Bee in front of him, he raised himself up on his elbows grimacing as he did.

"Here I picked this up for you on my way in." Bee passed a cup of tea across to McTierney.

"No beer, oh well. Cheers." McTierney took a slurp and then scowled at Bee. "This tastes foul. Are you trying to finish me off?"

"Thought you liked tea."

"I do, but not this muck and how many sugars?"

"Sugar's good for you when you're recovering."

"Hmm."

"How are the ribs?"

"Sore, but somehow they're still all in one piece."

"Good, then perhaps you can stop skiving and get back to the station. We've just picked up a complex case, which will need all of us to crack it."

"Not before Nurse Yeoh returns to change my bandages. She has the touch of an angel."

"You're clearly feeling better. Come on I'll give you a lift back to the station and I'll brief you on the case as we go."

McTierney pressed the button to call for the nurse.

"By the way, did you get a good look at the bag snatcher you were chasing?"

"Not really, a bit oriental in the face."

"Didn't get close enough to see him I guess."

"Only when he ambushed me. I think I'd recognise him if I saw him close up. I'll have a trawl through the station photos when I get back, but I'm not optimistic."

Their conversation was broken by raucous laughter from a bed further down the ward. Bee looked disapprovingly across the ward. "They don't seem ill, people larking around and wasting resources."

"What's got into you? You're never a bundle of laughs, but today you're acting like someone's stolen your favourite Sherlock Holmes book."

Bee frowned at his partner. "It's this place. It brings back plenty of memories of Jess's passing."

McTierney looked away and the conversation between the two men dried up. His eyes flicked around the ward but the pull from Bee was magnetic and McTierney returned to meet his gaze once again.

"The grief never leaves you. The best you can hope for is to bury it. But it always returns. There are just too many triggers." Bee turned and glanced around the ward and thought about the families that had lost a child; he didn't know how they could they ever forgive the killers. He knew he would never forgive himself for what had happened to his only daughter Jess. Ten seconds passed, then another ten. He pulled himself out of his reverie. "Another family has lost a son, or possibly a daughter, we're not entirely sure yet, and we must do our duty to find the killer and give this family some form of closure."

McTierney screwed up his face, "Son or daughter? Don't you know?"

"Not yet. The body was discovered in one of the caves under the town. It's been there a while, so the body's starting to decompose. I'd guess it's a young male, but we're waiting for Kelly to confirm. Looks like being a challenging case, so get your bits together and let's get cracking."

FOUR

IT WAS WEDNESDAY before Bee had his team together for a full briefing. McTierney's release from hospital had been delayed by the need for him to be assessed as fit for work. Bee found it hard to disguise his contempt for the delay believing there to be nothing materially wrong with the patient, despite McTierney showing him and anyone else who expressed even the slightest interest, his war-wound, a large purple bruise across the ribcage on his left side.

"Any higher and it could have damaged my heart," he told Itzkowitz.

"An assassin couldn't find your heart," she replied and Carol Bishop who had taken the seat next to her smirked.

"Kick a man when he's down," said McTierney feigning greater injury.

"Can we start?" said Bee flexing his fingers as he spoke.

The four detectives were sitting in the ops room in Reigate station. Although it was the room where major cases were discussed it was also a room that nobody owned and hence it felt unloved. It exuded a monotonous atmosphere with dull cream walls which absorbed any hint of vibrancy. The fluorescent lighting cast a pallid glow over the worn chairs. The lingering scent of stale coffee mingled with the hum of an outdated air conditioner. The centrepiece of the room was the main whiteboard which carried the mainstream cases. Ordinarily it would be decorated with images of the latest murder case to hit the town. But apart from two photos of the body, there was little else to define the case. Normally the victim's details would be written next to the photo; name, address, age, ethnicity, time, and location of death but on this occasion the photo was its own little island surrounded by a sea of white space. Nobody knew anything about the victim, they couldn't even get the year right for the time of death. McTierney summed up the situation, "What do we know? Anything?"

Bee sent a withering look in the direction of his DS. "Granted the board looks a bit sparse, but this is how all cases start. It's our job to fill in the details. Here's what we know. Two members of the Wealden Cave and Mine Society, who look after the tunnels that run under the town discovered a dead body on Monday afternoon. It seems it's been there for some time, perhaps four months, but possibly up to eight months. The tunnel is locked and sealed at the end of August, when the tourist season finishes and so the body could have been there since that date."

"Or even killed before that date and then hidden in the tunnel?" offered McTierney.

"Yes possibly but storing a dead body would be an unnecessary complication."

Bee paused and looked around the room as if expecting other questions, nothing was forthcoming, so he continued.

"McTierney's point goes to show how little we know about this case, and how much more there is to do. Dr Kelly, our pathologist is examining the body as we speak, and we should have his thoughts by this afternoon. In the meantime, here are a few items I want us to investigate."

The three detectives around the table instinctively pulled themselves towards the table and reached for their pens; this is where the day would start to get interesting.

"Let's start with the cave itself. What's the ground surface made of? Has a lot of blood soaked away, or perhaps the victim was already dead when brought to the cave? What are the access routes, how many ways are there into the cave? Who has keys and how many keys exist? Perhaps you can take those McTierney?" McTierney nodded.

Bee turned to Itzkowitz, "Find out what the cave temperature is like in the winter. Is it likely that the body would decompose quickly? There's no obvious sign that the body was dragged into the cave, so perhaps it was carried, suggesting a strong murderer and probably a man."

Bishop, can you do some general research on the caves, both the Barons' Cave and the Tunnel Cave. Let's see if anything interesting pops up."

The team picked up their notebooks, Bee closed the meeting and sent his troops out to attack the case, he closed the ops room door and made his way downstairs to the canteen. On his way he passed a couple of officers who immediately clammed up when they saw him approach. Bee had never been one to socialise heavily and he hated small talk. But since the death of his DC, twenty-one months ago a new poison had come into his life. Whenever anyone passed him on the stairs they would avert their eyes and truncate any conversations, it was as if he had become the fun police and he hated it with a passion. But what his colleagues didn't know was that the fallen DC had been Bee's own daughter, a terrible secret which only McTierney shared.

Shortly after lunch the team re-assembled to hear the thoughts of the pathologist, Dr Kelly, an overweight West Indian, who had lived all his life in the UK except for a year touring the southern states of the US in his pursuit of the perfect burger. Throughout his long training period and his near twenty years in the service he had never encountered such a case and his discomfort showed as he stood at the front of the room and began to address the team.

"This is a strange case and I fear one where our understanding will take time to evolve. I know you like to deal with precise facts, but I'm afraid we may not have many of those, at least not yet. It's fair to say I'd be much happier donning my cricket whites than my forensic whites at this point in time."

Kelly glanced around the room and looked back down at his notes, grimaced and returned to his audience.

"It's not going to be easy to determine either the age of the body, or the time of death. I'm hopeful of getting you the right month." Kelly laughed nervously, but no one joined in. "It's rigor mortis you see, it clouds the issue. Essentially there are four stages."

Kelly surveyed the blank faces and determined to push on.

"Stage one is putrefaction. This happens between day 4 and day 10 after death; you get autolysis, where the body cells start to break down, plus some skin discolouration, we're way past that. Second stage is black putrefaction, the skin turns black hence the name and bodily fluids are released. This takes two to three weeks, makes a horrible mess as you can imagine. After this we progress to stage three, known as butyric fermentation, this can occur anything up to fifty days after death. The remaining flesh is removed, butyric acid is formed and the body ferments and can develop mould. The final stage is known as dry decay and sees the hair and fingernails start to fall out and can take many months to complete. This is the situation we find ourselves in. I'd estimate that the deceased left us between five and eight months ago. As you will have gathered this is not an exact science."

"You can say that again." said McTierney.

Kelly bowed his head and glared at McTierney, who shrugged his shoulders and then mumbled, "Sorry Doc, still on medication from my trip to the hospital." McTierney rubbed his side to emphasise the point and extract whatever sympathy was available in the ops room.

"What a burdensome child you must have been," said Kelly, who had lost his place. He paused, looked down at his notes and continued. "If the body is in a low temperature area the process I've described will slow down, and that's what we have here. The temperature in the cave is a few degrees above zero, it varied between seven or eight when I was down there, and I understand it doesn't change much throughout the year. So, if you work on death occurring six months ago, you won't be far wrong."

"Okay, thanks Doc, I understand the challenges you're facing," said Bee.

Kelly looked across the table at McTierney but didn't say anything.

"Perhaps we can turn our attention to identification of the victim," said Bee.

"I can give you a start," said Kelly recapturing his enthusiasm. "The deceased is a male. I can be sure about that.

Unfortunately, there was no wallet left on the body, so I can't say much more at this stage. Although I'd venture to suggest that our victim might be Chinese, or at least Asian. The build would have been slight, and the eyes suggest he might be from that part of the world. We'll know more in the next few days. We haven't yet completed the postmortem so I can't give you a cause of death, but there's what appears to be a bullet wound to the back of the head, so I'll leave you to draw your own conclusions for now."

A couple of mouths fell open around the team as Kelly moved to sit down, then remembered something else.

"One other thing, he had one of those fitness watches on his wrist, so perhaps that suggests someone younger, we'll work through his clothing in the next few days."

"Thanks Dr Kelly. We're going to review our preliminary findings now and agree next steps, so you're welcome to stay if you wish. I think your input here could be invaluable, as we try to establish a few priorities."

Kelly nodded his acceptance and Bee continued. "We need to talk to anyone who might have seen anything suspicious around the entrance to the cave. If the killer carried the body to the entrance there's a chance someone witnessed it."

"How are we going to do house to house enquiries in a cave?" asked McTierney. Bee sighed inwardly and ignored the comment and turned to Carol Bishop.

"Bishop, help me bring some sense to the discussion, what have you found out about the cave?"

Carol Bishop was the fourth member of Bee's team having moved across from the drugs team. She wore her bottle-blonde hair scraped back into a tight bun, her clothes and

THE CAVE OF DEATH

shoes were taken from the comfortable rack in M&S. She was everything you'd want in a detective, smart, curious, and was able to think outside the box, but harboured little ambition. She worked hard and followed orders but rarely put her head above the parapet.

She smiled benignly at Bee and unfurled her notebook. "Sure. Reigate has two sets of caves, the Barons' Cave which we are talking about and the Tunnel Cave which is the larger of the pair and accessed via the tunnel in Tunnel Road which runs from the Market Stores pub up to the roundabout by Towers Watson." She looked around the room for some understanding and the team duly nodded.

"The caves are technically mines because for many years sand was excavated from them and used in the manufacture of glass bottles. When you get inside you'll see that the sand is very soft. Both are owned by Reigate and Banstead Council and the Tunnel Cave is rented out to a rifle club."

Bee perked up at the mention of the rifle club, "That might be an interesting lead, if nothing else, it gives us a bunch of people who know their way around the caves."

Itzkowitz scribbled herself a note and Bishop continued. "Visitors are welcome to both caves across the summer months, so it would have been easy for our killer to have researched the location without attracting suspicion. Also, occasionally they will entertain occasional out of season visitors to the Tunnel Cave, school trips, that sort of thing. But not to the Barons' Cave, where the body was found."

Bee lifted a finger, but Itzkowitz intercepted him, "I'll get a list of all the visitors for last summer." Bee nodded his approval.

Bishop smiled and ran her finger down the page of her

notebook, "I think that's most of the interesting stuff. Other bits are that the temperature in the caves is more or less ten degrees all year round. It rarely freezes, but I think Dr Kelly covered that. There's no connecting passageway between the tunnels, so our victim must have entered in the same way we all did." She flipped over her page. "They get bats in the winter in the Barons' Cave, they get in from the pyramid at the top, and that's the reason why the cave is left undisturbed throughout the winter. The Tunnel Cave is the larger of the two and was used in the Second World War to house people displaced by bombs."

Bishop began to flick across pages and sensed that she was losing her audience, "One more. The Tunnel Cave has an interesting claim to fame; it's the newest completed tunnel in the UK." She looked up and beaned at her audience, who looked slightly surprised. "Because there's been some new health and safety regulation which required an escape route to be built. But when the HS2 train route is finished, that will inherit the record."

"If it gets finished," said McTierney.

Bee nodded his approval, "Great summary. Thanks. How about you Itzkowitz, did you get far with the locks?"

He winced as he spoke and jabbed his finger into his mouth.

"What's up boss?"

"A touch of toothache, hopefully it'll pass."

"You should get yourself an appointment with a dentist pronto. Toothache is never good."

Bee smiled back at McTierney, then turned his gaze back to Itzkowitz.

"Yes, I've made a start. There's only one entrance for the

Barons' Cave, the route the bats use isn't feasible for a human. Ordinarily there are three padlocks on the door. Each of the keys held by different people. This is done to ensure that there's never just one person in the cave due to health and safety rules. But in this instance the locks had been broken and replaced. Unfortunately, there's no CCTV set up in the park, although there is some close to the Tunnel Cave."

McTierney appeared to be humbled by the responses of his colleagues, like a schoolboy who finds everyone else in the class has done the homework. He raised his pen and Bee prompted him to speak. "I think it's interesting that whoever dumped the body there, would have expected it to be discovered. These caves are open to the public every year so it's not the best hiding place, it's not like dumping the body out at sea."

"No, you're right, but maybe having a six-month lead time was enough for the killer to get away and hope that the trail had gone cold."

It was a point that brought a sudden silence to what had been a lively meeting. Bee allowed his team to mull over the challenge for a couple of minutes. Then he clapped his hands together.

"First priority; we need a face and a name. Once we have these, we can trace where they lived and where they worked, who they knew, where they went, what they believed and what they feared and that will start to give us a good sense of who may have killed them."

There was a murmur of consensus around the table. McTierney looked across at Kelly and said, "It's not going to be easy to do much before we get a name for the deceased."

"Clearly that will help," said Bee. "But don't dismiss this because we don't have much information at this time. If we apply good standards and we're structured and diligent, we will find something. We're all capable of that." His eye strayed to McTierney and he fought against saying anything direct, "Let's stick to our trusted process; focus on means, motive and opportunity and we can identify the victim and find their killer. We'll review each morning starting from Friday, but sooner if there's progress."

McTierney wasn't finished, "Do you think the Barons' Cave is significant?"

"Instinctively I'd say no. Maybe it was just a good place to hide a body, but for now I think we have to keep an open mind about everything."

With the meeting about to conclude, Dr Kelly began to pack his papers into his slim brown briefcase but paused, pointed at McTierney, and asked, "We've not had an outlandish theory from you yet that's not like you at all."

"I know, I don't think there are enough pieces of the puzzle available to conjure up anything remotely feasible. I presume our esteemed inspector would agree?"

But Bee wasn't listening, his thoughts were elsewhere, until he realised the room was waiting for him to speak. "Oh, sorry, what were you saying?"

"I had remarked on how strange it was not to be faced with an outlandish theory from McTierney yet, and he ducked the issue and passed the question to you."

"I see. I have a thought, but one that troubles me, and I wouldn't call it a theory."

Kelly and McTierney exchanged hurried glances.

"Come on spill the beans."

"No, I don't have any evidence to support it."

"That's rather the point of theories, I believe. My detective friend here, never has any evidence for his theories. That's the best part of them."

McTierney looked hurt.

"Maybe we need to be kind towards him, perhaps he's still suffering from concussion."

FIVE

Ron wandered into the kitchen, flicked on the kettle, and pulled open the fridge door, he paused, checked the date on the bottle of milk and tipped a generous splash into the nearest mug and then turned on the radio while waiting for kettle to boil. He was just in time to catch the eight o'clock news bulletin; a brooding serious voice announced.

'A major police operation is underway in Reigate to identify a body found in one of the many tunnels that run under the centre of the town. The tunnels are famous for their part in the signing of the Magna Carta'.

Scott arrived from upstairs and screwed up his face "That's not true. Some journalist has been overselling his story to get it up the list and be top dog for the day."

The announcement continued. "Police have asked members of the public to report any suspicious behaviour seen around the entrance to the tunnels over the last six months. Ron's face dropped, "Oh Christ! We'll have every Tom, Dick, and Harry coming in to the station with every bit of nonsense."

Scott wasn't impressed either, "I can't believe Beck would have asked for that, he knows the chaos that would cause."

"Not his problem though is it."

Scott shook his head, took some of the hot water for his

coffee and moved into the lounge to check the TV news.

It was almost two years since Ron had moved into the house of Scott Bee, initially on a temporary basis at the behest of Chief Superintendent Beck when the covid crisis had made it difficult for people to find accommodation and McTierney had come down on loan from the Norfolk constabulary. Although he had argued against the idea in the beginning, Scott had come to enjoy the company that Ron offered. However, their different lifestyles meant that on more than one occasion he would question his own judgement but on balance he felt his life was richer with his colleague as a tenant.

For his part Ron knew which side his bread was buttered; yes there were times when Scott could be a bit old-school but on the whole his life was as easy now as it had ever been, and he liked it that way. Together they lived in Scott's remote three bed house on the edge of Outwood a few miles outside of Reigate; it was far enough away from society to allow Scott some peace and quiet and it was close enough to the Bell public house to allow Ron to indulge in his favourite pastime.

Bee and McTierney drove into the station together, met Itzkowitz in the queue for coffee in the police canteen but then went their separate ways; Bee to check on the thinking of Superintendent Beck, McTierney to interview the secretary of the Reigate Rifle and Pistol club, while Itzkowitz took the short straw and contacted the Wealden Cave Society for a list of all their visitors over the last two seasons. Bishop, who was one of those people who liked to start early and finish early, was already at her desk continuing her research into the history of the Reigate caves.

★ ★ ★

BEE FOUND BECK in pensive mood staring out of the window of his third-floor office. It transpired that Beck had more on his mind than the simple discovery of a dead body.

"Headquarters are looking to shut us down, save money, squeeze us together with Leatherhead, create one superstation for the area. It's intolerable."

"In the name of progress?"

"Progress? No, I don't think so. It won't feel like progress when the public we serve, see their station closed down and the land sold for fifteen fancy new maisonettes each selling for a million."

"Maybe not sir, but can I bring you back to the case in hand and your announcement to the public asking for information."

Beck raised his hand. "Stop I know what you're going to say. What was I thinking? I know, but orders from above."

Bee raised an eyebrow.

"There's a feeling that the police force is too detached from the community and that we should be taking every opportunity to redress the balance. Speak to our community, get them involved. Evidently public trust is at an all-time low."

"But no one will remember anything of any consequence from six months ago."

"You don't know that."

Bee dropped his eyes to the floor.

"And besides the chief constable wants us to hold a press conference on Friday if the case is still open."

"Since when did a murder enquiry become a PR opportunity?"

★ ★ ★

McTierney had agreed to meet the rifle society secretary at the Tunnel Cave at 9am. He was surprised when a middle-aged woman with long black hair approached him and asked if he was a detective. He stumbled through his reply but recovered the situation.

"Let's slip into Gail's bakery for a quick cup of tea," he offered.

"Don't you want to see where we shoot?"

"Yes, but preferably with a cup of tea in my hand, by the way call me Ron."

It was fifteen minutes before the pair returned to the wooden door which opened into the Tunnel Cave and a further fifteen minutes before McTierney asked anything remotely connected to the case. He did ask plenty of questions about the rifle club but held back from testing his skills on the range on account of his ribs still being painful. But when the conversation did turn to the murder in hand it was evident that the rifle club lead was a cul-de-sac. There was no connecting tunnel between the two caves and nothing to connect the gun club with the Barons' Cave.

As McTierney walked away from the tunnel towards the town centre he noticed a CCTV camera outside the Market Stores pub. Believing this to be a sign from a higher authority that he should drop into the pub for a pint and a chat, he pushed open the door and made his way to the bar.

★ ★ ★

MEANWHILE ITZKOWITZ HAD contacted the Wealden Cave and Mining Society and was getting to know Julia Crampton who did most of the admin for the group. They had met outside the Barons' Cave, but Julia had forgotten to invite a second person with the required additional key to give them access to the cave. Itzkowitz wondered if this had been staged to demonstrate their commitment to security but let the point drift as Julia explained how the small band of volunteers spent their weekends scrabbling around underground. They started to walk around the park and up to the higher level where the pyramid entrance stood.

"We keep everything locked as best we can, primarily to protect the landowner from any liability should a member of the public break into a cave and injure themselves."

"Or get shot?" added Itzkowitz.

Crampton blushed, "Yes, my point exactly. Do you think there could be any comeback against the society?"

"We'll need to discover who the victim is first."

Crampton stopped in her tracks and the colour drained from her face. Itzkowitz touched her arm, "Don't worry, there's a long way to go yet and I doubt anything bad will happen to your club. Besides, they say all publicity is good publicity."

Crampton gave a half smile but didn't look convinced and their conversation dried up. They arrived at the site of the pyramid-shaped top entrance to the cave and this gave new impetus to their conversation.

"Here's where the bats enter the cave," said Crampton

pointing at the metal bars that blocked a small brick-built entrance. Itzkowitz nodded and pulled against one of the bars to convince herself that it would have been impossible for a human to enter the cave from here.

"I printed off a list of all the visitors from the last two years for you," said Crampton as she searched through her coat pocket and pulled out a sheaf of papers. Itzkowitz motioned for her to take a seat on a nearby bench, stretched out her hand and took the printout from Crampton.

She turned the pages over in her hands looking for a sign to jump out of the page, but nothing did.

"Sorry it's a bit slapdash but we're just a group of volunteers. I had to look them up last night and copied them over into a Word document."

"No problem, that's great," said Itzkowitz as she started to scan the list. "I'll take them back to the office and we'll make contact with each of them and see what turns up."

BISHOP PLOUGHED ON with her research and by lunchtime had compiled a dossier on the history of Reigate, or Ryegate as it had once been called, and the caves under the town, indeed such was the extent of her knowledge that she could have appeared on 'Mastermind' with this as her specialist subject.

Consequently, all of Bee's team brought interesting news to the progress meeting he had scheduled for that afternoon, but none could compete with the information that Kelly would deliver. Kelly had completed the postmortem and had two key facts to present to the team. The first of these was that the victim had died from a gunshot wound to the head, and Kelly had retrieved the bullet and announced that it had been fired by a Glock 17 pistol, standard issue for most police forces across the country.

"Are you sure?" asked Bee, looking concerned.

"Yes." Nodded Kelly. "I've checked it twice and I can also tell you that the gun is a fourth-generation model issued to the force sometime between its introduction in 2010 and the release of the fifth generation in 2017.

"But of course, it doesn't necessarily mean it was fired by a police officer," said Bee.

"Not at all," added McTierney. But a cold chill rippled around the ops room on the first floor where the group had gathered to hear Kelly's news.

"But it does gives us somewhere to start," said Itzkowitz.

Her colleagues all turned to look at her. "I'm not saying we investigate a police officer, but we can check previous murders and see if a Glock was used."

Bee nodded his agreement but shifted uncomfortably in his chair and looked down at his notes before Kelly came to his rescue.

"Shall I give you my second piece of news?"

"Please do."

"The postmortem shows that the deceased has had a kidney removed."

There was a murmur around the table, which Kelly ignored. "It's hard to tell with the skin deterioration but there could be incision marks on his lower back that would be reasonably fresh, all things considered. I'd estimate that the extraction occurred within the last two years, three at the most."

"Now we're getting somewhere," said McTierney rubbing his hands together.

"If I have your approval I'll bring in a specialist next week, someone who can rehydrate the skin. It will help us be more definitive about these incisions and may uncover a few other secrets."

"Until we have a name for the victim, I think we have to take some extraordinary steps, so yes go ahead. I'll inform Beck."

"Great. If I may, I'll just step out and call Professor Tidworth, I know he has a busy diary."

Bee acknowledged the pathologist's request with a nod and to fill the gap he invited his colleagues to update the group with any interesting developments from their mornings' work. McTierney offered an impromptu update on his time. He concluded by telling everyone that the Tunnel Cave was unlikely to offer much assistance in the case, which was underlined by the fact that the CCTV outside the Market Stores was routinely recorded over after seven days, and accordingly there was no video footage of anyone doing anything suspicious around the tunnel. He concluded, "Evidently it's too easy to dump footage onto a hard-disk and then record over it the following week. Apparently everyone's doing it."

Itzkowitz took up the baton and laid out the sheets of paper that she'd collected listing the visitors to the Barons' Cave. McTierney lent across the table and cast a casual eye over the list. "There's a Mr H. Kane from Nutfield, and a Miss L James from London, – I'll pay her a visit."

"I'll file that under predictable," said Bee.

Itzkowitz scowled at McTierney, but undeterred he carried on and ran his finger down the second page, "oh and on Saturday August 20th last year, a certain Phil Church visited the caves. I wonder if that was our own esteemed colleague taking a day off from the drugs team. I'll have to ask him."

Itzkowitz snatched the paper back and told them that she would work through the list of 375 names over the next couple of days. Bee's eyes turned to Carol Bishop, who smiled and assumed the mantle.

"Would you like to know something about the history of Reigate and the caves?"

Bee nodded, and she continued. "The Castle was built in 1088 as a consequence of the Norman conquest. William the Conqueror rewarded William de Warenne for his support with the land and in return Warenne built a castle and with it a cave. The cave was essentially an escape route from the castle if it was ever attacked."

"Traitor." Muttered McTierney.

"I didn't realise there was a castle here. I guess that's all gone now," said Itzkowitz.

"There's a few remnants, but 90% of it has gone."

"Anything on the cave?" Asked Bee.

Bishop flicked over a couple of pages in her notebook.

"It's basically a sandstone mine, a particular high quality soft sand, so we might get some footprints. It's damp in the cave so they might still show, we ought to take a look."

Bee nodded his acceptance.

"Finally, here's something for McTierney. This is where we get the phrase, *happy as a sandboy.*"

McTierney looked surprised as Bishop explained.

"Taverns in the Middle Ages were filthy places and young boys were paid, often in beer, to clear up the mess on the floor by spreading some of the fine Reigate sand over the mess and then shovelling it up. They earned the name 'sand-boys,' and because they were often inebriated they appeared to be happy."

"Really?"

Bishop nodded at him. McTierney was about to take the conversation into a new tangent when Dr Kelly returned to the room and his smile told them he had more good news.

"Tidworth will be here Monday morning."

"Excellent." Bee clapped his hands. "Now, priorities for tomorrow; let's start working through the list of cave visitors." He looked across at Bishop and then turned to Itzkowitz, "Follow up on that idea about footprints, while McTierney and I put our heads together on the implication of a kidney donor."

"And you get yourself to a dentist," said McTierney.

SIX

ON FRIDAY MORNING the ops room was abuzz with the revelations from Dr Kelly the previous afternoon. The possibility that a police weapon may have been involved was enough to stimulate a dozen wild theories and when that chatter died down on that subject, the noise soon continued with the idea that the victim had lost a kidney. It was only when Inspector Bee arrived at the door that the gossip stopped.

He signalled to McTierney and took him down to the canteen for a change of scene. Bee had been running that morning and wanted to share his jumbled thoughts with his number two. The two men grabbed cups of coffee and took them over to a quiet table in the corner of the restaurant.

"I want to run a couple of thoughts I've been having by you and see what you think."

McTierney sipped his coffee and nodded across the table.

"The first one concerns the crime scene; it's a strange one. It must be a planned action but why use a cave? I don't think a killer goes to the trouble of breaking into these caves and concealing the body there unless he, or she, is familiar with them. Even at night it's quite risky to take the body to the cave and dump it. There's a public footpath within two yards of the entrance and it's nothing like a five-minute job."

"No, not at all," agreed McTierney. "Which means their name may show up on the list that Itzkowitz is working through."

"Or they have some other connection to the caves, perhaps through the society that runs the visits on Saturdays. I'm convinced that it wouldn't have been the first time that our murderer had been down in that cave."

"Agreed. We're going to have to interview everyone who has a connection."

"Yes. Although these caves are in the centre of the town, I think they're a well-kept secret. I don't know anyone who has ever visited them, and that list only ran to 400 or so people over the space of two years."

"It was a new one on me."

Bee paused and pinched his lip as he absorbed the point, then changed tack. "Then why does a killer hide a dead body somewhere he knows it will be discovered." He let the question hang and then offered his own answer. "Here's a few thoughts; the killer knew he would be leaving the area, or even the country before the body would be found, so it didn't matter if the body was found."

"If you're right about the inside information that the killer had about the cave, then he could be fairly sure that the body wouldn't be discovered until now," said McTierney.

"Yes, fair point. Potentially that has allowed him three, four, maybe six months to clear the scene. Ample time to be long gone."

"Maybe this is a contract killer, who disposes of his bodies in a regular place, but for some reason that wasn't available six months ago and he had to improvise."

"That would work too, although I don't want to contemplate the prospect of another serial killer in the county." Bee raised his finger to make his point. "Here's another crazy idea that came to me as I was running this morning. Our killer is a member of a criminal gang but is uncomfortable within that gang and wants to expose his bosses or leaders, or the scam that they are running so he does something to attract our attention."

"Where did you get that idea?"

"I had Springsteen on random play in my ears as I was running and it threw up 'Jungleland', – worth it for the sax solo alone, but the song is about a girl killing her lover, but nobody notices, and that got me thinking."

McTierney shook his head. "You and Springsteen. He's your Doctor Watson."

Bee laughed, "Maybe. I'm convinced the answer to this question will lead us to the perpetrator. We have to get inside the mind of the killer. By the way did I tell you that Beck wants me to lead the press conference."

"No. Really? Has he changed his mind about it?"

"Don't think he was ever that committed. He told me the idea came from above."

"That's not good."

"Quite. Let's get back upstairs and add a few things to the white board. We need to get some momentum on this case. Something else we should do, is review the list of missing people. Logically our victim's name should appear somewhere on it."

"I'll get on it when we get upstairs."

Back in the ops room Bee picked up the black marker pen and stood in front of the white board. Five days into a normal murder enquiry he would have expected the board to be half covered with details of the victim, crime scene facts and ideally a suspect or two. But today, the only item on the board was a miserable photo of the deceased which didn't even look like a human. He didn't have a name, a time of death, or even a nationality. Bee pursed his lips, "I'm going to add something." He scribbled the words 'Barons' Cave' and added 'killer has a connection.' It wasn't enough. He scratched his head and added 'no kidneys' and finally 'Asian.' But then added a '?' and then put the pen down.

McTierney sensed Bee's disappointment and left him to doodle and popped his head around the cubicle of Itzkowitz to see how she was getting on. "Any joy?"

The tower of empty coffee cups told its own story and Itzkowitz rolled her eyes at him. Thus far she had sorted the list into alphabetical order, then constructed a generic email and begun writing to all the names asking the recipients to contact her at Reigate station so they could be ruled out of the investigation.

"The boss wants them all to come into the station so we can interview each one in person, he's convinced that the killer has an intimate knowledge of the caves and that our man is on that list."

"That's four hundred interviews, I'll have a home run by the time they're done."

"Better get started then," smirked McTierney as Itzkowitz reached for another strip of chewing gum.

McTierney pulled his head back from Itkowitz's desk and spotted Dr Kelly walking up the stairs. Something in the swift gait of the pathologist told McTierney that Kelly had good news to deliver. He leaned back, tapped Itzkowitz on the shoulder and the pair set off after Kelly.

They caught up with him in the ops room as he placed a dilapidated sports shoe on the desk in front of Bee.

"Good timing gang, you'll want to hear this."

Kelly turned around and smiled at the new arrivals. "I think we are getting somewhere with our deceased friend. I was examining his clothing and footwear hoping to build up an image of our victim and I discovered a lottery ticket carefully folded up and hidden in his shoe."

All the detectives leaned forward as Kelly revealed the ticket. "I took the liberty of checking the numbers and guess what? It's a winning ticket."

"Can we still claim the prize?" Asked McTierney.

"Sadly not. Any lottery ticket is only valid for 180 days after the numbers have been called and this one was bought for the week of October 8th, 2022. So that makes it 196 days today, you're a couple of weeks too late."

"But it does help us get close to working out the date of his demise. This would suggest the date of death as sometime between the purchase and the draw on the 8th," added Bee.

"Absolutely," said Kelly. "The deterioration of the body fits broadly with a timeline of six months."

"It gives us a few more questions," added Itzkowitz. "Not least, why would our dead body have a winning lottery ticket and yet not claim the prize?"

"Perhaps he didn't get the chance to claim it?"

"You think he might have been killed on October 8th?"

"It's a good reason for not claiming your winnings."

Bee nodded his approval.

"And if he knew he was in trouble, and might get searched, perhaps that's why he hid the ticket."

"Perhaps he was frightened."

"So that if he did escape he could still claim the prize."

"It's feasible."

Bee picked up the shoe, a sports trainer and twirled it in his fingers. "What's the brand on this? It's hard to make out, looks like A, something T, A. I'm not familiar with that."

There were blank faces around the room. "We must be able to Google something like that," said McTierney. Bee pointed at him and raised his eyebrow. McTierney nodded "I will."

"Good, and I'll follow up with the retailer who sold the lottery ticket, if we're lucky he may have a video recording system that will give us an image of our corpse."

"And possibly their bank account details if they bought the ticket using a card," added Itzkowitz.

Bee turned back to Kelly, "How about the clothing in general? Anything in the pockets, any other brands visible on anything."

Kelly shook his head. "Not much, there was nothing in the pockets of the deceased which suggests he was searched either before or after he died. In general, the clothes are bland, there's a label in the shirt collar, it's not something I recognised so I wrote it down." Kelly reached into his own pocket and pulled out a note. "Septwolves." He read it slowly to make sure he had the right name. He looked up at three blank faces. I ran it through Google and the first listing is a Chinese cigarette brand, followed by a Chinese clothing brand."

"That would fit with your suggestion that our victim might be Asian."

"Indeed so."

"Excellent, I feel we are making progress. But now I must

go and help our chief run a press conference.

★ ★ ★

DURING THE COURSE of the afternoon Bee's role changed from supporting Beck at the press conference to taking an active role and finally thirty minutes before it was due to start he found himself leading the event. He was not comfortable in front of a large audience and felt his palms start to warm as he joined the police press officer and together they made their way downstairs. As Bee approached the conference office he hoped Beck wouldn't ask how he was feeling. Mercifully Beck only played lip service to the wellbeing of his team and didn't care about how Bee felt so long as he tackled his cases effectively.

The press conference started at 5pm and the room was bustling with local and national journalists from newspapers, radio, and television. Bee could feel nerves in his stomach as he advanced towards the table. He kept his head down and reminded himself not to smile. He looked across to Beck who offered a supportive nod and not much else. Bee was happy with the minimalist approach. On the table in front of Bee were some glasses and a jug of water, alongside a pair of microphones placed there by some of the journalists in the audience.

Behind them on the wall was a banner depicting the logo of Surrey Police, an eight-pointed star surrounding a single rampant lion. Alongside this was also a large map of the castle site with a few key areas marked out, notably the entrance to the Baron's Cave and the access points up to the castle grounds from the town.

Bee took a deep breath and launched in. "This press conference is to update you on the case and to appeal to the public for any information regarding the discovery of a body in the Barons' Cave on Monday 17th of April."

"At this stage of the investigation we have more questions than answers, but we do believe that our victim was murdered in early October last year and that the body was concealed in the cave, until the management team re-opened it earlier this week. But there is much that we don't yet know, and this is where we would welcome support from the general public. Please get in touch with the police at Reigate station if you have seen anything or anyone acting suspiciously around the entrance to The Baron's Cave in the castle grounds."

Bee looked up, paused for breath, and noticed a few journalists tapping notes on their tablets.

"The period we are especially interested in is the weekend of October 8th. I know that's some time ago, so maybe I can jog a few memories by saying that the weather had been unusually warm during that week. The main news story of the day was a gas explosion in County Donegal in Northern Ireland, Liz Truss was still Prime Minister, King Charles III had ascended to the throne and Strictly Come Dancing was on the TV, so I'm told. Thank-you."

Bee spent the next fifteen minutes fielding questions about the investigation. He clarified his position as the SIO, dismissed the suggestion that the shooting had been gang related, although the thought sent a shiver up his spine and reiterated the need for any information no matter how trivial it may seem. As the journalists packed up their bits and began to filter out, Beck reached out and touched the sleeve of Bee, who steeled himself for the incoming advice and artificial concern. But Beck was beyond that, he kept his words practical and concluded with a warning not to spend too much on overtime.

By the time he walked away he knew he would be joining McTierney for his regular Friday night beer in his local pub.

SEVEN

McTierney made his way down the back stairs and out to the car park. Suddenly, Phil Church, the drug enforcement officer at the station appeared from nowhere, "Where have you been hiding today?" Asked McTierney.

"I'd like to tell you, but then I'd have to kill you Ron, classified information above your pay grade."

"Are you still pretending that the undercover drug action team is the most important team in the station?"

"Don't need to pretend. You know it's true, I know it's true, even your antiquated boss Sting knows it's true. Ask yourself who has the biggest expense account around here."

Ron laughed, "You really think you're in Miami Vice don't you."

Church smiled benignly. He had a rugged charm, with a hint of wisdom etched in his dark brown eyes. He offered an easy smile, "Although the word around the station is that you and the CID monkeys are working on the case of the century. Come on spill the beans, what's happening? I don't want the official blurb from the press conference, give me the inside story."

"Can't do that."

"Not like you to play hard to get, how about I buy you a pint?"

"Okay, but it'll have to be The Bell in Outwood, I've just agreed to meet Scott up there. I think he's had a tough afternoon running around after Beck."

The Bell was the nearest pub to the house where Scott and Ron lived. It nestled on a bend in the village and kept its rustic charm hidden from the main road. But once inside it offered a cozy embrace of worn wooden beans, a crackling fireplace, and the hearty aroma of home-cooked meals. None of that mattered to Ron, it was the beer that counted for him, and The Bell offered a wide range of real ales. He was sold on it.

Ron McTierney liked every alcoholic drink that had ever been brewed, distilled, blended, or matured anywhere in the world. This allowed him to always take the same drink as his guests. What would he do if one time a guest asked for a non-alcoholic drink? That had never happened. He chose his guests wisely and this Friday evening was no exception.

Twenty minutes later the two friends sat in the corner of The Bell a pint of lager placed in front of each of them.

"So, what can you tell me?"

Ron raised his hand, "Can't say anything until I've tasted the goods." He took a long draught and returned his glass to the table. "That's better. Now what do you want to know?"

"All that there is. Tell me everything you know."

"Not much at all, really. I think you might have overpaid." He beamed across the table but wrapped his hand around his pint. "We've got a body in one of the caves under the castle grounds. Kelly can't tell us much about it. He doesn't know who he is, doesn't know when he died, doesn't know how he got there, and we don't have a clue who might have shot him. Don't know much at all."

"You must know something. You've all been working on the case for a week. Even you lot would have unearthed something."

Ron took another gulp of his beer. "Oh yes, Kelly told us that he was shot in the back of the head by a Glock pistol. The same type as half the police forces in the country use, so there's a possibility that the killer is one of us."

"Wow. And you said you didn't know anything."

"Well, it's not going to be a copper is it, come on."

"You never know. Look at what some of those dickheads in the Met have been doing recently."

"Pff. It only really happens like that in TV dramas."

"That's because you used to live in Norfolk where the only crime is stolen apples."

Ron narrowed his eyes, took another swig and then a smile broke across his face, "Now I come to think of it, there's one other aspect. We've been running a check on all the people to visit the caves over the last couple of years. Bee has a theory that the killer wouldn't have dumped the body down there without some prior knowledge of the cave network. And guess what. Your name popped up on the list of recent visitors."

Church shifted uncomfortably in his chair.

"So, what were you doing down in the caves? A spot of reconnaissance?"

Church smiled weakly, "I know this is going to be a shock for you my friend, but I'm not the only Phil Church in the world. There's an imposter out there somewhere. But when you find him, throw the book at him."

At that moment, Scott Bee pushed his head around the front door of the bar, scanned the lounge for his friends and smiled once his eyes found them. "I trust you've not been discussing our sensitive case in the public domain with someone outside of our team, DS McTierney."

"Wouldn't dream of it Scott," said Ron, "and I'll have a pint please."

Scott rolled his eyes, "Anything for you Phil?"

"No thanks, I ought to be going."

Scott returned with the mandatory pint for his colleague, and they traded plans for the weekend. Ordinarily Scott would spend his weekends at home but on this occasion he had plans.

"You're going where?"

"It's the traditional early season BBQ at the house of Chief Superintendent Beck. You should come along."

"Jeez. It sounds ghastly – work talk on a Sunday and dozens of horrible kids screaming."

"There'll be free beer and free food."

"Tempting, but still no. Perhaps you'll get lucky, and it'll rain."

Ron and Scott tempered their beer consumption and enjoyed a quiet night, which for Ron still ran to four pints. This unusual behaviour was triggered by an impending football match featuring both of our intrepid detectives. For the last seven months Ron and Scott had been two key players in the Surrey Police football team and the following day represented the pinnacle of their season to date when they would turn out to play in the Surrey Intermediate Cup semi-final against East Molesey Wanderers.

The Police had home advantage with the game being played at their Hartswood ground, a mile to the south of Reigate. The sun peaked through the clouds, as if embarrassed to be caught watching the game, but the other fifty-odd spectators cheered as the Police team jogged out of the changing room in their orange and black kit to the sound of 'I fought the law and the law won.' by The Clash. That had been Ron's idea.

It wasn't a game to attract the television cameras, but it was a closely fought encounter, with left back Ron setting up three chances for Scott the tall centre-forward of the team. All three looped over the bar and as the players trooped off at half time, Ron offered some unwelcome advice to his colleague. "If you get your backside off the ground, you might be able to score!" Scott scowled at his colleague but didn't reply. Their manager, Gary passed around a plate of orange quarters and tried to encourage the team by talking about their fitness levels.

"Don't know about anyone else, but I'm knackered," said Ron torpedoing the pep talk.

To support his statement the second half began with the opposition's right winger racing past Ron and setting up a goal for East Moseley. Dean Grant, a new officer from the Caterham station berated Ron, but Scott wrapped his arm around his friend and whispered, "Prove them wrong" in his ear.

As the game approached the final whistle Ron made one last charge forward, a gap opened and he stole into the penalty area, Grant called for the ball and Ron looked to his right, feigned to pass but instead blasted the ball as hard as he could. The goalkeeper had shifted his weight to his left and couldn't get back across his goal and McTierney's shot rocketed into the goal. It was 1-1. Extra time followed. Both sets of players looked shattered, and play was focused on the centre of the pitch with the emphasis on not making a mistake rather than anyone going for glory.

As full time beckoned The Surrey Police had one last corner, nobody had the energy to trudge out to the wing to take the kick until Gary exhorted Ron to tramp over to the corner. He closed his eyes and thumped the ball across, Scott was determined to jump this time and leaped to head the ball. The central defender and the goalkeeper sensed the danger, and both jumped with Scott, they crowded him out and all three fell to the ground with no one touching the ball. Instead, the ball floated harmlessly over the tangle of arms and legs and landed in the goal, McTierney had scored direct from the corner. The Surrey Police team were in the cup final.

While Scott took his exhausted body home to celebrate the team's success on his own, Ron was keen to meet up with girlfriend Kate who had booked dinner for the pair in the Giggling Squid in Reigate High Street.

Ron arrived two minutes after Kate, kissed her on the cheek and flopped into the seat opposite her. "Where were you this afternoon? I was the bona-fide hero of the team, and you weren't there to see me!"

"Yes, it's nice to see you too darling and yes you look nice, thanks for making an effort for me." Kate flung the words across the table.

"Oh yes, sorry, you do look nice, you always look nice, but then you know that" said Ron immediately on the defensive.

"It's still nice to hear it now and again."

"Sorry," said Ron. He drew a breath. "You look gorgeous tonight; I am lucky that you have chosen to be here with me tonight."

"No need to go overboard."

"Sorry."

"And you don't need to apologise all the time. It's so irritating. You never used to apologise for anything."

"Sorry."

Kate scowled. "Let's order."

The waiter began to bring the food, but it arrived in dribs and drabs, Ron had scoffed a bowl of prawn crackers before his beer arrived and was almost gasping when his bottle of Singha eventually appeared. He turned to the waiter about to ask him for a second beer but stopped in his tracks. Did he recognise that face. The waiter seemed distracted, "Is there something I can get for you sir?"

Ron hesitated, "Can I get a second bottle?"

"Certainly sir," the waiter was about to move away, but Ron grabbed his sleeve. "Do I know you? Your face looks familiar."

"No, I don't think so sir. I'll just go and get your beer."

Kate kicked Ron under the table, and he spun his head around. "What?"

"You're making a scene."

"Sorry, I thought I recognised him from somewhere."

"There you go apologising again. Come on tell me about your football, I know you won't be happy until you have."

Ron smiled, "Well since you asked so politely, today was our cup semi-final against East Molesey, and we won. We won 2-1."

"So now you're in the final. Congratulations. I will make a big effort to try to come to the final."

"Please do. But I haven't told you the best bit yet." Ron

stopped and turned his head as he heard a waiter approach the table next to him, but it was a different waiter.

"Ron."

He turned back to Kate, "Sorry. Where was I? Oh yes, I scored both goals!"

"My hero. Really both goals."

"Yes. Thanks for the vote of confidence, but I do sometimes play quite well and today was one of those days. But we had to play extra time, another thirty minutes, so I'm shattered."

"So, it was a close game."

"It was. Although it didn't need to be. If Scott had got his head to any of the crosses I put in for him we could have thrashed them, but he had an off day. He's not been himself since we picked up the case of the dead guy in the cave."

"When is the final anyway?"

"It's on, sorry, excuse me a moment, I've just remembered where I saw that guy." Ron left his seat and walked into the restaurant. Kate's mouth fell open, then her face switched into a frown, and she plucked her mobile from her handbag. It was at least 10 minutes before Ron returned.

"What's going on?" she asked.

"It's him. The waiter who took our order. I'm sure he's the guy who stole the bag in the High Street last week, the one I chased, who then walloped me with the metal bar."

"Really?"

"Did you speak to him?"

"No, he seems to have disappeared. I couldn't find him in the restaurant, so I went to the manager, and she told me that he had told her he was feeling ill and had to go home."

Kate gawped across the table. "You really think that it

was him."

"To be honest I'm not sure, but given his reaction, I'm starting to think that it probably was."

EIGHT

MONDAY MORNING AND the ops room was a hive of activity, despite the slow start to the case, the end of the previous week had exploded with leads and work. Bee had adopted a divide and conquer approach with his team and after a short catch-up session, each was despatched to pursue different angles of enquiry ahead of a major review the following morning. Bee himself dropped in to see Dr Kelly and his new assistant Professor Ken Tidworth.

"Good to meet you professor," said Bee stretching out his right hand.

"Likewise."

Ken Tidworth was an overweight man of 50 plus years with a greying bushy moustache and equally greying bushy eyebrows. But where he allowed indiscipline to creep into his diet and his facial hair, his work ethic was immaculate.

"Interesting case you have here inspector. I can't guarantee you a result, but we'll give it our best. I've worked on a few of these in the past, one body had been concealed in a chimney for over thirty years, so this is quite recent by comparison, but you never know how it's going to take until we begin. We should have an idea if it's going to work by tomorrow."

"That would be useful. What is it that you do?"

"Essentially we take tissue samples and rehydrate them and then examine them under a microscope and tell you what we see."

"Perfect. I'll leave you in the capable hands of Dr Kelly, but if you need anything give me a shout."

Bee left the two pathologists to sort themselves out and went to find Bishop who had tracked down the retailer who had sold the lottery ticket to the victim. She handed the ticket to him, plus a separate piece of paper carrying the address. "It's a family run business in Redhill. I haven't spoken to them; I got the address from code on the ticket."

"Great I'll shoot down there now."

★ ★ ★

MEANWHILE MCTIERNEY HAD been given the task of cracking the footwear brand being worn by the victim and had created a mini spreadsheet depicting the letters and the possibilities that remained. He liked to shoot from the hip and his first thought was a five-letter word with A as the second letter. He wrote FANTA on the page in front of himself, but quickly crossed that out as it was already a soft drink brand. Then he thought that it wouldn't matter if it was in a different category, so he re-wrote it. But he'd never seen it used on a sports shoe. Time for some science, he typed 'popular footwear brands in the UK' into Google. He pressed the button and waited for the answer to appear. The first four were, 'Adidas', 'Nike', 'Tricker's', and 'Dr. Martens'. He scowled, "'Tricker's', can't be in the top four surely," he said in desperation. He pressed the 'show 6 more' button, and up popped, 'Veja', 'Clarks', 'Reebok', 'TOMS', 'Next plc', and

'Steve Madden'.

"What?" These couldn't be right. He lifted up his laptop and looked at the back, had someone sneaked in and added a bug. He didn't find anything untoward. Thinking that he may have mistyped his query, he started again, and the same result appeared. He looked left and right from his desk to see if anyone was watching him ready to jump out and ridicule him. All he could see was his colleagues busily working on the case. He took a deep breath and ploughed on. The list offered several options at the bottom and McTierney clicked on 'Who are the UK's biggest shoe manufacturer?' The answer flashed up with 'Hotter Shoes'. McTierney's eyes bulged. "I've never heard of them." He pursued the link and discovered that 'Hotter Shoes' made 1.3 million pairs of casual shoes each year in their factory in Skelmersdale and had been doing so for the last sixty years. "How many brain cells am I wasting on this," he muttered. "Time to apply some logic to this game." He changed his search to focus on the letters he had and discovered that there were eight sports shoe brands beginning with an 'A'. Aside from 'Adidas', and 'Asics', and a couple of variations of the word athlete, sitting quietly near the bottom of the list was 'Anta Sports'. "There you are you little bastard. You can run but you can't hide. McTierney will get you in the end."

A few more searches confirmed their Chinese origin and that they specialised in basketball and running shoes and had an exclusive distribution agreement with Foot Locker in the UK. Foot Locker had ten branches in the south-east, one in White City, one in Brixton, one in Shepherd's Bush, one in Bromley, one in Oxford Street, one in Brent Cross, one in Bluewater, one in Kingston, one in Sutton, and a final one in

Croydon. "All the nice places, – would it be too much to ask for one in Redhill?" He shook his head at the prospect of trawling around each of them on a wild goose chase.

Believing that he had done enough to move that particular strand of the enquiry forward McTierney got up from his desk and slipped out of the station and walked passed the grand houses of the main road into the town centre of Reigate. At the edge of the town is the entrance to Reigate College, as McTierney arrived dozens of students thronged the crossing; their chatter almost drowning out the traffic. McTierney crept around them picking up snippets of gossip as he went. Maths had been difficult that day; John was being a pig, and Taylor Swift tickets were the next to gold dust. He smiled; it was approaching lunchtime, and he hoped to catch the manager of the Giggling Squid restaurant before the establishment became busy. He was in luck as when he arrived he could only see one occupied table. A minute later he flashed his police badge to the manager, whose body froze when she realised he was talking to a police officer. McTierney noticed the apprehension and decided to take full advantage. "I'd like to see a full list of all the staff who work in this restaurant please."

"May I ask what the reason is?"

"I'm investigating an assault on a police officer and have reason to believe that one of your employees may have information that may help us."

"I can't imagine that any of our employees would attack a police officer. Or anybody else for that matter," the manager began to splutter.

"That's for me to find out, now could you get me that list."

"It will take me a few minutes, could you come back tomorrow."

"No. I'll wait. You can do it now, and I'll have a bowl of prawn crackers while I'm waiting."

The manager opened her mouth to speak but didn't say anything. She looked around the restaurant but couldn't find whatever it was she wanted. "Yes, right, okay. I'll just be a minute." She turned towards the bar and barked something in a language McTierney didn't understand and then darted downstairs. McTierney smiled at the bar tender, who looked away, but soon returned with a bowl of prawn crackers. "Would you like a table sir?"

"Thanks, I'll sit here," said McTierney making himself comfortable at the nearest table but keeping a view of the front door. He hadn't finished the bowl when the manager returned, she walked the last few steps with her head bowed and thrust a piece of paper onto the table where McTierney sat and then stepped back, "Here it is."

McTierney took another cracker from the bowl and chewed it slowly, before picking up the list. He read it slowly, looked up and beckoned the manager over. "You had a waiter in here on Saturday night who was looking after the tables over here on the left-hand side," McTierney waved his arm towards the area where he and Kate had been sitting. "Tell me which one is he."

"That would have been Carlos, the third name on the list."

McTierney looked at the list. "Carlos Hanbing of Goldworth Road, Redhill."

The manager nodded.

"Excellent. Reigate police thanks you for your assistance,

and the crackers."

★ ★ ★

TWO DESKS FURTHER along from where McTierney had been sitting on the first floor of the police station sat Carol Bishop, trying not to allow her colleague's antics to distract her from farming though a series of missing persons lists. The National Crime Agency maintains the grim database on behalf of the police. Bishop knew that the numbers were large scale, but also that the majority of people reported as missing were found within the first few days of appearing on the database. Despite that she was aghast to learn that there were currently over 600 unidentified bodies listed on the database and 180,000 people listed as missing. Even when she filtered it down to London and Surrey, the number was still huge. She found no comfort in excluding the two thirds of the total who were female. She switched her attention to adding their victim to the desperate catalogue but struggled to answer any of the mandatory questions. The system required a name, a photo and contact details, and if possible a DNA sample, details of any medical condition, and the names of close friends or relatives. Bishop clicked away from the website with a score of 0 out of 6.

★ ★ ★

ITZKOWITZ HAD ESCAPED the mayhem of the office and made her way back to the Barons' Cave with an appointment to meet Burgess and Ball. Both had regained their composure and colour from the last time she had seen them and didn't seemed to be affected by the prospect of returning to the cave. Together they stepped under the blue and white police cordon tape as Itzkowitz explained that she wanted them to examine the caves and identify anything that might have changed from their last visit when they had closed up the cave in October of the previous year.

"Not sure I'll be able to remember anything from back then," said Burgess.

"I understand that it's a bit of a long shot, but at the moment we're exploring every avenue," said Itzkowitz with a smile of encouragement. "Thank you for coming back in the same boots as you were wearing last week, we'll need them later."

They walked in single file along the edge of the tunnel into the central area of the cave and stopped under one of the bright halogen lamps. Itzkowitz turned to address her companions, "I understand that these caves are made of Reigate stone which is reasonably soft."

"It is." Agreed Burgess and Ball, exchanging surprised looks.

Itzkowitz smiled to herself. "And therefore, receptive to graffiti, scrapes and generally markings of any kind."

"It is." Agreed Burgess and Ball, who this time stopped to stare at their informed colleague.

"So, I want the pair of you to walk the length and breadth of these caves and examine the floors, walls, and ceilings for any new markings. I'm not expecting our killer to have left his initials carved into the wall anywhere, but it's probable that he carried the dead body down here and he may have inadvertently bumped into the surface and left a mark, or maybe some fabric."

Burgess and Ball nodded their understanding.

"Hopefully it won't take too long, but be thorough and when you've finished, please leave your boots up at the entrance with our duty officer, so our forensic team can identify your footprints and remove them from the search. I'll come back again on Wednesday, and we can review what you've discovered."

Eventually Burgess found his voice. "Certainly, I'm not convinced we'll find anything, but we'll give it our best." He turned to his colleague who nodded enthusiastically.

★ ★ ★

BEE SQUEEZED HIS old Mercedes in between two battered Japanese cars fifty yards past the B & D newsagent and walked back to the shop. The ground floor of two detached late-Victorian houses had been converted into a corner shop and he guessed that much of the upstairs acted as a makeshift storage area. Bee pushed open the door which triggered a bell on the back of the door and in turn an Asian man looked up from the counter opposite. The shop made Bee think of the Tardis, small outside but cavernous on the inside with aisles stretching back further than he thought could be possible. Every square inch of retail surface was in use, breakfast cereals next to tinned vegetables, next to cleaning chemicals, next to cooking sauces, next to magazines, next to confectionary. A Noah's Ark of small sized essentials, two of everything, an endless myriad of colour. Bee took a step towards the man behind the counter.

"Hello, I'm Inspector Scott Bee from the Reigate Constabulary. We're investigating the death of a man in the caves underneath Reigate; you may have seen the story on the news or in the papers."

"Oh, I know, very sad. It's here in the local paper."

"Quite."

"What can I do to help you?" The man spoke quickly, and Bee had to pause to process the words. "We found a lottery ticket in the shoe of the victim and the code suggests it was purchased from this shop in October of last year, and hence I'd like to know if you can trace the ticket to help us identify the purchaser."

Bee had wrapped the ticket in a transparent plastic wallet and passed it across to the shopkeeper who took it in his hand and held it up to the light.

"I can see that it's one of ours, but I've no idea who bought it."

"I see you have a security camera up there in the corner." Bee pointed to a concealed camera behind the tills. "Any chance that you may have a recording from October?"

"Sorry, sir. We only keep the recordings for a week and then we re-use the disk."

"Too costly to keep buying new disc space?"

"Yes that's right. Do you have a shop too?"

"No, but I've heard the same story before. No worries. Let me try a different approach. Many people who play the lottery are regular players, always playing the same numbers every week. Have you noticed the loss of a regular customer who no longer visits your shop. Probably a man of Asian descent perhaps aged between 20 and 40 years old and roughly 5'10" in height." Bee held out his hand beside him to indicate the size.

The shopkeeper paused for a moment and then shook his

head, "Sorry, I can't think of anyone."

Bee tutted and nodded in disappointment. "Take my card, if anything comes to mind, please give me a call."

NINE

ALTHOUGH THE CASE had been running officially for a more than a week, it was only in the last few days that any of the detectives had felt they were starting to make any progress and consequently, the ops room was electric with excitement that they might be on the verge of a major breakthrough. Bee was downstairs conducting the first of many interviews with people who had visited the Barons' Cave in the previous two seasons. His absence allowed McTierney to conduct the pre-work debate, which this morning focused on clothing.

Kelly had given McTierney a Chinese own-brand label from the shirt that the victim had been wearing and McTierney had since discovered that the shirt was at least six years old. Armed with this insight he had started a conversation about how frequently the team updated their wardrobes.

"I don't try to follow the fashions," said Itzkowitz. "I buy something new maybe every month, but if there's nothing that catches my eye, then I'm equally happy to save my money."

"Yes I'm a bit the same," said Bishop. "I have my favourite shops and I tend to look around them when they have a sale on, but I can go weeks or months without buying anything. Although I do try to keep a clean jacket for work. I think it's important to maintain a smart appearance."

"What do you do, Mr Fashion?" asked Itzkowitz looking McTierney up and down. "Doesn't look like you're keeping too many tailors in full-time employment."

McTierney offered a look of disdain. "I'm a boy, I only buy clothes when I need to, it's not a lifestyle choice for me, it's a purchase of necessity. One pair of trousers falls apart, I go and buy a replacement."

"So, you're no better than our Asian friend."

"I don't buy own-label clothes. I try to buy stuff that is going to last."

"To make sure you get your money's worth."

"Nothing wrong with that."

Itzkowitz smiled at him but decided to back off and that allowed McTierney a second wave. "I'm willing to bet that Bee will be the one who keeps his clothes the longest. Since I've shared a house with him I don't think I've seen him go clothes shopping once."

"I happen to think that Inspector Bee always looks very smart," said Bishop before blushing and turning away. "But I have work to do, I'm working through this list of missing persons and there are hundreds of them, no thousands. It's really quite sad."

"At least you can do that at your own speed, I've got to go and join our beloved inspector and interview some of these tourists who visited the caves last summer. How tedious is that going to be?" He looked across at Itzkowitz. "And before you say anything smart, you're coming too."

The two detectives left Bishop to search through the missing persons list. Before she began her work she flicked back to the boy she had spotted on her first visit; Michael

Jones a 15-year-old boy who had been missing for over 30 years. A lump came to her throat as she looked at his photo, but what good was that photo, Michael Jones was now a middle-aged man and would look nothing like the boy on her screen. She wondered what could have happened to make this teenager walk away from everything he knew. Would he still be alive, maybe he had a 15-year-old son of his own. Maybe, but probably not. Not many of these stories had a happy ending. But maybe this one would, she returned to the task at hand. Once she had filtered out non-Asians and women she was pleased to see that her list had shrunk down to less than 100.

By half past eleven Bee, McTierney and Itzkowitz had completed twenty-five short interviews. Itzkowitz escorted the last person out of the building and returned to find her colleagues slumped in one of the interview rooms. Bee raised his eyes, "I'm starting to regret this approach of bringing in every person who has visited the Barons' Cave."

"Agreed," said McTierney, "This feels like an endless round of futile questions."

Bee ran his hand through his short black hair "I think part of the problem is that we don't really have a starting point. There's no angle to work from."

"It's like one of those Rubik cubes. You keep turning it around in your hand and each face looks as impenetrable as the next."

"Actually, I was always able to crack that cube."

McTierney raised his eyes to the ceiling. "I did think we were starting to get somewhere at the end of last week, but we're still lacking a decent lead. All we've got are a few half-ideas."

"It might be better to cross-check the names against our database and focus on the ones who have some criminal history," suggested Itzkowitz. "I interviewed an old lady earlier and there's no way she could have carried a dead body down into that cave."

"You're right, that would be a smarter approach," said Bee. "I'm not thinking straight today, I've got a toothache and it's clouding my judgement."

"Maybe Dr Kelly and his new friend can give us something to identify the victim, I think once we have a name or a face we'll be able to make some progress."

"That should be after lunch, let's hope that new professor is earning his corn."

★ ★ ★

IT WAS A little after 2pm when Dr Kelly tapped on the open door of the ops room and brought in Professor Ken Tidworth.

"Can we interrupt and update you on what we've discovered?"

"Please do," said Bee jumping up from his seat to welcome in the two pathologists. McTierney, Itzkowitz, and Bishop sat and nodded towards the professor as Bee introduced his team. Tidworth looked around the room and his eyes fell on the whiteboard in the corner of the room, he squinted at a couple of words and offered a weak smile. As if reading his mind, Bee picked up the gauntlet. "Early days in the case," he said offering his palms to the professor, "We're hopeful that you may be able to provide us with some new insights."

Tidworth smiled benignly and turned back to Kelly to allow him to lead.

"Firstly, I need to tell you that some of the work we've been doing is experimental to say the least. We are fortunate to have Professor Tidworth here who is at the forefront of some of the advances being made in this type of work. For example, we may be able to extract a set of fingerprints from the body, but the work is not foolproof and probably it would not be admissible in court."

Tidworth leaned into the table and added, "They never have been yet, but we live in hope. DNA analysis started this way and nowadays it's commonplace, but it wasn't always so."

"Since we're only likely to use any fingerprints for the purpose of identification, we should be okay this time around," said Bee.

Kelly smiled. "Either way, we should have a set of prints, or something close to it by Thursday. The hydration process takes a little longer when we require a lot of detail."

"What is the process?" asked McTierney, "Are we allowed to know or is it top secret?"

"Let's see if I can remember from yesterday," said Bee looking at Tidworth for his cue. The professor waved his arm. Bee rubbed the back of his neck, and then coughed, "It's a rehydration process, which brings human tissue cells back to life." He looked across at Tidworth for his approval.

"Not bad inspector. Yes, in its simplest terms all we do is re-hydrate dry cells and in so doing the tissue displays previous markings that may have been lost."

"Does the body still have to retain some moisture of its own to allow the process to work?" This time it was

Itzkowitz.

"Actually, no. We can go back for many years, even centuries. A couple of years ago I went to Egypt to work on three mummies."

A mischievous grim shot across McTierney's face, "How do Egyptian mummies take their coffee?"

Bee scowled at him, but it didn't have any impact, three seconds later he produced the punch line, "De-coffin-ated!"

Tidworth lowered his gaze and exchanged looks with Kelly. "I think I warned you about DS McTierney, "He likes to enjoy life."

"Too short not to," said McTierney.

Kelly gave a clipped smile, "Back to the case in point. Aside from the fingerprints which are pending and also an identikit image that we hope we can produce for you; we do have three discoveries that we believe will be helpful to you. Opening the batting is an estimated age of the deceased as somewhere between 28 and 35 years. This is consistent with what I've said before, but this time I can lift the confidence level to something like 90%. Professor Tidworth has assessed the cartilage on the leg and noted that much of it has turned to bone which is consistent with a body in their late 20's, at least."

The group looked at Tidworth for confirmation who mustered a faint smile but said nothing.

"Additionally at the other end of the age spectrum there is no evidence of arthritic degeneration, so the body is most likely to be under middle age, probably not yet 40 years old. Finally, there is little deterioration on the teeth, only one molar is missing from the left side. There hasn't been any significant dental work, but then little has been required. All of which supports our belief that the victim was in his late 20's, maybe early 30's."

Bee looked pleased but didn't say anything.

"Once we get a name, if we do, then we can try to locate the dental records of the victim and that may show something new."

"That's positive and your second point?" asked McTierney.

Kelly turned to Tidworth, "DS McTierney likes to keep us on track. I believe he was a lyrical child, kept his mother busy."

Then he turned back to the main audience. "Yes our second item is the confirmation that the deceased has had a kidney removed, his right sided kidney as it happens, and probably within the last 12-15 months."

A murmur of appreciation rippled around the room. "We examined the state of the tissue around the incision and where the kidney would have been and there is an indication that the body has healed well and therefore it was a few months before death occurred that the kidney was removed. It was also a neat and tidy job. So, if you are going to try to track down the surgeon, I'd suggest that it wasn't the first time that he, or she," Kelly smiled at the two ladies, "had performed such an operation."

Bee nodded his approval and added something to the notebook in front of him.

"Thirdly, and this is totally new. Professor Tidworth spotted a couple of marks on the left arm of our victim which, once hydrated suggest that our deceased friend was most likely a drug user." The murmur that had greeted the previous item was swamped by the babble that followed this revelation.

"Heavy user?" Asked Itzkowitz.

"Hard to say," said Kelly, "but almost certainly a regular user, there's one clear set of needle marks and probably a second, but it's hard to be precise with tissue this old."

"Again, this wouldn't be admissible in a court, but we felt it would help you identify the victim." Added Tidworth.

"No, that's fine. Thank you," said Bee.

The chatter around the table continued for a couple of minutes, then McTierney raised his voice to ask a question. "Maybe we should bring Phil Church into this group as he's our undercover expert on drugs around here. Who knows this might be a dispute between drugs gangs over turf."

"Yes, maybe," replied Bee, but his mind was elsewhere. He turned his head to Kelly and lifted his finger, "You mentioned DNA a little earlier, can I ask if we can expect to use DNA in our attempts to identify our victim?"

Kelly blanched and looked across at Tidworth for support. The professor titled his head and Bee thought he noticed a smirk flicker across his lips.

"Good question inspector," said Tidworth. "I understand that DNA is the Holy Grail for detectives these days, but I'm afraid you may have to go without it here. Yes we can extract some, but in my experience DNA comparisons are tricky because the tissue is very degraded. I don't think I can't recall a single case when we've found a specimen that has worked."

"Not to worry, you've given us a lot to digest and I'm sure this will help us in our quest to both identify our victim and find the killer."

The group stood up to leave and a couple of small conversations started as they stepped out into the corridor. Most people were keen to get down to the police canteen in the basement before it closed but Bee wasn't one of them, He was troubled by this case, he wasn't able to get it into his head as he would normally do, he had found it difficult to stand in the shoes of the victim. Maybe it was the lack of a name or even a face that was preventing him from engaging with the corpse. It was now more than a week and he knew he'd made no progress whatsoever. He stopped to wonder if he was the right man for the case. He'd achieved nothing from the lottery ticket, nothing from the sports shoes and what would he do with today's information. Perhaps he should go to Chief Superintendent Beck and ask him to re-assign the case. He walked over to the window and looked down on the two pathologists as they stood in the car park. He watched them shake hands before Tidworth got into his grey Jaguar and swept away from the building.

"Pull yourself together man." He said as he marched over to the white board and picked up the marker pen to update the white board with today's information. He added 'drug user?' and then an arrow off to the side with 'drug gang killing?' in one corner. Next he wrote 'kidney transplant', added another arrow to a second corner with a pair of addendums, 'rogue doctor' and 'black market organ killing'. That idea necessitated two question marks. He mused *this case has a bit of everything.* Reluctantly he added 'police weapon', something he knew he should have added four days ago. This time he finished the line with an exclamation mark and put all of this in the bottom corner.

TEN

"I'VE NOT BEEN to one of these fancy London dinners before, is it posh?"

"Super posh." Kate lowered her kindle and looked directly at Ron. "You'd better behave tonight, there will be some mega people at this ceremony. People who shape the industry, people who could be very influential in my career."

"No worries, darling, I'm on the case."

Kate rolled her eyes. "Don't get drunk, you're too loud when you're drunk."

"Come on, you can trust me."

"Hmm, the trouble is there's free wine on the table, and I know what you're like. Promise me, you won't go crazy."

"You have my word."

Ron and Kate were on a Southern Rail train rattling its way into London Victoria station, each dressed in their finery; Kate in a long black dress with a red diagonal stripe across the front reminiscent of David Bowie's 'Aladdin Sane's' alter ego face and Ron in a standard, but smart black dinner jacket. They were en route to the 2023 Audio and Radio Industry Awards, known in the trade as the ARIAs and considered by the radio industry to be the Oscars of their world. Kate was representing BBC Radio Surrey.

They grabbed a taxi from Victoria across London to the

Grosvenor Hotel in Park Lane, where the event was being staged in the Great Room. As Kate stepped out of the taxi, she nudged Ron, "Get a receipt and then I can claim the fare on expenses."

Ron thrust a piece of paper into his jacket pocket and scuttled after his girlfriend, "Do these expenses run to a beer or two?"

"Within reason, they do."

"I'm starting to like this event."

They passed through a series of swing doors and into a cavernous atrium awash with bright lights and mirrored surfaces everywhere. The hotel combined the hustle and bustle of a Sunday car boot sale with a regal ceremony. Fancy jewellery was in evidence everywhere, not only gold earrings and diamond necklaces, but nose studs and tiaras as well. Kate smiled at a well-dressed couple as she and Ron crossed the hall.

"Who's that?"

"Not a clue, but he nodded at me as if he knew me, so I thought I should acknowledge him."

"Tell me again, what's happening?"

"It's the annual showcase event for the industry, the night when we get together and celebrate excellence in the UK radio and audio presenting industry. We'll have a sumptuous meal, enjoy a comedian, I think it's Dom Holland this year, and then there's 25 or so awards to recognise the best talent across the industry. It should be a spectacular night."

"I guess anybody who's anybody will be here and wanting to be seen."

"Yes, a bit like your Sports Personality of the Year programme that you made me watch."

"Are you going to win anything?"

"Unlikely. Producers don't win. All the limelight is on the talent; the producer might, should, get a mention in the thank you speech, but that's about it. We have a shot at the station of the year, but I'd be amazed if we won. If it was on the cards then the big boss would have come instead of sending me."

Ron and Kate collected a couple of cocktails from the bar and made their way through to the Great Room, by way of an enormous seating plan chart. They took their place on table 46, about 40 yards from the main stage.

"This place is enormous; you could get an ice-rink in here."

"The marketing spiel that came with the invites said it's the largest public dining room in the country."

Kate was correct in her assessment of the venue and her prediction for the evening; the three-course meal featured the ubiquitous chicken, this time in a Cajun style. She ate it all and approved of the taste and the tiramisu dessert which followed surpassed her expectations. Dom Holland made her laugh, especially his monologue about his wife having a new man in her life, called John Lewis. But on the down side, the speeches ran on far too long, and Ron drank much more than she'd hoped. The wine waiter took up residence behind their table and Ron made sure he earned his money for the night.

"I think you've had enough wine for one night and will you stop pointing at people, it's embarrassing."

"Sorry, but it's exciting. Who's that over there in the green dress?"

"I think it's Lily James."

"Can we go and say hello."

"No. I don't know her. Christ this is like bringing a three-year-old to a sweet shop."

Kate topped up her own wine glass and prepared herself for the awards ceremony to begin. One more hour and she could head home. The committee had employed Jack Whitehall to compere the event and he took to the stage and opened with a couple of snappy one liners about radio programmes and then began to work through the awards. Each category had five nominations and then Whitehall announced the winners in a bronze, silver, gold format, all of which flashed up on a giant video screen behind the speaker. The winner was then welcomed to the stage and given a large silver trophy in the shape of a radio microphone.

Kate breathed a sigh of relief as the first winner, for News Coverage, waved the trophy in the air but didn't make any attempt to give a speech. This pattern continued through Podcast of the Year, Specialist Music Programme, and Best Sports Show. It wasn't until the sequence got to Best Audio Dramatisation that the pattern was broken. This award was won by Dear Harry Kane a Radio 4 special that hadn't been rated and the writer decided to grab her moment in the spotlight and went full 'Gywneth Paltrow' on the audience. A new pattern had been established and now each winner presented the audience with a snapshot of their family tree.

One award rolled into the next and Kate started to wish that someone had curtailed the number of categories but that changed when Whitehall read out the nominations for Entertainment Production of the year. Better still when the winner was announced as Craig Charles which was followed by the biggest cheer of the night. Ron turned to her excitedly, but she beat him to the punch, "No, we can't go and meet

Craig Charles." Ron turned back to his wine in disappointment.

Craig Charles was followed by the last mainstream award and the one in which Kate felt her station had a small chance of victory, but to no avail, Best Local Station of the Year went to Vectis Radio on the Isle of Wight. "Bugger," she muttered under her breath, Ron reached across and put his arm around her shoulder, and then ruined it with his words, "Getting beaten by the Isle of Wight – how embarrassing."

The evening finished with a special Pioneer Award to Tony Blackburn to recognise his sixty years in broadcasting. He appeared shocked and delighted at the award and gave a short speech which culminated in one of his favourite jokes. Kate saw Ron scribble it down, and grabbed his arm, "Don't, his jokes are worse than yours."

The return cab glided through the traffic on the return journey to Victoria, Kate felt tired and slumped against the seat, but Ron found a second wind and engaged the driver in a lengthy debate about the price of a pint of beer in various London establishments. Kate rubbed her eyes and wished she'd taken up her manager's offer of staying over in the hotel after the event. Once out of the taxi they stomped across the concourse of the station and joined the throng of people waiting by the overhead signs opposite the last tranche of platforms.

"How can there be so many people leaving London late on a Tuesday night," moaned Ron but Kate ignored him. She was tired and wanted to get home, then a human stampede began, she raised her head and saw platform 19 had been designated for their train. She and Ron trudged along behind the crowd and squeezed onto the train, everywhere she looked people were spreading out trying to occupy two or even three seats and deter others from sitting in their area. Eventually they found a space and sat opposite two youths. Each had a bag of fast food, and they began munching through their contents as soon as Kate and Ron had sat down.

Kate tried to bury herself in her kindle but knew Ron was irritated by both the smell of the food and the sound of it being consumed. She sensed that a wine fuelled Ron was about to produce his warrant card and make a statement, she grabbed his sleeve, and her eyes warned him. Ron changed his tactics and started a discussion on the best way to secure a seat to yourself.

"You know the best way to keep others away is to bring some food into the carriage, the stinkier the better." Kate scowled, but Ron continued. "A close second is the fake coughing fit, preferably with sniffing to give the impression that you have Covid."

She shook her head and closed her eyes, forty minutes to go. The train emptied out as it left the capital and soon it trundled over the bridge which spanned the M25 motorway.

"Ron, I think you should get off here. I'm going to stay on the train to the next station and get a cab back to my place."

Ron looked perplexed. "What did I do?"

"I'm sorry, but I think we've reached the end of the line, and this is your station." With that Kate stood up and walked to the next carriage.

ELEVEN

BEE HADN'T SLEPT well on Tuesday night; his mind wouldn't release the idea that a police weapon may have been used in the killing of a civilian. Aside from the simple horror of any such occurrence the possibility brought back too many memories of his own recent experience with a gun. As a result, it was a little after 6am when he found himself walking up the back stairs at Reigate station. He slipped behind his desk and turned on his computer and watched the Surrey Police logo spin slowly on the screen. He had a mountain of admin to catch up on. His paperwork included crime reports, intelligence reports and even documents connected with the shift administration and overtime, all needed attention and all would reappear within days. But he couldn't concentrate on any of it. Instead, he opened a restricted access file which listed 'Unsolved UK killings' and filtered the file by type of weapon so it would show him only deaths involving the Glock pistol, then he applied a second filter to show only the county of Surrey. He double-checked the filters to ensure there was no possibility of mistakenly retrieving the data that would mention his own name, as bad as it was, it couldn't be classified as 'unsolved'. There were plenty of words Bee would use but it was no secret. While the screen flickered into action, he walked along the corridor to the nearest coffee machine, he wanted some protection from what he was expecting to see.

He tipped the first two cups away, knowing that the water would be tepid, and took the third and fourth back to his desk. His computer had finished shuffling the data and had produced the answer he expected but had hoped he wouldn't see. Two other unsolved murders were suspected of involving police issue Glock pistols in the area; one in Croydon and one a little closer to home in Caterham. The first one was thirteen years ago, when Bee was a fresh-faced PC in Northampton, the second was three years later, shortly after his transfer to the region. He hadn't been involved in either case, but he knew officers who had been, and the anxiety that the cases had generated. He made a note to find a quiet moment to discuss the cases with Beck, who had been in charge of the second investigation.

The next of the team to arrive was Carol Bishop, who spotted Bee's old Mercedes in the car park and took the opportunity to walk up to his office. She tapped on the half-open door and stuck her head around the door. Bee had been lost in reading something on his screen but jumped up when he saw her.

"Good morning sir, I wonder if you have a couple of spare minutes, there's something I discovered last night that I'm not comfortable with and I'd appreciate your thoughts."

"Certainly Bishop, I've always got time for you."

Bishop blushed and stepped away from the door, "Maybe I could show you on my laptop downstairs."

Together they walked down to the communal area on the first floor where Bishop had a desk. "It concerns the list of visitors to the Barons' Cave."

"Oh yes."

"I've been able to contact most people but some of the email addresses that the Wealden Cave Society gave me had been obscured so I asked our technical team to uncover them. There weren't many and I think they tracked the IP address to identify a user in each case."

"That's sounds about right," said Bee pulling up a chair and looking at the screen.

"But one of them appears to be Phil Church from our own team. I mentioned this to McTierney, but he said he's spoken to Church and that it wasn't him. But I don't think our technical boys would make a mistake like that. I'm not sure what to do."

Bee pinched his lip, "You've done the right thing bringing it to me. Can you print off that page with the address confirmed as Church and I'll talk to him myself. No need to mention this to McTierney, I'll take it from here."

★ ★ ★

AWAY FROM THE station Itzkowitz was following up on the task she had left with Burgess and Ball at the Barons' Cave. They were waiting for her outside the cave as she arrived.

"I've brought along one of our forensic team today to help us interpret anything you may have spotted. This is Stephen Capon. He's the one who borrowed your boots to remove them and hopefully you from our investigation. The three men exchanged pleasantries, while Itzkowitz popped a stick of gum into her mouth. Picking up on the sudden silence Capon spoke.

"Perhaps footprints is a good place to start. The cavern

floor in these caves is sand and damp sand to be precise and that is a highly receptive surface to footprints so we're fortunate. Over here we have a couple of prints that are unaccounted for, and therefore quite probably belong to the perpetrator."

Capon stepped across to the side of the entrance wall and shone his torch on a couple of prints in the sand, while the others gathered around it.

"It's a standard boot, probably a size 10. That's around 11% of the male population but we've managed to pull a couple of quality impressions. It looks like our perpetrator was conscious of leaving footprints, because throughout the rest of the cave he has dragged the edge of his boot through any prints. But he seems to have forgotten to smudge a few here at the entrance, maybe he was distracted by something when he entered."

"Impressive," said Itzkowitz. "Are you sure it's a he? You sound convinced."

"I'd say there's a 90% likelihood. The size of the print is a strong indicator; you probably don't know this, but generally men in the North have slightly larger feet than their counter parts in the south, by 7%. Edinburgh is known to have the largest feet in the UK. Additionally, men's feet are usually 3 sizes larger than women, Milton Keynes being the home of the largest female feet in the country. So, putting that together it seems highly likely that these prints belong to a man."

Itzkowitz gawped at her colleague. "Are footprints your specialist subject?"

Capon blushed and dropped his eyes to the floor.

"What else did you find?" Itzkowitz turned her attention

to the pair of cavers.

"Not a lot to be honest, nothing as impressive as your colleague," said Burgess. "It looks much the same, and it's hard to remember exactly what the cave looked like eight months ago," added Ball, "But we think one of the corners has been marked."

"Can you show me?"

The group walked forward thirty yards to the junction between the main tunnel and the principal arterial tunnel in which the body had been found. Ball stopped and pointed to a few marks on the corner.

"What do you think Capon?" asked Itzkowitz.

"Could be."

"So, in summary we have evidence of footprints from an unidentified person, probably a male wearing size 10 boots, with further evidence of him trying to cover his tracks and entering the cave after it had been secured for the winter season."

"More or less."

"More or less?"

"It's not the most convincing piece of forensic evidence I've ever seen, but it does hold together."

"Good work, guys. You can give them their boots back now."

★ ★ ★

BACK AT THE station McTierney had arrived at his desk; he had only an hour to kill before he was due to attend a follow-up appointment at the East Surrey Hospital and it didn't seem worthwhile getting too engrossed in a lead. He turned on his laptop and immediately flicked across to the BBC sports page, but before he had read the first article Bee appeared in front of him. McTierney sighed and slowly closed the laptop lid.

"I've been thinking."

"Dangerous habit."

"If our victim gave up his kidney then quid pro quo, it follows that somebody else must have it. Maybe if we could find that person, then perhaps we could find the surgeon and that might give us some more background on our man."

"Sounds like a long shot."

"Right now, all we have are long shots. While you go off to the hospital to get yourself checked out, I'll start working through the donor lists and waiting lists and see what I can find. Although something about this makes me think it might have been an illegal transplant."

AFTER BEE HAD helped Bishop resolve her problem with Church on her list of cave visitors she had now contacted every name on the list and had appointments set for all but three of the names. This allowed her to switch her attention to the list of missing persons.

She started to run a new set of filters based on the information that Kelly and Tidworth had been able to share on the previous day. Once she had restricted the original list to men, people reported as missing after October 2022, people of Asian appearance and people aged between 28 and 35 years as given by Kelly, she felt she was making some progress. She looked back at the list of 'facts' provided by Kelly and cursed the system for not including height as one of their factors.

Nonetheless her list was now down to five sheets, and she hoped that their man was somewhere in those pages.

★ ★ ★

ONE OF THE interviews that Bishop had arranged fell on Wednesday morning and Bee joined Peter Seymour in interview room 1. Bee knew within two minutes that this person wasn't a suspect, but it still took him a further eight minutes to conclude the session and escort the man from the building.

While he was on the ground floor, Bee decided to rattle the cage of Phil Church. Bee knocked on Church's door, didn't get an answer and was about to walk away when he thought he heard a sound inside the room. He pushed the door open, and Church was sitting behind his desk, feet up on it.

"Didn't you hear me knock?"

"I was busy."

"I can see."

"What do you want Bee?"

"You told McTierney that you'd hadn't booked a tour of the caves last year, but the tech boys checked the email on the booking and it's yours, so what's going on?"

Church stood up and walked around his desk and stared out of the window. Bee thought Church was going to ignore the question, but it seemed he was weighing up how to respond. Eventually he turned back to face Bee and grunted. "Good work detective, thorough as always. Yes I did make the booking, but I did it on behalf of a friend who was coming to visit and wanted to take the tour, but then couldn't make it."

"What's your friend's name?"

"Anne, she lives in Copenhagen."

"I'll check."

"Be my guest."

"Do you have her contact details to hand?"

Church glared and strode back to his desk, pulled open a drawer, plucked a business card from it and tossed it towards Bee. "Here, knock yourself out."

Bee turned to leave, then turned back. "I've been doing some digging on this case."

He paused waiting for Church to bite, but he didn't. "Off the record, can I check that you've not been running some 'clean-up campaign', taking out the trash on the streets?"

"No. And off the record, can I say fuck off. Close the door on your way out."

★ ★ ★

McTierney parked his car in the giant car park that surrounded two sides of the hospital and reached in his pocket for the appointment card he'd been given with the details of where to find Dr. Knowles. But it wasn't there. "Damn!" he yelled as he remembered placing it flat on his laptop before he'd slammed the lid closed.

He scurried into the hospital and stopped at a giant map of the building posted to one of the walls near the retail area at the entrance. None of the ward names rang a bell for McTierney and he turned away in disgust biting his lip at the same time. Next to the map was a colour advert alerting people to the signs of autism and suggesting some ways of spotting the symptoms of the disorder in friends or family members. A strange thought crossed his mind, and he stood staring into space with his brow furrowed. At that moment a petite blonde nurse walked by and paused momentarily to check he was okay. McTierney broke out of his reverie and smiled, and the nurse continued walking. In a flash McTierney turned around and decided to follow her. Three paces along the corridor she stopped and confronted him "Can I help you?"

"In more ways than you can imagine."

"Excuse me!"

"Sorry. DS Ron McTierney," McTierney flashed his warrant card towards her.

"You're a policeman."

"Yes."

"Sorry, I thought you were a pervert."

McTierney laughed, "I've been called worse."

"What can I do for you DS McTierney," said the nurse crossing her arms.

"Three things." She looked aghast, while McTierney read her name from her badge,

"Nurse Jenkins. Number one I'm looking for Dr Knowles. I'm an outpatient and I have a check-up with the doctor following an affray in Reigate town centre when I was trying to apprehend a bag thief and got walloped across the ribs for my trouble. I was in here for 3 days, then released and now I'm back to be assessed."

"How are you now?" Nurse Jenkins looked down at his ribs in search of a sign.

"Bruised ribcage, but yes I think I'm fine."

"It must be tough on the front line."

"You have no idea."

She rolled her eyes. "What about number two?"

"I was reading this poster about autism, how common is it?"

"Not very, about 1% of the population I think."

McTierney paused mulling over another question which never arrived.

Jenkins glanced at her watch, "You said three things, what's the third?"

"I'll save it until I see you the next time."

"How do you know you'll see me again?"

"I've got a feeling I will Nurse Jenkins, and I'm prepared to take the risk."

Thirty minutes later McTierney walked back down the same corridor, this time with a greater bounce in his step, not only had he been signed off by the doctor, but he had a date for Saturday night. Now to make his morning complete he drove up to Redhill in search of the waiter who had left the restaurant so abruptly last weekend. It was a short drive into Redhill, but there was always congestion on the A23 and especially around the train station roundabout. The address he'd been given was Goldworth Road on the north side of Redhill. It was a newish estate where the developers had made the most of the land and each resident lived in arm's reach of their neighbour. He parked a few doors away and walked back and knocked on the door of number 77. There was no answer and he knocked again, Then looked through the letter box, no lights, no radio, the place looked deserted. No matter he would return.

TWELVE

"BUY ME A cup of coffee and I'll allow you to tell me how you got on with the donor goose chase yesterday."

"Do me a favour."

Bee and McTierney had arrived at the Reigate station and walked in through the rear entrance of the building. But despite his outburst Bee succumbed to the offer and the two detectives stopped for coffee. The police canteen was set in the basement and relied on three rows of fluorescent ceiling lights; the walls were painted in light neutral tones with the occasional motivational poster praising the work of the police. The serving area was organised along one side and displayed an array of food options from sandwiches to hot meals, but at this time of the morning most of the visitors wanted coffee. Hence the air was filled with an aroma of freshly brewed coffee and the hum of conversation as colleagues caught up on last night's tele.

Bee led them away from the hubbub and into a quiet corner.

"I recruited Bishop to help and together we sifted through pages of material about kidney transplants on the internet. Took us most of the day."

"But you can bundle it up into a short five-point summary."

Bee smiled, "I can. Point one, kidney transplants are a personal issue with a high degree of privacy around the involved parties, so an investigation won't be easy."

McTierney pursed his lips.

"Point two, kidney transplants are complicated; it takes time to find a match, takes time to recover, the survival rates are low."

"Didn't know that."

Bee smiled, "Point three, there are not many operations per year, about 2,500 in the UK, so we have a chance of finding our boy."

"A 1 in 2,500 chance," added McTierney.

Bee frowned, "Point four, all the operations are completed in only 20 transplant centres across the UK, which greatly improves our chances."

McTierney nodded, "Okay, a 1 in 500 chance."

"And point five, demand outstrips supply by a factor of 3 or 4 to 1, which creates the opportunity for suspicion."

"Gold star for effort, but where do we start?"

"Bishop already has. There's an endless task of cross-checking between lists. The good news is that both donors and recipients have to provide a lot of personal data to enter the programme so it's relatively easy to be sure you're got the right person. For now, I've asked her to contact all the 20 centres and collect all the names of the participants in the last two years. I'm expecting our boy's name will appear somewhere on the list."

"Go to the head of the class. Teacher Beck will be impressed."

Bee dipped his eye towards McTierney and finished his

coffee, "Instead of mocking the good work, tell me what you've been up to."

"I'll give you my theory."

"I don't think that counts as work but go on."

"I'm still leaning towards some form of gang fight or vendetta. It's the only thing that makes sense for the killer to leave the body somewhere he knew it would be found."

"Don't you think gang warnings are usually a grislier affair. It doesn't need to be a horse's head, but if you're making a statement it's typically quick, bold, and public. But this is slow, cowardly, and delayed." Bee paused as if assessing his own comment. "You may be right, but I'm not convinced it's a gang."

"Perhaps we should run the idea by Church, he ought to know if the county is on the verge of a turf war between rival drug groups."

"He ought to, but for now let's leave him out of our conversations."

McTierney screwed his face up. Bee looked around the canteen and leaned in closer to McTierney, "He lied about visiting the Barons' Cave. When you challenged him last week, he brushed it off, and yet the tech team here proved the e-mail address that was used to buy a ticket belonged to him."

McTierney's eyes widened, and Bee continued to whisper. "I confronted him with the evidence yesterday and he grudgingly admitted it and offered a flimsy excuse. I'm not saying he's the killer but there's something awry there, so I don't want to involve him anymore than is necessary, and right now it isn't necessary."

It was another morning where Bee's investigative team were spread thin and wide. He and Itzkowitz were working through the last remaining interviews with members of the public who had visited the Barons' Cave in the two years before; Bishop was engrossed in creating a spread sheet of kidney donors and recipients and McTierney trekked across Redhill in an effort to locate the elusive waiter from the Giggling Squid.

McTierney drew a blank and couldn't even find a neighbour willing to speak; Bishop created her list but felt a pang of disappointment at the shortage of Asian names on her list. On the upside it wouldn't take long to interview each of them, but she'd hoped for a bigger pond in which to go fishing. Success was also in short supply on the ground floor, where Itzkowitz and Bee spoke to twenty-five people between them without ever once ticking the box of possible suspect against any of the names.

AFTER FOUR FRUITLESS mornings all members of the team trudged a little wearily into the ops room to hear the second instalment from the forensic team. This time Tidworth took centre-stage.

"Good afternoon everyone, thank you for giving up your time, I hope you'll think it's worthwhile. We're going to share with you an identikit photo of what we think your victim looked like at the time of his demise."

The mention of the word identikit was enough to awaken the group and immediately a murmur of expectation rippled around the table. Everyone knew that a good photo of their victim would represent a significant step forward in the campaign to identify the dead body and ultimately to find his killer. Tidworth also knew the significance of the photo and allowed the buzz to rise before bringing the room back to order. "To recap, our process uses a special re-hydration solution to bring the skin back to life. It's a slow process where we submerge specimens of the damaged tissue but one that can reveal changes or markings on the surface of the tissue that would otherwise be lost."

"What's in the solution?" asked McTierney.

"Can't tell you that, it's a trade secret."

"Like Coca-Cola?"

"Something like that," smiled Tidworth, who nodded towards Kelly who in turn passed around 4 A4 sized colour images of the identikit that they had created, an additional copy popped up on the screen behind the professor.

The bubble quickly deflated, as all detectives took in the image before them; an average looking, easily overlooked Asian man of middle years with no distinguishing features.

"He's a bit dull," said McTierney. "No outstanding marks of any kind."

Tidworth lowered his gaze, "That is partly due to the process, inevitably we can only rehydrate very distinctive marks, so anything slight gets lost, but also I suspect that this face will appear more complete to someone more accustomed to seeing Asian men. I'm willing to bet that you don't meet many in this neighbourhood."

"No, we don't, fair point," added Bee. "But it's a photo, and we've been craving an image for days so this will be a great help to us." He picked up the photo, "Whoever this is, they have family, and they have friends and each of them deserve to know what happened to their loved one. And we are going to find out."

"It's something to help me when I'm sifting through the

library of missing persons, so thank you very much professor," said Bishop.

"And it will surely assist us when asking the public, a face makes a huge difference, great stuff, professor," said Itzkowitz.

Bee, Bishop, and Itzkowitz all turned to look at McTierney.

"Yep, even I can take it around to the Footlocker stores," conceded McTierney.

"Good to see that we've made a difference," said Tidworth. "I'll be packing up shortly and leaving, but I'll look out for developments in the press."

"Looks like we all know what we'll be doing tomorrow," added Bee. "But right now I need to seek out Maria and find some painkillers, my toothache is going into overdrive."

"I told you, get yourself along to a private dentist. They'll take care of your ache within a day or two."

Bee rolled his eyes at McTierney and got up to leave the room. As his colleagues left, McTierney grabbed Kelly by the shoulder, "Thought you'd like to know I've developed a theory now."

Kelly cast a sidelong glance and hurried away.

THIRTEEN

TIDWORTH HAD EARNED his fee; his work to rehydrate the face of the victim to create a usable image had revitalised the team and they all approached Friday with renewed vigour. Bee began working through Bishop's spread sheet of kidney donors and recipients, McTierney raced around his tour of the Foot Locker branches of southern England, Itzkowitz completed the final interviews with visitors to the Barons' Cave and Bishop returned to the list of missing people armed with a secret weapon, a photo.

But sometimes an enquiry needs more than enthusiasm and this case was proving to be one of those. None of the branch managers of the Foot Locker outlets recognised the face that McTierney placed in front of them, even when he shoved it into their face. As he left the last store he weighed up the futility of the task. Both the ANTA brand and each of the Foot Locker outlets specialised in two sports, basketball and running. He knew from the analysis performed by Tidworth as well as his own first hand viewing of the corpse that their victim was not tall enough to be a basketball player, at least not a very good one. That left running, maybe he should try contacting a few of the running clubs in the area and see if they've lost a runner recently. He didn't feel he was any closer to the finishing line.

Itzkowitz's enthusiasm evaporated even quicker; she had three final discussions to complete but even the additional item of the identikit image didn't spark any memories from her interviewees. Plenty of apologies, a couple of shakes of the head, but no sudden realisation that the man in the photo was Jim, or John or perhaps more likely, she struggled to think of an Asian name, hopefully he'd anglicised the name to Jake. Whatever his name was, nobody knew him.

Carol Bishop was a steady worker, she never got too involved in a case, and found it easy to leave the investigation on her desk when she got up to leave to go home, and she rarely if ever worked beyond 5pm. But this morning she felt a tremor of excitement run through her fingers as she picked up her mouse and clicked on her Excel file of missing people. Methodically she went back to her list of possibles and removed hundreds of 'impossibles' from the list when Tidworth's recreation ruled them out. Although she retained a cautious approach as the image was far from definitive, the number was getting manageable and if she applied the local geographic filter she was down to single digits.

While his team continued to pick away at the enquiry Bee sought to jump start the case and dropped down to see to Maria, Beck's secretary and asked her to get the photo issued to every local newspaper. "If you can get them to take it, and place it on a page near the front, I'll do a press conference if need be, much as I hate doing those kind of things, but we need a name to give this enquiry some impetus."

"I think the local media will lap this up, their coverage has been getting a bit stale of late, in fact some of the editorial has turned against us, suggesting we're not making much progress."

Bee looked disappointed. "Exactly the type of commentary that drives Beck crazy."

Maria nodded.

"I suppose it's too much to hope that he hasn't seen it?" Asked Bee.

Maria nodded again. "I'm afraid so."

Bee returned to his office and dived back into Bishop's analysis of would-be kidney transplant recipients. He ran his cursor down the first page, not really reading what was on the screen but stopped at the first highlighted name. Bishop had added a comment to the individual cell, 'this person dropped off the register, but has no record of ever receiving a kidney, isn't listed as continuing with her dialysis treatment and lives in Reigate – might be worth a visit.' Bee grabbed a 'Post-it' note, scribbled down the address and set off to the north side of Reigate.

He turned onto Friths Drive, high on the hill overlooking the town of Reigate, a leafy cul-de-sac where any of the properties would have estate agents salivating over the potential commission to be earned from a sale. He parked his car opposite the address he was looking for and dodged an Ocado delivery van as he walked across to the mock-Tudor house with the double garage, manicured front lawn, and mini statuette and rang the doorbell.

Bee was greeted by Sarah Rowe, who nervously welcomed the police officer into her kitchen and offered him a cup of coffee. Everywhere there were signs that this was a family home; drawings on the fridge door, a pile of children's clothes stacked on the ironing board in the corner and a Roald Dahl book open but face down on the sofa.

Bee took a seat at their island unit, "We're investigating

the death of a man last year whose body was discovered in the caves down in the town centre."

"I read about that in the news."

"At the moment we are following a number of different leads, and it would be useful to understand why your daughter's name has dropped off the waiting list for a kidney transplant."

The woman's mouth fell open, and she spluttered, but didn't answer.

Bee prompted, "I assume that she no longer requires a kidney, is that because she has acquired one."

"Things have changed a little."

But before Bee could press her for a fully answer, Mr Rowe, who had been working from home came down the stairs and marched into the kitchen. Relief washed over the face of his wife.

"Alistair Rowe, can I help?"

Bee repeated his position and Rowe allowed a smile to flicker across his face, his body relaxed, and he took control of the conversation. "Thank you for your interest inspector, but I can tell you that our daughter received a kidney from her Australian cousin who we brought over to the UK specifically for the operation."

Bee allowed the comment to dangle, hoping that either Rowe or his wife would add something to the explanation, but nobody did. He returned his gaze to Mrs Rowe who offered a thin smile which only served to convince Bee that they were lying.

"May I know the name of the cousin?"

Rowe scowled, "I don't see how this can be at all relevant. None of our family has anything to do with the death of this man you're investigating."

"You'll have to take my word that it is. Clearly there are components of our enquiry that I'm not at liberty to disclose. But I can assure that it's an important element."

Rowe didn't bite.

"Additionally, I can tell you that none of your family are under suspicion in this case, but the name would be helpful."

Rowe looked around the kitchen as if searching for an escape route from the conversation, but found none, "Joanne Shepherd, but she's already returned back to Oz."

"Thank you," said Bee, taking a moment to record the name in his notebook.

"Now if you wouldn't mind leaving us, I have work to do, as does my wife."

"Certainly sir." Bee got up from his chair and stepped towards the hallway, but stopped in the doorway, "Your daughter exited the waiting list three weeks ago yesterday, so that implies that her cousin has made a rapid recovery following her operation. I hope she continues to prosper."

He saw the colour drain from Rowe's face and knew that he would be back in this kitchen asking more questions soon.

FOURTEEN

Before Bee could return to question the Rowe family further, the weekend intruded into his investigation and not any weekend, but a Bank Holiday weekend. When Bee arrived back in the station he could sense his team winding down for the break. It happened every time there was a public holiday, he had to remind the team that they didn't work regular hours, they worked the hours they needed to work to solve serious crime and to keep the public in Surrey safe.

He brought the team together and gave the speech he had given on countless Fridays when the team were expecting an extended break. "I know this is a Bank Holiday weekend but don't forget that we have a serious murder on our hands, and we need to keep the pressure on."

There was a general groan around the room and Bee's shoulders drooped in disappointment, he knew what was coming. McTierney started the challenge, "Now we have an image of the victim, we need the general public to help us identify who he is, and they won't be around to talk to us on Monday. It'll be a waste of time."

Bee held up his hand to stop the moan becoming a clamour. "The image is going to appear in the paper and on the local news tomorrow and we need our phones manned as usual across the next few days. If someone recognises the face, they will call in, especially if they are close to the victim. The opportunity is too good to miss."

They all knew Bee was right and the noise quietened down, as he passed around a roster for the next three days.

"Obviously if we get a name, I want it circulated to this group immediately."

The team nodded their understanding.

"Consider me on call from now until we solve this murder."

★ ★ ★

SCOTT HAD DESIGNATED the Saturday as on call for both himself and Ron, although as far as Ron was concerned that was code for a day off. Scott had spent the day hunched over his laptop reading reports, reviewing interview records, and researching donor transplants on the internet. Whereas Ron had enjoyed a leisurely brunch, watched a football match on the TV over lunch and had even done some washing – anything rather than police work. None of this bothered Scott until late afternoon when he wanted to use the bathroom and found Ron was still occupying it. Eventually Ron emerged from the room. Scott narrowed his eyes as he pushed passed into the washroom. Ron was dallying in the kitchen when Scott returned.

"You've got enough spray on you to drown a sailor, Kate is going to need a gas mask."

"Not Kate anymore. We agreed to go our separate ways after her awards dinner on Tuesday."

"Oh." Scott jerked his head back. "Are you okay about it? Wait what am I saying you're like an overendowed dog. Of course, you're okay. Where are you going tonight and why all the preening?"

"To heaven. I have a hot date."

Scott rolled his eyes.

"I'm the Rizzler."

"What?" Scott frowned at the word.

"I have charisma. I bounce back, I'm not the type of person to sit at home and mope about. It's all a state of mind, you like the quiet life, but I like the high life."

Scott shook his head in bemusement. "Okay see you Monday, – but we're working on Monday, no bank holiday for you I need you on the case."

"Can't you let me off? I told you; I've got a hot date."

"No. You know the rules."

A cloud momentarily hovered over Ron's demeanour, but nothing was allowed to rain on his parade on this day.

"Who's the lucky lady?"

"Becky She's a nurse from East Surrey."

"Someone to take care of your injuries."

"Hopefully I'll be confined to bed for at least a week!"

"I can't take any more of this, just remember work on Monday."

Scott shook his head and wandered back to his laptop in the lounge and left Ron to continue his grooming ritual. One hour later Ron called out to Scott as he headed out for the evening, but Scott didn't hear him he was engrossed in his work and scribbling away furiously on his notepad. But his industry didn't prove fruitful. Scott was disappointed. Nothing shouted out at him about the case. It was like an overly wrapped Christmas present from Aunt Sylvia with no obvious way to open it – all the ends were sealed. He must have missed something, he would sit here all night and go back through the evidence, look at every photo and read every statement. He needed something to click.

Five hours later Scott was still absorbed in his work, when Ron pushed open the lounge door. "Still working?"

"Yes. Look at this." He beckoned Ron over. "I think I might have found something around this kidney donor piece we've been working on."

Scott was sitting in his favourite armchair in the lounge working on his laptop. Ron couldn't see Scott's face, but he knew from the tone of voice that he would be frowning, but then that was Scott's default look. It looked like he hadn't moved since Ron had been out, a plate and an empty glass were on the floor around him.

"I don't know why you keep pursuing this kidney transplant angle, it's a complete red-herring."

"Humour me. Bring your bottle of beer over here and read this article."

Ron moseyed into the kitchen took a cold beer from the fridge and sauntered back to lean over Scott's shoulder and started to read the article that had so excited his friend.

Under the general heading of kidney transplant, Scott had followed a trail that had led him through the causes of kidney breakdown and on to the details of the actual operation. Ron read the following, 'Recovery time varies from person to person but generally requires a full week in hospital. Complete recovery can take several weeks even months, during which recipients need to follow a strict regime of medication and attend regular check-ups. It's important to allow the body to adjust and the immune system to accept the new organ. Similar recovery times and regimes are necessary for the donor.'

"Yeah, okay so it's an intense operation."

"Keep reading."

Ron looked testy but did as Scott asked. 'Medical practitioners use medicines to suppress the immune system to prevent it from identifying the new kidney as an alien object and thereby rejecting it. But supressing the immune system makes the patient more susceptible to other diseases especially cancer, and all medicines, of which the popular examples are tacrolimus or ciclosporin carry side effects of the medication.'

He paused for breath. "With some challenging post op conditions."

"Exactly, and one that demands both parties to the transplant take it easy after the operation."

Ron still hadn't caught up, so Scott took over. "So, you shouldn't get on a plane for a twenty-hour flight to Australia, within a couple of weeks of your operation. I knew they were lying."

"Why would parents lie about their daughter's kidney transplant operation?"

"Because they've got something to hide."

"But what?"

"That I intend to discover. Perhaps it was a black-market transplant."

Ron raised his eyes.

"Looking at their house I had the impression that they were not short of a penny or two."

"So, you're suggesting that Mr & Mrs Rich became bored waiting in line to get their precious daughter a transplant and so they paid some lowlife a few quid to buy his kidney and jump the queue."

"Exactly. Now it's not easy to do, because you need a willing donor and a surgeon and his team to perform the operation, but it does happen. Money talks."

"In Nigeria."

"Maybe here as well. One of the other things I read on Google is that if you have too much dialysis you become unsuitable for a new kidney, so the clock is ticking. If you wait too long, you get timed-out. Not everyone on the waiting list for a kidney is fortunate enough to receive one. Imagine your little girl is running out of time, what would you do to give her the chance of a new life?"

Ron began to engage in the conversation and took a seat on the sofa and put his bottle down on a coaster. "When you put it like that I can understand the motivation, but it's still costly, difficult and against the law."

"Without doubt."

Ron pinched his nose and Scott could see his mind turning, then Ron offered a theory. "So, you think our boy in the cave was killed after he sold his kidney to Mr & Mrs Rich."

"It's possible."

"But why?" Ron answered his own question, "Maybe he didn't willingly agree to the transaction and threatened to turn whistleblower."

"Yes maybe."

Ron took another swig from his beer bottle, as he started to buy into the theory, "Or, he demanded more money."

"Equally possible and likely to end in the same result."

"Ah no. The dates don't work do they? Damn!"

Scott looked bemused.

"The dates, they don't work. You said the operation for Miss Rich was a few weeks ago, so our cave boy was already dead by then."

Scott grimaced at the revelation.

"Have you sat there all-night reading Google and developing your theory? What a waste!"

"Most of it. I did stop to grill myself a steak and open a bottle of Malbec." Scott dropped his head and sighed, "The bottle's in the kitchen if you want some, it's not bad."

"I know I tried it when I came back through the kitchen earlier."

Scott shook his head and mumbled something inaudible, then he closed his lap-top and put it down on the floor. "That's enough for one day." Then in a louder voice, "Pour me a glass of that Malbec if you've left any."

A couple of minutes later, Ron returned to the lounge with two wine glasses and handed one to Scott. Scott took a large gulp and turned back to his friend. "What kind of mad promises were made in the heat of the night then?"

"None. I wouldn't let her."

"Not her. You!"

The pair began to laugh. Ron broke the laughter "You know the excitement you get when you discover a new app or a video game, that buzz when you think this is going to be fun. It's like that, I love first dates."

Scott look blanky back at his friend.

"Okay, in your terms; you know the buzz you get when a new bulletin comes in from head office or when Beck says he wants a closed-door meeting with you."

Scott smiled, "Okay, I get it. Anyway, tell me, how did you two meet?"

"She found me in East Surrey Hospital reading a poster about autism."

Scott blanched, and the smile left his face "An autism poster, what on earth were you doing there?"

"It was an accident really, I stumbled on it, but it started me thinking."

"Reading and thinking in the space of a couple of minutes, are you sure it was you?"

"Ha, maybe it's not been diagnosed, but you have a lot of the symptoms."

"I don't think so; it's just we have a major enquiry on our hands, and I get a bit anxious."

"You don't even know which symptom I'm talking about."

Scott fell silent. Ron put his bottle down and lowered his voice, "I think you find it hard to express your feelings and emotions and you become anxious about upcoming social situations. You find it hard to make friends and prefer to be on own, look at this weekend."

Scott didn't reply.

"I'm not saying this to make fun. When I read the poster last week, I immediately thought of you. I'm trying to help. Becky says you've probably only got level one autism."

"You discussed me with your new girlfriend! Someone who's never met me!"

Ron squirmed in the chair, "Yes, but it's how we met. It was totally innocent."

An uncomfortable silence settled in the room. "I haven't said a word to anyone else about this."

"And please keep it that way."

"While I'm out here on this limb, I may as well tell you that you need to talk about your grief over Jess. Learn how to handle it, to share it."

"I don't want to share it," snapped Scott, "It's mine. It's all I have left of her."

"It doesn't have to be that way."

Scott sat staring at the window; he hadn't drawn the curtain and there was nothing but blackness outside, blackness and his own dark thoughts. Then suddenly whatever he'd been thinking about returned to him, he shivered and then started to speak.

"When I was a boy, my comic 'Whizzer and Chips' was delivered every Saturday morning before I was awake. Dad would bring it into my room and put it on my bed so that it was there when I opened my eyes. It remains one of the simplest and most precious memories of my childhood." He paused. "Most weeks, I would only read the stories that weren't my favourites before I got up so that I had something to look forward to when I went to bed again on Saturday night."

"I don't know whether to laugh or cry."

FIFTEEN

ONCE SCOTT AND Ron had sobered up there was no mention of the meaningful conversation they had shared on the Saturday night. The weekend continued in much the same way as it had begun; Ron relaxing and Scott working, and when he wasn't working, Scott was running around the fields that surround Outwood with Springsteen playing through his air-pods.

It wasn't until Monday that things changed; Scott and Ron shared a car to go into the office and out of the blue Scott made a statement, "It isn't that I don't like people, it's just that I'd prefer other people to take responsibility for talking to them. It's a great benefit of having you as a friend. Nobody has ever said so, but I'm sure that, in social settings at least, I must have often been perceived as rude, aloof, ignorant, odd, a combination of these, or, quite likely, much worse."

Ron turned his head and opened his mouth to speak.

"No, don't interrupt. When I've allowed myself to dwell on the subject, it can feel like quite a serious flaw, but I always seem to find something to mitigate my discomfort, an escape route seems to appear whenever I need it. Getting along with people in a social situation just isn't a priority for me at all, and I'm not very friendly in person unless I know and like someone. I won't make any more effort in a social interaction than I'm in the mood to make. I don't think it impairs the way I do my job, in fact in some ways I think it helps."

Scott paused and Ron opened his mouth again as if ready to speak but chose not to.

"And just so you know; it's Asperger's syndrome not autism, at least that's what they used to call it, now it's all just ASD."

"What's the difference?"

"Asperger's tends to be less severe, and rarely affects language ability, so I have a full vocabulary to describe you."

"Magnificent will do."

Scott shook his head. "No, I don't think so."

Their chatter was broken by a groan from Scott as his tooth woke up and joined the party.

"I don't know why you don't book an appointment with a dentist and get that fixed," said McTierney.

"There's a long waiting list at my dentist's surgery."

"So go private. You can afford it."

"I don't believe in private healthcare. It's not right that people should get better treatment just because they're fortunate enough to have more money than others."

"What? You need it to help you think clearly and that will help you crack this case. Then everyone can feel a little safer."

Bee grimaced at his partner.

"So really you owe it to the community. You'd be doing them all a favour."

McTierney continued his argument as they arrived at the station and walked into the building. Bee continued to ignore him but couldn't quite shut him out and was pleased to see Itzkowitz. She offered them a potential name for their victim, Michael Winter believed to be living in Redhill. "We've had 6 calls over the weekend and this is the only one which sounded both plausible and meaningful; two were timewasters and the others had no conviction."

"Fair enough," said Bee, "McTierney and I will go along to the town centre and see if anyone recognises the face."

The heartbeat of Redhill town centre is in fact the bustling street market which sprawls around the central paved area a short walk from the railway station. The market is alive with a vibrant tapestry of colours, sounds and smells. Tucked beneath a canopy of makeshift stalls, vendors proudly display an array of goods from exotic spices and handcrafted trinkets to fresh produce and aromatic street food. The air is thick with the symphony of impromptu bargaining, raucous laughter, and sizzling delicacies. Crowds weave through the precinct exploring the diverse offerings and absorbing the energetic atmosphere. A young boy picks up a football hat, while his grandmother feels the quality of a lavender jumper, before sniffing, tutting, and moving on. Each stall tells a story, inviting the visitor to immerse themselves in the other world of the market. Yet Bee sensed that no one would be keen to tell a story to him. At the end of the line is a stall with magazines and newspapers, Bee spotted the local paper, 'The Surrey Mirror' and bought a copy. The story he wanted was on page three; they had reproduced Tidworth's identikit photo but added their own provocative editorial bemoaning a lack of success by the police and calling for "a serious investigation' to be undertaken by The Met. Bee pursed his lips, closed the paper, rolled it up and dropped it neatly into the nearest bin. Meanwhile McTierney was deep in conversation with the owner of a cake and pastries stall. Bee's mood lifted at the prospect of McTierney developing a lead, but that evaporated rapidly when McTierney turned around and walked towards Bee with a doughnut in each hand.

"If you buy two coffees from Charlie, these will be free. Don't forget I'll have two sugars in mine."

Bee snatched the bun from McTierney's hand and went over to complete the transaction.

"Rather than stuffing your face with freebies, you could have asked him if he recognised the face."

McTierney took the paper cup from Bee, took a long draft, and said, "I did." Then he took another bite of his doughnut to make Bee wait. "And he thinks he recognises the face. He wasn't sure about the name until I offered him Winter, but then he said he thought it was Wing or maybe Winger."

Bee stood ashen faced.

"Your apology is accepted. Charlie also suggested talking to some of the taxi drivers down by the station, he thought they would likely know more."

"Good. Why don't you do you that and I continue asking questions around the market and we can meet outside McDonalds in an hour."

"Will do."

The two detectives took their different approaches and walked off in different directions seeking the one name that would help them with this case. Bee approached each stall holder in turn, introduced himself, showed the identikit photo and explained the background of the case while listening intently to the responses from the market traders.

The first fifteen vendors offered a selection of blank expressions and head shakes, a couple of 'dunnos' and a surreptitious 'sorry, no'. Bee's next target was manning the fruit and veg stall, an Asian lady who seemed to know everybody in the market. She had seen Bee coming and had moved to the other side of the large stall to keep her distance. Bee ducked behind the stall and appeared on the far side and took her by surprise. Her cheery demeanour melted away in the face of authority and Bee wondered if she had all the right permits to be operating on the street, but that was a topic for another day. He pushed the image into her hand and watched as she recoiled. Her eyes darted across to the man who was working on the same stall as her. Bee thought there had been a sudden signal between the two, but he couldn't be sure. The woman pushed the photo back and said, "No sorry, now I have to work."

The man was equally dismissive, but Bee knew he had found something. He watched as the woman busied herself around the back of the stall, another customer approached the stall and distracted the man and Bee took his moment, "You know this man don't you?"

The woman ignored Bee.

"Is he your son?"

The woman dropped the crate she had been emptying. "Please go away, I can't talk now, my boss won't allow it."

"I will but call me. I can help." Bee slipped his business card into the crate of carrots that the old woman had been handling.

★ ★ ★

TWO HUNDRED YARDS away McTierney pushed open the glass door of the waiting room come office of the Roadrunners taxi company, a place he knew well. He surveyed the scene with a kind eye; three men were slouched across two sofas, one flicking through the racing pages of that day's paper and two fiddling with mobile phones, behind the desk sat Julie who manned the phones and kept the place operating. She offered her radiant smile, the one that made him feel like he was the only person in the world. The trouble was she had already beamed that smile at three people that day. She followed it with something closer to McTierney's heart; "the kettle's just boiled if you want a brew."

He nodded his appreciation and clapped his hands to awaken his would-be audience.

"Who saw the Man United game at the weekend?"

"Ha, they were lucky to get that win and should've been beaten by Spurs on Thursday night."

"Never," argued McTierney.

"And you'll get mashed in the cup final."

"You need to be careful Dave, if you carry on talking rubbish like that I'll have to arrest you and put you in the cells for a night just for your own safety."

"Still feeling sore after that spanking you picked up at Anfield are you?"

"Last warning."

"Go on then, you must want something, what is it?"

McTierney pulled the image of the dead Asian man from his pocket and passed it around the office. "Take a good look, it's not the best image, it's been recreated from what's left of the kid we found in the caves over at Reigate."

"In a bit of a mess was he?"

"Wasn't pretty, our doctor chap reckons he'd been there for 6 months before we found him."

The first driver handed the photo to the one called Dave who handed it back, "Sorry, can't help you."

McTierney walked it over to Julie who studied the photo, she was ten years younger than either of the drivers.

"Yeah, it might be Mickey Wing."

McTierney's ears perked up, "Really? Not Winter?

The third driver sauntered over to take a look, he twisted the photo around to face him, "Yeah, it could be. But his name's not Mickey, it's something longer, he uses Mickey as a nickname."

"Do you know where he lived? Or worked or anything else about him. Right now, we don't know anything."

The girl was the first to speak. "If it's Mickey I used to see him outside McDonalds a bit. Don't know where he lived. Or where he worked, he seemed to do odd jobs."

"He just turned up out of the blue one day." It was the second driver, who McTierney didn't know well. "Don't know where he lived though, don't recall ever giving him a lift anywhere."

"Well, that's a start, I'll pop back in a couple of days in case you think of anything else." McTierney reclaimed the photo, "I'll walk over to McDonalds and see if anyone there recognises him."

As he reached for the door handle, Dave grabbed his shoulder, "Go easy over the road, it can be a rough place, especially for the law."

McTierney nodded his thanks and pulled up his jacket collar.

"And chuck a few quid on Popmaster in the 3:15 at

Ascot, he's a dead cert," added Dave as McTierney stepped out through the door.

Inside the fast-food restaurant he didn't encounter any roughness or any antagonism at all. Nobody offered any response of any kind; a few shrugs and grunts but nothing useful at all. He stepped back outside and looked at his watch Bee was ten minutes late.

When he arrived, Bee was impatient, "Let's walk back and I'll show the stall to you and maybe you can drop back sometime and speak to the woman. I'm sure she knows something. It wouldn't surprise me if this man was her son."

McTierney nodded his agreement and the pair walked back the few hundred yards into the hubbub of the market place, but as they turned the corner Bee could see that the produce stall had been closed and vacated. Bee cursed and looked to the heavens. "It was here." He said pointing at the large wooden skeleton, "I'm sure they've gone because they didn't want to talk."

A beep arrived to indicate that their What's App group had received another text from Itzkowitz, both men reached inside coats to retrieve their phones. They had the same message. 'Three callers, all anonymous, giving the name Michael Wing, one suggestion that he was a rent boy in Redhill.'

"Lovely," said McTierney.

"He's still someone's son," added Bee, and I think we've found his mother.

SIXTEEN

BY TUESDAY MORNING the general public had offered the police four different identities for the victim of the cave killing. Bee wrote them up on the ops room whiteboard in order of their popularity, at the top was Michael Wing, below was Michael Wang. Then Mike Li and finally Muchen Liang.

Bee felt compelled to add a question mark to each name.

"Julie, called him Mickey, not Michael," said McTierney. "That might be a crucial difference."

Bee scowled at him, but changed the name, "I bet his mother christened him Michael."

"Probably not if she's Chinese," said Itzkowitz sympathetically. "And interestingly Wang is the Chinese equivalent of 'King'." Her colleagues all turned to her. "It is. I knew a guy in Brooklyn one time, and he had the name Wang. He told me it meant King."

"I think we'll file that under 'interesting, but unimportant'," said Bee.

McTierney smiled and said, "And I'll file it in the waste paper bin." He then pointed at the whiteboard. "Perhaps our boy's got a police record, what with the suggestion that he's a rent boy. Right now, that would help to fill in a lot of gaps."

Bee added McTierney's suggestion to the board and

complemented it with his own; get medical records, employment records, social media profile and phone. He looked across the room at Carol Bishop offered a nervous smile and added the initials CB next to the list.

"At least we're starting to build a picture of this guy," said Itzkowitz as Bee began a list on the left-hand side of the board.

A) Return to Barons' Cave and check cancellations.
B) Ditto re new face.
C) Go back to Foot Locker outlets with identikit photo.
D) Start a door-to-door campaign around Redhill with identikit photo.
E) Go back to market and talk to produce lady.
F) Check new names on police computer.
G) Start a public appeal using the new names and identikit photo, – possible TV?
H) Go back through missing persons list with new names.
I) Go back through kidney donor list with new name.

As he got nearer to the bottom of the board Bee began to write smaller and smaller to enable him to squeeze the last item on. Then he stood back to admire the list.

"If you move your back side out of the way, maybe the rest of us can read the list," called out McTierney.

Bee duly obliged and the team read the list in silence.

"There's a lot there," said Itzkowitz.

"And the most important item of the week is football training on Wednesday night, don't forget we've got a final to play in a couple of weeks."

Bee rubbed his ear as if checking that it was still functioning, "No, that's not the most important item here, not even for you."

McTierney shrugged his shoulders, "Okay, but can we prioritise some of these?"

"The priority is finding the killer of this guy Wing, or Wang or whatever his name is. I think everything on this list is important."

Nobody felt inclined to disagree, but Bee still sensed some discomfort around the room. "Let's spend the next two and a half days tackling each of these points and then we'll have a group review on Thursday morning, when we've got a better sense of what's working and then we can perhaps drop one or two. There wasn't a lot of buy-in, but Bee pressed on.

"McTierney you're best placed to work on C, and can you take the lead on D?"

"Itzkowitz can you take points A, B, and back McTierney up on D, and have a go at a poster campaign for G?" she nodded.

"Bishop, could you pick up points F and H, plus come back to the market with me to take care of E.

"I'll take I, help out on D, and go back to the market with Bishop on E, and get the chief on board with doing something around a public appeal now we have a possible name and a face."

"When you're talking to the chief get him to free up some extra bodies to help with the door-to-door stuff or we'll have very little to show on Thursday morning."

"Will do. I think he'll be on board with what we're doing."

Bee left his team to work out their own next steps and ventured up to the top floor to put his theory to the test in the office of Chief Superintendent Beck.

Beck's office was on the top floor of the station, but it was more than the extra flight of stairs that separated it from the day-to-day police work. It was an opulent affair with mahogany furniture, subdued lighting, and a pair of recliner chairs at the end of the office positioned to look out over the centre of Reigate.

Every time he stepped into Beck's office; Bee felt inadequate. It didn't matter that the chief regularly praised his detective, Bee never felt confident in his presence. He knew he should be more assertive, but he started each meeting on the defensive and felt the discussion run away from here thereafter.

"This case has been running for two weeks now, why don't we have a suspect or even a name for the deceased? It's ridiculous."

Bee felt himself step on the familiar office merry-go-round and spent the next five minutes making excuses and offering apologies. Eventually he made his points, brought an end to the tirade from the chief and explained his need for a public appeal and more resources. Beck stood up and wandered over to the window while contemplating the request. He blew out his cheeks and walked back. "Damn shame, this cave business. But I guess we'll have to do something. Very well then."

"Thank you sir."

"But don't go crazy on the overtime, we're on a tight budget," said Beck as he reached across the table for another chocolate biscuit.

★ ★ ★

BEE DECIDED TO call for an early lunch and skipped down the stairs to collect the rest of his team on the way down. He pushed open the double doors to the canteen and caught the end of a conversation of two traffic officers who were leaving, "of course he's delighted to have Sting back, he's been in love with him since he…"

The officer blanched as he saw who was facing him but ducked his head and kept walking.

"What did he say?" asked McTierney but Bee didn't seem to have heard and didn't answer him.

The group each collected a hot meal option from the main counter and congregated around a table in the corner. McTierney was quick to open the discussion.

"I'm thinking of getting a new car, I won't have a Ford, but apart from that I'm not sure what to get. I'm bored with my Jaguar and want a change; anyone care to recommend their car? That question doesn't apply to you, boss, I've seen enough of your old heap."

Bee frowned at his colleague but didn't challenge him. It was Itzkowitz who took him to task. "You should be buying an electric car and help the environment."

"My landlord doesn't have an electric charging point."

"Don't blame me, you could always pay to have one installed."

"They ought to have charging points here at the station," added Bishop. "Come to think of it the police and all the other emergency services should be leading by example and switching over to electric vehicles."

"I'm not sure it's very practical for the emergency services. We would require a near second fleet of vehicles constantly on charge while the others are out on the roads. We'd need much more space to accommodate them all and as you know there is no room around the station to expand."

Bee's comments meet a sea of nodding, yet glum faces.

"In fact, that may be one of the reasons that the chief constable is looking at merging our station with the one over in Leatherhead."

"I didn't know that." said Itzkowitz.

"Well, you didn't hear it from me," said Bee firmly. "Although I don't think it's a secret."

"It isn't now," added McTierney.

Bee scowled across the table, "I imagine the same goes for all the other emergency services; you just never know when a vehicle is going to be needed, so each machine has to be ready to go at a moment's notice."

"Can you imagine the scene when Starsky and Hutch are in pursuit of some dastardly criminal and their car runs out of juice. How embarrassing."

"Exactly, but it doesn't stop you from making a positive step for the environment."

"But it does. You've just highlighted a key requirement for my next car. I have to be able to put my foot down and chase after a bad guy at a moment's notice."

"When did you last chase a bad guy?"

"Two weeks ago! Don't you remember coming to check on me in the hospital after some thug had clobbered me with an iron bar."

"Oh yes, how could we forget," sighed Bee.

"Have you fully recovered?" asked Bishop.

"More or less."

"His tongue has," said Bee.

"Did you get anywhere trying to identify your attacker?"

"No, I must go back to the address I was given."

Itzkowitz had dropped out of the conversation for the last few minutes and was Googling something on her phone. "It seems all the police forces are struggling to adopt electric vehicles; it says here that across the UK the police operate 30,000 vehicles, that includes cars, vans, bikes, everything and the number of electric ones is less than 3%."

"Wow," said Bishop.

"That was the picture last year, so it may have changed a bit."

"It won't have changed much," said Bee.

"We're not the worst force though, Kent has that honour, it has only 10 vehicles."

"I remember watching a programme about it some while ago, I think it was on Panorama it was comparing the UK against China. It claimed we have a highly expensive, yet poorly designed power grid that is not fit for purpose whereas China have more charging point stations than regular fuel stations. They're building hundreds a week."

"When the Chinese set their mind on something, they do get on with it."

"All very interesting but none of this helps me decide on a new car."

"Stick with the Jag – it's a nice colour."

SEVENTEEN

WITH A PLATE overflowing with potential leads it was essential that someone should make a fast start. Itzkowitz, with her can-do approach was the ideal person to have on the team and she decided to tick off two of the actions assigned to her that afternoon. She arranged to meet Julia Crampton of the Wealden Cave Society at the station to clarify the outstanding issues relating to the Barons' Cave.

The best thing that could be said about the subsequent interview was that it didn't take long, but even at 30 minutes it wasn't worth the time and certainly not worth the tea and biscuits she had given to her guest.

Crampton had politely explained three things to Itzkowitz; firstly, that on visitor days it was common practice to print off a list of expected visitors, but they didn't collect a list of non-attendees. Most people turned up, some didn't. "We've got their money, what do we care, we're only volunteers." It was perfectly possible that someone bought a ticket and didn't turn up. Itzkowitz smiled as she wrote her notes, this wasn't a disaster, but if it came to court this wouldn't suggest a watertight process.

Secondly, if the booker ordered multiple tickets her group only kept the email address of the booker, there would be no record of the other attendees. Itzkowitz stopped writing

THE CAVE OF DEATH

and helped herself to a stick of gum. Thirdly, if a tour isn't full and someone turned up out of the blue and offered to pay cash, then it would be gratefully accepted, and the unexpected visitor would remain unknown to the world.

Of course, why wouldn't they, the society ran on a shoestring. Itzkowitz crossed out all that she had written. And the icing on the cake was that Crampton didn't recognise the face that Professor Tidworth had re-created. No matter how she looked at it, Itzkowitz knew this lead was in a blind alley.

★ ★ ★

MCTIERNEY'S HEART WASN'T in the task of re-visiting all the Foot Locker outlets with the new identikit photo. He knew it would be a wild goose chase and he was fairly sure that Bee would agree, at least in private if not in public. He decided to make a couple of calls and then ambush Bee with the 'waste of time' plan when he was relaxing. The challenge would be finding a time when Bee was relaxing.

The next question was which of the branches to visit, he flicked through the list, Oxford Street – no, too busy, Brent Cross – no, too much traffic, Sutton – that store had an attractive manageress, but in the end he settled for the Bluewater store. If he remembered correctly there was an HMV store in the shopping centre. McTierney had several addictions, one of the more acceptable was his addiction to vinyl records, although when friends discovered that this invariably meant heavy metal records a few deemed it totally unacceptable. But that didn't matter to McTierney, he had started to rebuild his vinyl album collection, and this was a good opportunity to increase it further. He needed something to counter the growing omnipresence of Springsteen who seemed to be a permanent fixture on Bee's Spotify playlist.

★ ★ ★

McTierney knew he had to take the door-to-door campaign seriously. A door-to-door campaign organised by the police involved officers systematically visiting residencies in a specific area to gather information related to an investigation. Officers would politely approach residents and inquire about any observations. The objective being to gather an eyewitness account of the incident, as a bonus a strong and proactive approach featuring direct engagement with the community would often build trust.

McTierney and Itzkowitz sat in the canteen and started mapping out the brief; they allocated a few officers and drafted a couple of opening questions before McTierney threw his pen down on the table. Itzkowitz raised an eyebrow. McTierney grimaced. "The problem we have is a combination of a bland generic photo and a name with four variations, no one is going to be able to help us."

"I know it's a shitstorm" said Itzkowitz, "but the boss is doing his best."

McTierney let out an exasperated sigh.

"Could you do any better?"

"I want to work in and then manage a team where I can dictate the philosophy. Can't be too high up the organisation. A team that works together and helps each other but one that enjoys the process and doesn't take itself too seriously, a group of people who can and will take the mickey out of each other and will keep their collective feet on the ground. A group of people who are happy to drink a beer together on a Friday night after work but who will also muck in and help each other when there is a deadline. No room for anyone to be pompous."

"Doesn't sound like any police force I know."

"I can't help being a visionary."

Itzkowitz rolled her eyes "Meanwhile back on planet earth, how do you see this campaign working?"

"We should focus this around the Asian and Chinese communities in the area."

"Is there a Chinatown in Redhill."

"Not the sort that you're used to seeing. But we can focus on the cheaper housing areas. Mostly around the railway station and either side of the main London Road as it passes through Redhill."

Together they produced a set of questions and compiled a list of the streets to cover and assigned them to the three officers that had been made available for the campaign. They concluded with a couple of streets each and nominated Wednesday as the day to execute the plan.

McTierney gave himself Baxter Avenue and Fairfax Avenue situated alongside the railway line as it cut a swathe between Rehill and Reigate. He recognised that it was the closest assignment to the station, and he hoped it would be suitably quiet. The two roads combined to make a rectangle and McTierney sniffed as he reached the halfway point; he wasn't sure if it was the faint smell of diesel that irritated his nose or the selection of dog turd that he carefully stepped around as he negotiated the broken pavement. Thus far he'd received every variation of "no, nope, no way, and never seen him before, mate," that he considered it possible to say. He pulled his coat a little tighter as a gentle breeze flexed its muscles and pretended to be a gale. Two used Costa Coffee cups raced across the road towards a group of garages where an old Ford Escort stood, partially jacked up and with one wheel missing on the driver's side.

McTierney turned his head to try and make out a colourful image left by a street artist but gave up and began counting the number of Sky dishes visible. There seemed to be more dishes than there were houses. 15 more addresses to call on and then he could head back to the station. The next door was a part wood, part glass combination where the wood had recently been painted a deep shade of purple and the painter had allowed some of the paint to dribble across the glass. He knocked on the glass and took a step back. A short lady with jet black hair opened the door and looked him up and down. Once McTierney had explained his visit and she had looked at his badge the woman launched into a rant about the police. McTierney gave her 30 seconds and then moved on to her next-door neighbour, where the colour scheme had jumped to black. Both the front door and the carpet in the hallway.

The occupant was another woman, a few years older than her neighbour with similar Asian features. She took the photo in her hand and began to speak. McTierney knew he should listen to what the woman was saying but he found his attention wandering. He couldn't help it; he had a low boredom tolerance and there was a lot of repetitive police work which he found boring. You asked people questions, they said, 'no sir, I can't help you' and you moved along to the next person. You only needed to pay attention when they said 'yes, – I do know that man', and if that happened, you invariably asked a follow up question, so you could listen to the detail on the second pass.

Besides this woman could bore for England – she had switched her brain to broadcast and hadn't paused for three minutes. How could she say so much? And then suddenly she stopped. McTierney cursed in his head, had she said, 'yes' or 'no'? He didn't want to listen to the whole tirade again. He was contemplating the best option when the woman took the initiative.

"Did you hear what I said? I think this is Mickey. I haven't seen him for a while, but he used to keep his bike in that garage over there, the one with the graffiti across the door." The woman pointed to the garage McTierney had been staring at. "He put that mess on the door – little bleeder. Someone ought to clean it off."

★ ★ ★

AT FIRST GLANCE one of the simplest tasks on Bee's list was the checking of the new names on the police computer, made slightly more complex by the potential variation of the surname. But the thing about computers is that they remove the variables, they are binary machines which work in the definitive; when it asks for a surname, you can't type 'it might be X or it might be Y', You can only enter one name and in this case 'Wing' was the name entered by Bishop. The name generated 22 responses, and once filtered down to Michael, Mickey, or Mike this reduced to two, but neither response came anywhere near to the description she was hoping to find. She repeated the process with variations of the name including Wang, Li and even Muchen Liang but with less success. It seemed that Michael Wing if that was his name was unknown to the police before now.

The same principles and approach applied to Bishop's search through the list of missing persons. To no great surprise she produced the same answer. She started to wonder if Wing had completed slipped through the net or whether he had only been in the country for such a sort time that he hadn't made it on to any list. She jotted down a note to herself to search the register of births to see if he could be found there, but before she could contemplate the size of the task, Bee called her to discuss how they would approach re-visiting the market in Redhill.

★ ★ ★

BEE HAD CLEARED the idea of a new public appeal with Beck who thought the idea might re-energise the few mediocre leads that Bee had presented. The benefit of Beck's support meant that the station would throw everything at the campaign as Beck liked the idea of speaking to his public. Hence he had instructed his secretary Maria to orchestrate the programme, and she was busy organising social media, a new press release and the icing on the cake another press conference. The principal challenge revolved around which details to disclose and which to hold back, not least was the problem of the precise name of the victim. Opinions were split on whether they should offer the public a selection of names, a game of multiple choice as McTierney expressed it, or focus on one single name, as Bee preferred. Maria raised her eyebrows and determined to give the decision to Beck. Within a couple of days, she had the campaign prepared and ready to go. The key decision was when to press the button. Maria was acutely aware that the town was feeling nervous about the idea of a killer on the streets and that a dose of re-assurance from the chief superintendent would be both appreciated and critical to encouraging people to come forward. She hoped that the decision to make the radio broadcast at tea-time on Friday wouldn't get lost amongst the plans being made for the weekend.

★ ★ ★

BEE HAD EXPECTED his team to challenge his decision to add kidney donor to their list of priorities and it was this fear that had driven him to assign it to himself, that was probably the same reason why no one had complained about it. Bishop had unearthed another name for him of a local girl who had dropped off the donor waiting list without getting a new kidney, at least not officially and this time the dates fitted with their timeframe, and it was another Reigate address.

Bee pulled up outside the house in Manor Road. An imposing brick-built five-bedroom property, it was set back from the road with a semi-circular drive which allowed cars to pull in from one direction and leave by another without the faff of reversing. The house had been re-furbished, Bee tried to remember the façade before the upgrade but couldn't. Manor Road wasn't a street where the police had cause to visit very often. As Bee parked his car on the loose gravel drive he imagined the owners looking down at his weather-beaten Mercedes and believing that it had been abandoned on their drive. The doorbell boomed and brought a petite brown-haired woman to the door who was dressed ready to go to lunch and greeted Bee with a Colgate smile. Bee presented his credentials and was welcomed into a spacious and modern kitchen where he was offered a fresh coffee from the percolator sitting on the counter.

Bee took a sip of the coffee, pulled out his notebook and started the conversation; "I'm investigating the death of a man last year whose body was discovered in the caves in the town centre."

"I can't imagine that has anything to do with us."

"Maybe not but at the moment we are following a number of different leads, and it would be useful to understand why your daughter's name has dropped off the waiting list for a kidney transplant."

The woman's eyes bulged, and the rest of her body froze, all her earlier chattiness evaporated.

Bee continued, "I assume that she no longer requires a kidney, is that because she has acquired one."

The woman swallowed heavily, "We haven't done anything wrong inspector, I think I'd like you to leave now."

"This is a murder enquiry, and I need answers. We can either do this with a discreet off the record chat here, or I can caution you, take you to the station and you can have a solicitor join us but you would have to face the same questions."

The woman looked aghast, pulled her hands to her face, and flopped down on one of the high stools that surrounded her kitchen island worktop. Bee took another sip of coffee and allowed her a couple of minutes to come to the right decision. She started to whimper, and Bee thought that it wouldn't be long. Another couple of minutes and she brushed away some tears, wiped her hands on her designer jeans, took a deep breath and started to speak.

"Penny has suffered from liver problems all her life. She has more hours of dialysis than she's had days at school. The doctors said that her systems were being weakened by the process and that she needed a transplant quickly, but she's a rare blood type and they couldn't find a suitable donor. We had to do something. So, we did. We found a doctor who would help her jump the queue. It saved her life. It's no different from having private medical care and getting knee surgery ahead of time. People do that all the time. I don't think we've broken any laws but to tell you the truth I don't care if we have. Penny probably wouldn't be here now if we hadn't done something. If I was faced with the same situation again, I'd make the same choices. As a parent, it's your duty to do your best for your child."

Bee thought back to his own daughter and knew that he would have given anything to save her. He was relieved that he hadn't been faced with this kind of dilemma.

"I understand your position Mrs Trimble, all I want from you are the details of the doctor you used to organise the surgery."

EIGHTEEN

A ROUND THE SAME time Bee had invited Bishop up to his office to share his plan for speaking to the woman he'd seen at the fruit and veg stall in Redhill market. Despite her initial reticence Bee had encouraged and finally persuaded Bishop to help. She would walk up to the stall and buy some pears, then with the woman off-guard she'd ask her about the missing man. It wasn't a complex plan.

Bee had parked in the multi-storey carpark on top of The Belfry shopping centre and together with Bishop they walked down the stairs and through the arcade on their way to the market. Bee noticed that Bishop's pace was slow and slowing further, she had her head down and wasn't speaking. As they passed through the automatic doors at the exit Bishop looked up at him with puppy-dog eyes.

"Are you okay?" asked Bee.

"I'm not comfortable doing this. I know it's an important case and all that but suppose something goes wrong. Suppose I mess it up."

Bee reached out to touch her sleeve and forced himself to look at her, "You won't. I'll be there if anything goes awry. You know I'll always have your back."

Bishop offered a weak smile and took a step forward but stopped again.

"Okay deep breath. Let's do this." She marched toward the market stalls leaving Bee in her wake.

The Redhill open market sits in the centre of the pedestrianised area at the cross of Station Road and the High Street and stretches for sixty yards in each direction. The stall they were targeting was ten yards along Station Road, Bee took a position on the junction and lent against the façade of the Lloyds Bank, he pulled out a bottle of carbonated water from his jacket pocket and took a sip while watching the action. He never used the market, he remembered being taken to a market in his home town of Northampton by his mother, she loved the bustle of the place and he'd enjoyed those days, probably more so because he was with his mother than being at the market. These days he distrusted the place; it had lost its charisma for him. The advent of food regulations had made him doubt the quality and freshness of the food on sale, for him the home delivery service of Ocado met his needs perfectly.

Bishop approached the old woman who was heavily layered against the cold, but her hands were free and weathered, she offered a welcoming smile to Bishop and the pair quickly began chatting. A paper bag of pears was passed across the stall and soon followed by another with broccoli. Bee smiled at the exchange and strained his ears to hear the conversation but couldn't pick up anything. A third bag followed, peaches this time and a fourth, carrots. Bee's smile faded, what was happening? Had Bishop bottled it and was now doing her weekly shop? He slipped his phone into his shirt pocket, but before he could move, the shopping stopped and was replaced by an earnest conversation. Bee couldn't hear the words, but he could read the expressions; concern and empathy leapt from face to face. Bishops laid her paper bags on the stall and walked around the side to meet the woman who seemed to be crying, they embraced. Bishop pulled the old woman close and slowly turned her around until she could see Bee and beckoned him over. He stepped forward but reluctant to break up the couple, he stood there embarrassed. Bishop smiled weakly at him and then pulled herself away from the woman. "This is my colleague Inspector Bee, tell him what you just told me, he can help you."

The woman dragged her sleeve across her face to wipe away her tears, sniffed and shuffled her shoulders as she looked Bee up and down working out whether or not she could trust this man. She decided she could.

"The photo is my nephew, little Mickey." Bee winced at the name, knowing that McTierney would brag about getting the name right. "He went missing last September. He was here one day then gone the next, no one knows what happened to him, but I know it was something bad. I can feel it. Is it true what she says that he's dead? Say it's not true."

Bee blanched at being faced with the stark truth. He didn't need to answer, the woman read his face and burst into tears. Bee stood dumbfounded. He glanced around the market, his undercover operation was starting to attract attention, people turned their heads to see what was happening. Out of the corner of his eye he caught sight of a young boy soaking up what was happening and then running off to a doorway further along the street. He thought he darted into an alleyway or an opening somewhere beyond the Costa Coffee shop. A lookout he supposed.

"Don't worry, we can find out what happened to him. I

have friends who can help. Lots of friends."

The woman grabbed the sleeve of Bee's coat and said, "Promise me you'll find the person who did this. My little soldier, he didn't deserve this, he's always been a good boy, worked hard at school. He came for a better life, we all did, but what did we get? This…" The woman looked around the precinct and shook her head. Bee didn't know how to respond.

"His mother is sick and still in China, promise me you will find out what happened."

"We will, you have my word. Can I ask you to tell Carol everything you know, and we'll take it from here."

Bee nodded towards Bishop and let the women talk. He wanted to be ready to intercept whoever the boy had gone to fetch. He didn't have to wait long. The young lad he had seen burst back out from the doorway he had disappeared into followed by the heavy-set man; Bee had seen at the market stall the other day. The boy pointed towards the fruit and veg stall and Bee watched the man march purposefully across the street and steeled himself for the encounter.

"We don't want you here. Get away!"

Bee raised his hands and faced the man directly, "We're the police, we're here to help." Bee fumbled for his badge and presented it slowly to the man, who paused to read the name.

"I don't care Copper; we don't want you around here. We've done nothing wrong. Leave us alone and go away."

Then he turned his attention to the old woman, and spoke firmly in a foreign tongue, the woman bowed her head and stepped away from the stall without a word. Next he waved at the young lad and with a simple click of his fingers the boy ran forward and began packing up the stand. The man grabbed a couple of crates and began packing away the fruit and vegetables acting as if Bee wasn't there. He offered a phrase of encouragement to the boy, but Bee didn't understand what was said.

Bee could see that within a couple of minutes the whole stall would be cleared, and his potential witness disappeared and gone. He had to do something.

"Sir, excuse me, sir."

The man continued to pack away carrots, oblivious to Bee's protestations.

"Sir, we can help."

The boy had packed three quarters of the produce onto a wheeled trolley, it would all be disappearing in a matter of minutes.

Bee took a sharp intake of breath. "Sir, stop, or I'll arrest you." Bee thought the man paused for a second, perhaps considering the threat but quickly returned to his task.

"I believe you are obstructing us, the police, in our duty as we investigate the murder of a young man. If you continue to ignore me, I will have no choice but to arrest you."

It would be a gamble, but Bee supposed that the man didn't have a solicitor to hand. If he could get him down to the station for a few hours it might give him or Bishop the opportunity to make some progress with the old woman, and who knows, maybe he could make this man see sense and co-operate.

The man turned back to face Bee with a battle-weary expression on his face, Bee interpreted it as surrender and took his chance. "You've had your warnings, now I'm placing you under arrest."

NINETEEN

BEE HAD EXPECTED the Chinese man to put up a fight after he'd been arrested, but instead he sat quietly in the back of Bee's car chuntering away in Mandarin. Bee felt convinced that he was calling to some dark spirits with the objective of setting a curse on him, Bishop, and the entire police force. But as they marched him down to the first empty cell no evil spirit had yet appeared.

Bee bounded up the stairs and found McTierney at his desk, where he was drafting a warrant to search the garage. "McTierney, I need a favour."

"No can do. I need to get this warrant issued. I think we've discovered where this Mickey lived."

"Have you?" Bee looked disappointed, but quickly recovered himself. "Excellent, but that will have to wait. Bishop and I have found his aunt and I think she's ready to talk."

Bee lifted McTierney out of his seat and escorted him downstairs, giving him the brief as they walked. "Use your legendary people skills and see if you can unlock this guy. He won't speak to me; he hates me for interfering with his family and that's before we think about his reaction to being brought back to the station. He might be scared; he's probably hiding something or he's mistrusting of authority or a bit of all three. Have a chat with him put him at ease and see what you can discover. Give him a few of your biscuits. But don't release him for 24 hours, I need as much time as possible to find the woman who says she's the aunt of our victim. She disappeared when this chap came running. I'll call you when I get something. Friday's beers are on me."

With that Bee slapped his colleague on the back and sped off out of the back door.

At last, McTierney smiled. But the smile didn't last long. He took the prisoner up to the first interview room and fetched them both a coffee. He stood the plastic cups on the table and looked across at his adversary. The man had a bulbous red face which made McTierney think of a boxer, a bad boxer with thinning black hair, jet-black eyebrows and a cauliflower left ear. This could be a long bout.

McTierney read the man his rights, explained the case they were investigating, cracked a joke, threatened him all to no avail. The man had a full repertoire of shrugs, grunts, and glares but not a single useful word passed his lips. During the silence McTierney's mind wandered. He was irritated that he'd been asked to babysit this lump of Chinese granite. He wanted to pursue his own part of the case. He had slogged around for the best part of two weeks following lost causes and now as soon as he'd discovered the victim's garage, an Aladdin's Cave of possibilities, here was Bee pulling rank on him and dumping this crap on him. Sod that! He knew this guy wasn't going to say anything useful. He'd give him his phone call and pass him back to the desk sergeant so he could continue with his warrant. Imagine Bee's face when he brought in a major lead from this garage. What might he find? Stolen goods, drugs, cash, weapons the possibility was endless. But before he could do any of that he needed to offload this loser.

McTierney decided that the interview from hell was a development opportunity for Itzkowitz, so he stepped out of the room and went to find her. He visited her desk on the first floor, then scoured the upper floors all without success. Then kicked himself for not starting in the canteen, but that too was devoid of the American officer, but he did meet Church.

"Have you seen Itzkowitz?"

"Not recently. Why?"

"There's a silent Chinese guy in the cells that Bee brought in. He's not saying a word to anyone, I'm not even sure if he can speak English. Bee wants someone to find out if he's connected to the cave-boy case."

"Mind if I take a look?"

"Be my guest."

The pair walked up from the basement to the interview rooms and Church took the chance to casually ask McTierney how the case was progressing. McTierney readily told him about his garage discovery before he remembered Bee's words of caution, as they arrived at Interview Room 1 he clammed up, but Church didn't seem to notice.

The room had a two-way mirror which allowed officers to watch the interview without the participants being aware. McTierney took Church into this adjacent room to show him the Chinese man as he told him about Bee's wish to keep the man off the streets for 24 hours.

"Don't suppose you know him do you? You who knows everybody in the town."

Church smiled at the empty flattery, "No, I can't say I do."

But when McTierney returned to the room he felt sure he'd seen a flicker of recognition in the face of the Chinese man when he spotted Church enter. McTierney left the pair together and made his way back to his desk. But as he got to the corner of the corridor a thought knocked on his mind and he tip-toed back to the surveillance room. He stared through the one-way mirror at the exchange that was taking place. It looked like the two were talking. He reached for the volume button and turned it up just in time to catch a few words, "and say nothing." Church had advised the man to say nothing. Suddenly it seemed that Church did know him, but less than five minutes ago he'd denied any knowledge of him.

McTierney hadn't been able to ascertain who owned the garage with the colourful graffiti, when he was on the street but in the scheme of things that didn't matter much. With a shiny new warrant in his hand the police would force entry and presumably the owner would come running and screaming and they would waive the warrant in his face and tell him it was a murder investigation and would he like to assist their enquiries down at the station. That would shut him up. So, when McTierney arrived at the question on his warrant application asking for the name of the property owner, he typed in Smith.

Bee took thirty minutes to complete his task of delivering the Chinese stall owner to the police station, briefing McTierney and returning to the scene. He ran across from the car park at the railway station to find Bishop loitering outside the bank where he had stood before. As he approached he saw that she was shaking and biting her lip.

"Sorry I think I've messed up." Bishop kept her head down and couldn't look at Bee.

"Why? What happened?"

She peered up at him, saw that he looked anxious and quickly dropped her head. "Just after you left, another Chinese man arrived and spoke to the woman and the young lad who was here, and then everyone scattered."

Bee looked at her, trying to hide his disappointment but didn't say anything.

Bishop felt he needed a fuller explanation and continued to utter incoherent statements. "In different directions. It all happened quickly. I started to follow the woman but thought the man might be more use. But then I couldn't find him. I came back and the woman had gone too. I'm sorry I don't know where any of them went."

Bee's jaw dropped; they'd managed to lose every one of their possible witnesses in the space of half an hour. They'd snatched defeat from the jaws of victory. He looked up and down the four boulevards that led away from the paved junction where they'd been standing. There was no large neon sign to tell him which way to go. Damn! He rubbed at his eyes, and avoided Bishop's face, he didn't know what to say to her. They stood together for thirty seconds which seemed like thirty minutes to each of them. At last Bee blew out his cheeks,

"Let's recap on what we learned. The boy went to fetch someone from a flat or something up there." He spun and pointed along one of the avenues.

Bishop nodded, still unable to string words together.

"Let's see if there's anyone there now."

Together they walked the two hundred yards along the street until they arrived at the doorway which Bee believed to be the one where he had seen the boy and the older man emerge. He rang the bell and hammered on the door. Nobody answered. He tried the door handle, it was locked. "I'll get a warrant tomorrow, we'll come back then." Bishop nodded.

"Last throw of the dice. Let's talk to the other stall holders and see if anyone can offer any light on our elusive fruit and veg seller. If that doesn't work then tomorrow you can contact the local council and find out who issues licences for these stalls, and we'll get a name and address from them."

For the first time in fifteen minutes Bishop smiled and they walked back to talk to the other vendors. Nobody offered any useful information. Eventually, Bee called time on their pursuit, this woman, or aunt wasn't going to be found. He wanted to remain positive but couldn't escape the feeling that they were on the verge of a break-through but had allowed it to slip through their fingers. But at least they still had the taciturn Chinese man back at the station. It wouldn't be easy to get him to talk but perhaps Bee could explain the situation to him in a way that might encourage him to talk. As he said goodnight to Bishop and walked into the station, he consoled himself with the thought that a few quiet hours might have inspired the man to co-operate. When the desk sergeant informed him that Church had released the man he hit the roof.

TWENTY

WHEN THE TEAM congregated on Thursday morning there was a buzz of excitement in the air. Each person knew that they were on the verge of cracking the case; after what had seemed like weeks in the detecting desert they had finally stumbled on an oasis of leads, and each felt that a happy conclusion was within reach. Hence everyone wanted to speak and to present their own private success. The sense of anticipation was palpable, and the belief radiated around the room. it wasn't a common experience in the ops room of Reigate police station. The cacophony of the different conversations grew until Bee clapped his hands to draw a close to it. Everyone stopped except Itzkowitz who rattled off the conclusion of her story.

"...and most amazing of all, my friend told me that yesterday was the first day when all six escalators were working in Redhill Sainsbury's."

"You're making that up – there's always at least one undergoing some form of maintenance," said McTierney.

"Not that you ever see the people doing the maintenance," added Bishop.

"Can we get back to the case in hand?" asked Bee. "We make the most progress we've made since the case opened and all you three want to do is talk about the damn supermarket."

His three colleagues all looked admonished and turned their faces to the front with a smattering of apologies.

Bee moved to the front of the room and cleaned a space on the white board. "Let's summarise what we think we've learnt so far this week. McTierney I know you were happy with your discovery on the house to house so why don't you kick us off?"

One by one each of the team relayed their personal adventures of the past two days, there was so much detail that Bee's arm began to ache with all the scribbling, and he traded places with Itzkowitz, although the rest of the group complained about her handwriting. But 90 minutes later they had a full board and most importantly a name for their victim, Mickey Wing.

Bee resumed his position as task leader, "With a name we can do things, lots of things let's get cracking. I want details on his bank account, his mobile phone, his work life, social life, his love life. That will do for a start although we may get some of those answers when we get the warrants through to search the flats in Redhill and the garage on Baxter Avenue."

Around the table there was a moment of collective back slapping.

"In light of the progress we've made this week, allow me to buy you all a coffee in the canteen," offered Bee.

"And cakes?" asked McTierney.

"Do you ever give your stomach a rest?" said Bishop.

"And cakes," said Bee.

No sooner had the group taken their seats in the corner of the canteen than Bee saw Church push open the main door, jut his head inside and scan the room. As soon as he spotted Bee he withdrew his head and let the door swing. Bee had been saving his ire for Church and was up in an instance to follow him. He caught him on the second flight of stairs leading up from the canteen.

"Church. Tell me why did you release my prisoner yesterday, when I and then McTierney left express instructions that he should be retained for the maximum 24 hours."

Church turned slowly and rolled his eyes, "This isn't your private prison, you can't detain innocent people on a whim, you need a reason, some evidence. Didn't they teach you anything at detective school."

"You know we're investigating a murder here, and you also knew that he might be an important associate of our victim. He could have helped us understand the man's background. This case has been tough enough already."

"Don't blame me for your inadequacies."

"There's nothing inadequate in my team." Bee spat the words at Church. "I've a good mind to report you for obstructing our enquiry."

Church took a step back and sneered at Bee. "Piss off. I don't work for you. If you can't control your team don't come crying to me. I report to Beck and Beck alone."

"Are you sure he's the only one?"

"What's that supposed to mean?"

"You know exactly what it means."

Church took a step forward and stopped in front of Bee's face and prodded his lapel.

"You want to be careful, inspector, that quick wit of yours could get your lights punched out."

Bee's nostrils flared as he pushed away Church's finger, he clenched his fist but before he could strike a group of traffic officers filed out of the canteen doors and onto the stairs, their chatter evaporated, and they stopped abruptly as they took in the sight in front of them.

Both Bee and Church took a step back from each other, traded glares and Church turned and walked up the stairs leaving Bee to smile weakly at the officers as they continued on their way.

★ ★ ★

LIKE RED BUSES the two warrants they had wanted both arrived at the same time and Bee decided to split his team; he took Bishop to search the two flats that sat above the printing and copying shop on Station Road, Redhill and left McTierney and Itzkowitz to strongarm their way into the garage on Baxter Avenue. The two properties were less than half a mile apart and it was easy to conceive that they could be linked.

McTierney opted to bring along a couple of uniformed officers to his search as he anticipated that there could be an adverse reaction to the garage being forced open, but in the end nobody came to the show. The first officer took a set of bolt cutters to the lock and then slowly pushed up the steel door, it creaked as it moved, suggesting it hadn't been opened for a while. The team were hit by the odour of stale air, McTierney brushed the smell away from his nostrils. a shaft of sunlight flashed across the floor and illuminated a dilapidated wooden wardrobe resting against the backwall and an old pine chest of drawers.

McTierney plucked a pair of purple forensic gloves from his pocket and tossed another pair towards Itzkowitz. "Better use these in case we find anything significant."

THE CAVE OF DEATH

She nodded her agreement, then her attention was caught by a rustling at the back of the garage, a rat scampered across the concrete floor, stopped to look at the intruders then darted through a small hole in the side wall to the next garage.

"Maybe we'll need something stronger than these," said Itzkowitz holding up the purple gloves.

"No, they won't go for your hands, they'll shoot up your trouser leg," replied McTierney with a laugh.

"Don't say that."

Itzkowitz nudged McTierney in the back and allowed him to take the first steps, "Come on, this is your baby."

He stepped forward, narrowly avoided a large oil stain on the concrete floor and brushed away some cobwebs from around the wardrobe and pulled open the door. A number of garments hung on hangers in the wardrobe, he flicked through them with a disinterested hand, then scowled and turned on the torch on his mobile phone for a closer look. "Wow. Hey, come look at these." Itzkowitz joined him at the door and together they gawped at a row of fanciful costumes that could have been worn in sex games. Below these on the shelf at the bottom of the wardrobe lay a couple of whips, and a box of sex toys.

"That's a bit more like it. This makes it worth filing the paperwork for the warrant. Bee's never going to find anything this good in his crappy flat."

Itzkowitz picked up a pot of lubricant and a crimson red wand, she turned it around in her hand, and offered it to McTierney, "How would you use this?"

"Don't know, never had to resort to these kind of things. But I'm looking forward to seeing Bee's reaction."

"It seems our little poor boy victim, wasn't so innocent after all."

"Not many men are innocent."

Itzkowitz rolled her eyes, "Why do men feel the need to pay for sex?"

"Maybe they were lonesome and in need of comfort."

"That's a bit out of character for you," said Itzkowitz lowering her gaze.

"Just for the record, I don't frequent brothels."

"No, I meant getting all poetic on me."

Itzkowitz left McTierney and his imagination to wander and turned to a pile of boxes on the side. She pulled a sheet of tarpaulin away from some junk leaning against the side wall and exposed half a dozen framed paintings, some large, some small, all marked with the initials MW, and a couple of tatty mattresses. Meanwhile McTierney had more luck with the chest of drawers revealing a kilo of amphetamines, a knuckle duster, a box of photos, and a locked box. Itzkowitz peered over his shoulder. "We've cleaned out the Vegas jackpot here."

Meanwhile half a mile further toward the town centre Bee pressed the buzzer rather than begin with the battering ram and was relieved when a woman answered the call. But his optimism was short lived. The staircase led up to two small, aged, and battered flats. One flat housed an Indian family, the other a Chinese family, although Bee doubted whether all the residents were related. There was a strong smell of curry, and some other foodstuff Bee didn't recognise. Both odours permeated across both flats and mingled in an unsavoury combination at the top of the stairs which irritated his nose. Bee left an officer in the second flat to deter the residents from dumping anything incriminating and started his search in the Chinese flat. It was a tortuous process, the rooms were jam packed with stuff, ornaments, boxes, books, clothes, plus some packaging that would suggest they were wholesalers of fruit and veg. As he moved into the first bedroom a huge oil painting of the Hong Kong harbour caught his eye and while distracted he stepped on a label from a big bag of carrots. He was convinced there was a connection between the inhabitants and the fruit and veg stall but when he questioned them, nobody admitted anything. None of the individuals he'd seen the previous day were in the flat, in fact he didn't recognise any of the occupants, and to complete the picture of innocent and ignorance none of them recognised the photo of Mickey Wing. He left Bishop and another officer to complete the search and walked down the corridor to the second flat.

Again, the place was overloaded with junk and mess. *Didn't these people ever put anything away?* There seemed to be more people than it was possible to accommodate in the place. Bee wondered if he had arrived during a mid-afternoon party of some description. The icing on the cake for him was the noise, everyone seemed to be in the midst of a long conversation while the TV had the volume turned up to loud in one room competing with a radio blasting out of another room. Bee suspected it had all been orchestrated to deter the police. Unfortunately, they didn't know that they were dealing with the most fastidious detective in the county who would relish the challenge. Bee started in the largest bedroom and systematically opened every drawer, every cupboard and searched under every bed. The search took him four hours and despite finding numerous weird and wonderful objects it didn't reveal anything suspicious. All in all, it had been a fruitless search. He concluded by taking the names and contact details of everyone present, and bid them farewell with a cheerful, "We'll be back again tomorrow." He didn't have any intention of returning but he wanted to keep them on their toes.

Bee's extended search of the two flats meant he was late arriving at Hartswood for the Police Team football training session; all his team mates were already kicking balls around when he ran on to the pitch. He was greeted with a chorus of abuse, principally from Dean Grant, "What happened to you, did you get lost or use the local roads? If you don't want to play in the biggest game this team's ever had, just say, we won't miss you."

There was always an edge to anything Grant said, and Bee looked abashed but didn't reply. The team coach stepped in to intervene, not wanting his players to fall out prior to the important game and Bee was duly dispatched to run two circuits of the pitch to warm up. When he returned the coach took them through a series of runs, drills, and set plays all designed to foster team work and build a group spirit ahead of their big final. After an hour the coach looked out at an array of sweat soaked shirts and focused faces all attesting to the intensity of the session. He brought them over to the side of the pitch to run through some set piece tactics and concluded the session by telling them that he had lined up a practice match for the coming Saturday. The news was met by a chorus of moans as no one wanted to risk injury ahead of the game.

After the training session Ron offered Scott the opportunity of a beer in their local pub, The Bell at Outwood.

Scott readily accepted as he wanted to talk through the events of the day which would help him fully digest all that had happened. But Ron didn't have work on his agenda. He bought the first pint and as soon as Scott had taken a mouthful he hit him with his request.

"I'd like to invite Becky over to dinner on Saturday night and cook her a meal. Initially I thought I'd ask you to go out somewhere, but then it occurred to me, we could make it a foursome."

"A foursome, how?"

"You could invite Carol Bishop. I'm sure she'd come."

Scott sat bolt upright, and his eyes widened.

"Don't pretend you don't like her; everyone knows you do."

Scott opened his mouth but didn't speak. Ron took another gulp of his pint.

"Don't ever play poker for money. Now how about it? What's the worst that could happen?"

"She wouldn't, I wouldn't, I couldn't."

"Of course, you could, and I'm sure she would. She follows you around and hangs on every word you say."

Scott screwed his face up and looked at Ron in disbelief but didn't challenge the notion. He sat still and quiet for a moment and then burst into life. "No, it wouldn't work. I can't do it. I can't."

Ron took a moment to place his beer carefully in the centre of the beer mat in front of him and then looked up to meet Scott's eye. "Okay, here's the deal. You handle the food and I'll take care of the company, and the drinks. Oh, and the music, nobody wants to listen to Springsteen all night."

Scott moved his mouth to protest but didn't speak. Ron

thought he was more likely to object to his attack on Springsteen, than anything else, but decided not to push it. He lent back in his chair to enjoy the moment.

The silence lasted a couple of minutes before Scott spoke. "When Springsteen finally hangs up his guitar and I find myself searching the Surrey Hills for a caterpillar I won't miss Holly Willoughby on Good Morning, I won't hunger for steak or oysters, but I will pine for avocados."

"That reminds me, we'd better have a chat about your conversation topics before Saturday night."

TWENTY-ONE

IT WAS BACK to work for the dynamic detective duo on Friday morning as Bee scheduled a team review to ensure everyone knew what had happened in the past couple of days and what would be the priorities going forward. A couple of minutes after 9 o'clock the group shuffled into place around the large table in the ops room each armed with a coffee or in Itzkowitz's case a peppermint tea.

Bee took the lead. "It's been an action-packed week but let's spend some time reflecting on what we know and what we need to focus on over the next few days." The electricity that had buzzed around the room the last time the group met was still present, people were leaning into the table and eager to join the debate. McTierney kicked it off. "I think we proved that our victim is known as Mickey Wing. Not much doubt about that." He beamed around the room as he spoke.

Bee rolled his eyes but deflated the bubble. "Yes that's the name people knew him by, but his passport, uses the name Michael Chen Wing. You were the one who discovered the passport, didn't you look inside it?"

McTierney mumbled something and Bee smiled, "Let's call that a draw, there's enough good stuff here, no reason to argue. Either way we have a name."

Bishop raised her hand, "If you give me the passport, I'll

run a check with the Home Office and see if and when he's travelled overseas. I guess we're thinking that he's travelled from China."

Bee flicked the passport open to the page with the personal data. "This tells us that he was born in Shanghai, so it's likely that he's been to China at some point. And we've just missed his birthday."

"May 1st?" asked Itzkowitz.

"A month out, April 1st."

"Wonder if the Chinese believe in April Fools' Day," said McTierney.

"We celebrate it," said Itkowitz, "One of the many bits of junk you Brits shipped over to us."

"You're welcome, and by now we seem to be equal."

Itzkowitz stuck her tongue out at McTierney.

"Returning to the case in hand," said Bee sternly. "Now we have an identity, we need to piece together the last movements of Mr Wing. We need to discover who was the last person to see him and where he had been in the last moments of his short life. Let's recap what we know." Bee moved back to the white board and picked up the marker pen.

"Our best guess for time of death remains as October 7th – 8th 2022." This was greeted by a murmur of approval around the table.

"Obviously we don't know the killer, but we have learnt a lot more about our victim. McTierney can you update the group."

McTierney provided a 5-minute summary of the items they had discovered in the garage in Redhill and passed around a couple of photos he had taken while at the scene.

THE CAVE OF DEATH

Bishop stared open mouthed at the images. McTierney seemed to read her mind, "I know, not quite the young innocent we thought we had when we first found his body."

Bee wrote 'drugs' and 'sex trade' on the white board. "I want to focus on these two strands, so would you two be okay if I write 'Itzkowitz' against the drug line and 'McTierney' against the sex trade?"

Both officers nodded their acceptance. McTierney had already decided that he would focus on the garage and whatever leads that offered. It seemed to him that there was enough work there to keep him busy for at least a couple of weeks. He broke out of his reverie and added "We also collected a locked metal box, which we haven't opened yet and I expect that to reveal more secrets about our friend Mickey."

Bee nodded at McTierney and resumed control of the meeting. "I don't want to leave you out Bishop, I know you'll follow up on the passport, can you also conduct some desk research on his DHSS records, employment records, maybe even a police record given what we've discovered."

"Sure, I can start this afternoon."

"One other thing let's see if we can come up with a phone for our mystery man. Given the colourful life he seems to have enjoyed, his personal directory might contain some interesting names."

"I'll add it to the list."

"Good. All of this is positive stuff, but regardless of what McTierney's box of secrets reveals we still have a major problem."

"Where was he killed?" suggested Itzkowitz.

"Exactly a crime scene would be useful, although I must

confess, I don't know where to begin looking."

It wasn't often that Bee didn't know where to start, he looked at his team and was greeted by a sea of blank faces. McTierney looked around at his colleagues to see who might speak, nobody was looking likely, so he launched into the conversation.

"If I wanted to kill someone, and there's been a few people knocking on that door recently, then I'd go for somewhere quiet in a wooded area out of the town and late at night."

Bee wanted to support the discussion and offered a half-smile before adding, "Yes, I suspect it's likely to be Reigate or maybe Redhill or one of the surrounding villages."

An uncomfortable hush started to develop in the room as if the detectives had been challenged to answer some impossible quiz question. Then Itzkowitz broke the silence, "Does it matter much?" She shrugged her shoulders. "In my opinion the benefit of securing a good crime scene is the evidence that it offers. I think that even if we did find the crime scene this time around, it's been so long since the actual murder, what is it, 6 or 8 months in this case, and we've been through winter, surely in that time any forensic evidence will have been washed away long ago, so the value diminishes greatly."

McTierney nodded his approval.

"That may be true but there is one significant benefit," said Scott, "It will help our case when it comes to court." He let the point settle with his audience. "If we can't explain where the murder took place any defence counsel worth his salt is going to tell the jury that we have an incomplete case and suggest that they should give the defendant the benefit of the doubt."

A moment passed while everyone digested Bee's point, before McTierney perked up, "I don't disagree with the point made by Itzkowitz when she says most forensic evidence is likely to have been lost by now, but maybe not if he was killed under cover or out of the way. Although with what we've discovered this week, it wouldn't surprise me if Mickey was killed by a crime gang to stop him. The bullet in the back of the head is an execution style killing."

The comment was greeted by a thoughtful silence from his colleagues, but McTierney had one more thing to add. "I can't remember who said it, but when we started this enquiry someone suggested it might be a turf war killing."

Bee offered him a pale smile. "It was you who said that."

"Oh yes so it was, I nearly forgot."

Bee shook his head and brought the meeting to a close. "It's been an interesting few days; we started the week with an unknown innocent victim, and we are ending the week with the idea that Mickey Wing had his finger in several criminal pies and may have been murdered by another criminal who felt he was getting too big for his boots. I think I need to persuade Beck to change the tone of his press conference."

★ ★ ★

"How did the press conference go?"

Ron was sitting on a bar stool in their local pub and pushed a pint of lager across the bar to Scott. "Okay, I think. But I don't want a pint. Can you get me an OJ with lemonade?"

"Lemonade? Come on, I've got a reputation to maintain,

I can't be seen buying a man a lemonade." Scott lowered his eyes and Ron relented. "Don't tell me you're taking it seriously ahead of tomorrow's big football match."

"Of course. It's a proper game and I don't want to let down my team mates. Or myself," he added after a momentary pause.

"Does that mean you'll be there in the morning helping put the nets up and making sure all the corner flags are in the right place."

"Someone's got to do it. It wouldn't hurt you to chip in once in a while."

Ron screwed his face up at the idea. "Anyway, back to my original question, what happened at the press conference? Did our chief make a hash of it?"

"No worse than usual, but he did seem a bit off."

Ron put his pint back down on the bar and tuned into what Scott was about to say.

"I went to see him before the broadcast and told him we were making progress on the case and actually had a name for the victim. But instead of being pleased he was a bit nonplussed."

"Strange."

"I know. He gave the impression that he didn't think we'd get anywhere and even to the point that he would be happy if we quietly closed the case. To be honest I'm a bit worried."

"And there was I thinking you'd be more worried about tomorrow night's dinner party."

"What? Shit, Did you actually organise something? I thought it was just a wheeze from you to get me to allow you to have Becky stay over."

Ron looked offended. "No. Well yes it was originally, but you seemed to like the idea, so I thought why not. I asked Bishop this afternoon and she's up for it. A little over eager if I may say so, but anyway she's coming. I told her 8:30pm. Give us time to finish the match, have a couple of beers with the lads and get home in time for you to bung something in the oven for all of us."

"What?" Scott's jaw dropped. "Please tell me this is one of your less than funny jokes."

Ron shook his head slowly. "All true. You can thank me later."

"Thank you? I should bloody strangle you." Scott started to hyperventilate.

Ron looked surprised.

"Dinner in my house, I'm not ready for it. I've no idea what to cook. Oh no. She'll see how I cook, the smell, the mess, everything. You!"

"Calm down, she'll be more nervous than you."

Scott stopped and looked over the rim of his glasses at Ron. "Maybe I will have that drink after all."

"That's the spirit." Ron signalled to the barman for another couple of pints, while Scott started to mumble to himself about all the things that could and inevitably would go wrong during the following evening.

TWENTY-TWO

RON ROLLED OVER and blinked at this alarm clock as he tried to focus on the time. The clock said it was 7:20am, but his brain couldn't accept that. It was Saturday morning the day didn't start until 10am, so it couldn't be something beginning with a 7. Then his senses were assailed by a horrible throbbing sound, what the hell could that be? They lived in the countryside, the nearest property was 500 yards away, Scott didn't allow people to come within a hundred feet of the house so what could be making that dreadful racket. Ron pulled the pillow over his head but couldn't block out the noise. He rolled back, cursed, clambered out of bed, and shuffled to the door. Ron's bedroom was on the ground floor in a recently added extension. As he opened the door the source of the noise became clear.

Scott was in the middle of a cleaning frenzy and was hoovering the entire house. He had his back to Ron who stood in the doorway shaking his head. As Scott systematically worked his way around the hallway his eyes fell on the dishevelled figure, he silenced the vacuum. "Come on, there's lots to do today. Get yourself dressed; I've written a list of jobs for us to get ready for tonight."

Ron scratched his head, "No, you're kidding. Nothing needs doing at this hour," and with that he slammed his bedroom door.

A more equitable Ron emerged from his cavern three hours later, he helped himself to a breakfast of orange juice, coffee and cereal and ate it sitting at the kitchen table. As he did he read the task list from Scott. He grunted as he worked his way down the items, but it wasn't as bad as he'd feared. Scott had wisely assigned the majority of the work to himself. Ron's tasks were limited to clean the downstairs loo, clean all the cutlery, polish the wine glasses, buy some napkins and a dessert, and sort the drinks – NOT ALL BEER had been added in capital letters. Ron smiled at the addendum, maybe Scott was coming round to the idea of the party. It would do him good. He was contemplating what he might buy for dessert when Scott skurried into the kitchen.

"Good, you're up. I wanted to pick your brains on what to cook tonight. I was thinking of either roast breast of duck with a honey sauce or perhaps lamb tagine, they're both dishes which aren't too time sensitive."

Ron titled his head as he considered the option, "Yep, I like both, I don't mind."

"Not you, donkey, what does Becky eat?"

"Oh her, yes. I don't know. She'll be fine, I don't think she's veggie or anything like that."

"Veggie! Shit. What does Bishop eat. I've never asked her. Maybe she's a vegetarian. What did she eat in the canteen last week? I can't remember."

"I think she had coffee mid-morning and later a salad, but you can't serve coffee and salad."

"No, I agree. Maybe I should stick with chicken, everyone eats chicken."

★ ★ ★

THE POLICE TEAM coach had organised a friendly game against another police team from Croydon, but the problem with lower league football is that a friendly only exists on paper, once the two teams get out on the grass pitch it only takes one rogue tackle or one poor decision from the referee and the match can quickly spiral into a blood and thunder contest.

None of that bothered Scott, he had too much on his mind with the impending dinner party and an evening with Carol Bishop. Was it really going to happen at last? His head wasn't in the game at all, and he was two yards off the pace, something that was particularly bad for his team. Scott played as centre forward and was expected to win headers and nod the ball on for his willing team-mates running from midfield hoping to benefit from his headers and charge through on goal. By half time the team was playing poorly and were two goals down against mediocre opposition that they knew they should be able to beat. The team trudged slowly off the pitch to the changing room where a few heated opinions were exchanged. Scott was the target for much of the abuse. The coach let them vent for a couple of minutes but stopped it getting out of hand, he added a few thoughts of his own and sent them back out. "If you could have as much passion out there as you have in here, you wouldn't be getting beat, now get out there and show me why you deserve to be in the team for next week."

But Dean Grant had a wide competitive streak in him, and he was still seething about Scott's performance and decided to take matters into his own hands. Ordinarily he would play behind Scott in the formation and be one of the players to run onto flicks made by Scott. But with Scott not winning many headers that wasn't happening, so at the next opportunity Scott felt he had to win the header, Grant jumped for it too and bundled into Scott knocking him flat across the pitch. It wasn't clear what Grant was trying to achieve, when the players talked about it afterwards there was a quorum who thought he was trying to injure Scott, but in the end he only injured himself; a flailing arm had smashed across his nose and broken it. Now he was a doubt for the cup final. Grant sat in the changing room raging at Scott for deliberately breaking his nose. Scott's mild indifference only served to aggravate him more. "If he's in the team next week, I'm not playing," said Grant as he stormed off to the local A and E.

★ ★ ★

"Can't believe you're offering our guests mushrooms stuffed with garlic and cheese as a starter, poor old Bishop is going to be fretting all night thinking that her breathe stinks and you won't want to kiss her. Schoolboy error my friend."

"Shut up Ron and do something useful like polish the wine glasses on the dining table."

It was a little before 8pm and Scott was in hurricane mode in the kitchen trying to do ten things at once. He was fiddling with his mushrooms, while stirring rice, steaming broccoli, and punctuating all of this with regular checks on the chicken he was roasting in the oven.

"I think we might be all right. Thanks for your help, I

don't know what I would have done without you!"

"I did buy the cheesecake, and the wine."

"Well done Man Friday. Did you remember the napkins?"

"Ah, no forgot them."

"What? One job, that's all one job and you couldn't get that right!"

Ron was about to defend himself, but his speech was broken by a knock at the door. Ron returned a minute later with Becky and introduced her to Scott and then took her on a tour of the house. They had just returned when a set of headlights illuminated the kitchen window and shortly after Carol Bishop knocked on the door.

She had put her hair up in a bun and was wearing a little black dress; if she looked casual in the station, out of it she was stunning. Even Ron took a double take. She smiled, pushed a bottle of wine into his arms and asked "Where's the birthday boy? I bought him a present."

"I bet you did," muttered Ron under his breath, "He's in the kitchen fussing over the meal."

Carol looked surprised but stepped past Ron and walked into the kitchen. Scott spun round, brushed his hands on the apron he was wearing and made to stretch out his hand as if offering to shake Carol's hand, but thought better of it and quickly withdrew it.

"Thanks for coming Bishop, good to see you."

"Oh, please call me, Carol."

"Right Carol." Scott paused momentarily and Ron stepped into the kitchen and around Carol. "You should call him Scott when he's off duty, like tonight. Or Donkey that works just as well."

Carol smiled weakly at Scott and handed over a wrapped present tied with a bow, "Someone told me this was a party for your birthday, so I thought I should bring you a gift."

Scott blushed as he took the present, "Actually it's not my birthday, that was in March." It was Carol's turn to blush.

"Sorry, you must have misheard me," said Ron then he nudged Becky, and they wandered off into the lounge.

"Am I a bit early? What time are the others getting here?"

"Others? I think it's just us four."

Carol smiled, gave a little laugh, and looked at the floor, "I must get my hearing checked next week."

"Sorry. I don't know what the little sod said. He lives by his own rules. I hope you don't feel you were tricked into coming here. But I can't imagine there'd ever be many people here. I don't know a lot and I hate socialising in big groups. I'd understand if you wanted to turn around and leave."

"Oh no. It looks like you've gone to a lot of trouble with this meal. Let's enjoy the evening of your non-birthday."

Scott smiled his agreement but panicked as he remembered the mushrooms. While Scott checked on the food, Bishop wandered around the room admiring it. "I've always wanted a kitchen with real wooden beams, they give such character to a place."

"They do," said Scott with his mind elsewhere.

"And this place is deliciously remote but not totally isolated. It must be so peaceful."

"Only when our favourite comedian is out of town."

"Can you see another house from here?"

"Only one. It is serene here; I can't imagine living anywhere else."

Despite Ron's predictions of doom, Scott's starters and main course were welcomed by everyone and once the quartet had moved to the dining room the evening began to flow – as did the wine. If Ron had failed with the napkin job, he excelled as the sommelier. The more wine she drank the more Becky laughed. She laughed easily and laughed a lot. Ron always liked girls that laughed and even Scott decided that he found this an attractive quality. There hadn't been much laughter in Scott's house in the last 2 years and not much before that when Scott lived alone. Suddenly Becky was the life and soul of the party, and everyone loved her. Carol was a little guarded to begin with but by the time Scott presented his 'Chicken Seville' so named because of the oranges he added to the dish, she began to relax.

So, neither Scott nor Ron took her seriously when she screamed, "Is that a mouse, – I hate rodents."

Scott glared across the table at Ron, who jumped up, "I'll go and sort it. He returned two minutes later with a broad grin across his face.

"Did you fix it?" asked Scott.

"I did. I sprayed it with WD40. It won't kill it, but you won't hear it squeak anymore."

Becky burst into laughter, Carol followed suit and Ron mentally patted himself on the back. Now he was on a roll, "Did I ever tell you about that time I got one of Scott's sausages stuck in my throat? I had to dislodge it with a cold beer. I called it the Heineken manoeuvre."

Becky snorted and collapsed in hysterics. Carol laughed and turned to Scott. "You know he's actually quite funny out of the office."

"Really? Do you want him? It could be arranged."

The evening meandered on until Ron was cajoled into delivering his dessert. He made his way into the kitchen and began clattering about.

Scott frowned, "I don't know why he's making so much noise, it's only a cheesecake he bought this afternoon, all he needs to do it release it from the cardboard box. I'd better go and see what he's doing."

He arrived to find Ron hunting through the drawer looking for a knife to cut the cake. Ron spun round, "No get back. Don't leave the girls on their own."

"I didn't know what to say, I was outnumbered." Ron shook his head.

Left alone for a couple of minutes, Becky lent across the table, "So how long have you and the inspector been an item?"

Carol looked flustered, "Oh no we're not, just friends. Good friends I hope."

★ ★ ★

DESPITE MCTIERNEY'S EXTENSIVE attempts at comedy the evening never recaptured it's earlier sparkle and it was a little before midnight that Carol Bishop elected to call a taxi to take her home. That was no surprise to Scott, although he did raise an eyebrow when Becky asked if she could share it.

Left to their own devices a subdued couple of friends wandered into the kitchen to tackle the mountain of washing up. Subsequently Ron started to replace a couple of the larger pots on a set of wooden shelves on the wall close to the back door.

"Go easy with the pans on those shelves."

Ron turned and looked quizzically at Scott, "Why?"

"Unlike all the other fixtures in this room, I put those shelves up a few years ago, so their imminent collapse is well overdue."

"There you go showing that streak of self-confidence again. You should give yourself a break."

Scott offered a weak smile, "I think it's hereditary. My father was terrible at DIY. A gentle and kind man fulsome with his praise, even when there was nothing to admire, but he displayed dizzying levels of practical ineptitude around the house."

"You know you can be a good person, and you are a good person, without achieving lots of things. It's not only the guy that wins the gold medal who gets to make his parents proud. There's plenty of people struggling in poor countries all around the world who live good, wholesome lives."

Scott shrugged, "Yes you may be right," and then took a seat in the kitchen.

Ron walked across to his friend and laid his hand on his shoulder. "Might as well put your Springsteen music on now, he's probably got a song for a depressing Saturday night."

"A song? He's got a whole album!"

Ron smiled. "A Springsteen for every occasion. I presume you expect one of his songs to be playing when you get to heaven."

Scott laughed, "Firstly, I don't believe in heaven, and the afterlife and all that. But I suspect the traditionalists would suggest classical music of some description, perhaps Mozart or Tchaikovsky."

"You don't think St Peter is at the gates manning the turntables taking requests from the new arrivals?"

"If it's a good as they say, perhaps God has worked out some clever system where everyone gets to hear whatever they want, wherever they want."

"He didn't do much of a job working things out for tonight." Ron opened the fridge for a last consoling bottle of beer.

"Everything happens for a reason."

"Stuff that!"

TWENTY-THREE

Come Monday morning McTierney had forgotten all about his disappointment of Saturday night and was excited by the prospect of forensics returning the mystery box to him that he and Itzkowitz had found in the garage. It was standard practice within the team to pass any locked containers over to the forensic team upon acquisition to allow them to check the item for possible booby-traps. McTierney thought it was a pointless exercise but was aware that either evidence could be damaged, or personnel injured if a case was opened recklessly. He filled the void by drinking coffee in the canteen and flicking through the sports headlines on the BBC website.

Bee decided to leave McTierney to enjoy his moment of glory and set off to pursue the doctor who had made the kidney transplant for Penny Trimble. Her mother had said that the operation had been conducted at the Gatwick Park Hospital, a private establishment situated in Horley, roughly 10 miles south of Reigate. Bee pulled into the car park and thought how little the building looked like a hospital, and much more like a hotel or spa facility. As he walked towards the entrance there was no noise, no hustle and bustle, no queue of ambulances, no huddle of patients outside in their dressing gowns grabbing a quick smoke. He mused that this was probably the kind of image Aneurin Bevan had in mind when he launched the NHS, a peaceful combination of countryside and medical professionals, only here they had swapped the hills of Ebbw Vale for the rolling hills of Surrey – not a bad trade.

The automatic doors swished open and allowed Bee to pass, he reflected on how easy it was to gain access to a private hospital and how difficult it was with public hospitals. All you need is a big bag of cash. He stepped past a fancy overlarge pot plant and felt his resentment towards the private healthcare system growing. His troublesome back tooth seemed to sense the location and woke up and gave him a stab of pain. He shoved the base of his thumb against the tooth to quieten it down and made his made to reception. The lady on the desk apologised and informed Bee that Mr Dickinson only worked at this hospital on a Friday. Bee smiled to disguise his disappointment and looked around to survey the plush surroundings.

"Can I take a name?"

Bee was about to give his details but had a sudden flash and decided to keep his powder dry. "No that's okay, it's easy enough for me to pop by again later in the week."

Bee got back to his car and picked up two messages, one from McTierney and the other from Carol Bishop. McTierney sounded excited while Bishop sounded worried. Instinctively he knew who he would prioritise when he returned to the office.

He found Bishop at her desk in the open-plan area and pulled across a chair from a neighbouring desk to sit beside her. She turned and looked pleased to see him, but then a look of worry settled back on her face.

"I got your message. How can I help?"

Bishop smiled sheepishly and reached down to her large black bag which was sitting on the floor. She fumbled inside it and then pulled out a brown paper bag and plopped it on the desk between them. "I think it's for you."

Bee frowned and delved into the bag, pulling out a pear. He held it up and looked surprised. "A pear? Not really my favourite."

"No not the pear, there's a message inside the bag. But I didn't read it until yesterday."

Bee looked again and extracted a folded piece of paper, he opened it and read the note. It appeared to be from the woman at the fruit and veg stall. Although the writing was difficult to follow it seemed that she wanted to meet Bishop in the Memorial Park at 2pm on Friday.

"I'm so sorry, I don't really like pears either, goodness knows why I bought them last week when we were in the market, but I did. It wasn't until yesterday that I thought I ought to get them out."

"Bee smiled, "No worries, we can file that under unfortunate incidents."

"I did pop into the park yesterday at 2pm, but she wasn't there, no surprise really as it was the wrong day."

Bee gave a short laugh, "Never mind. The positive thing is that she wants to make contact. That's a great sign, but I imagine she's wary of that other man finding out, which is why she tried to do this discreetly."

"Yes. A bit too discreet for me. I guess she must have sneaked the note into the bag of pears when we were talking on Wednesday."

"You know what this means?"

Bishop shook her head.

"You'll need to go back for some more ghastly pears this week."

Bishop laughed.

"Or maybe some fruit that you do like."

"Okay."

"Let's strike while the iron is hot and get back there as soon as possible. Maybe tomorrow, but this time hopefully catch her on her own."

Bishop nodded her acceptance and Bee wandered off to see if McTierney's wave of excitement had abated.

It hadn't. Bee found him sitting in the ops room with Itzkowitz smiling like a Cheshire Cat.

"What's this exciting news then?"

"Forensics opened the box for us and it's a gold mine."

Bee could see the black metal box resting on the main table, but it was the contents that provided the excitement. Sitting in front of McTierney and Itzkowitz was a small book.

"Mickey kept a diary, and it seems to be a record of all the dodgy deals and trades he was ever involved in. An A to Z of every criminal in the district."

McTierney pushed the book across the table and Bee picked it up. He flicked through a few pages his eyes widened on several occasions. "Wow. What a life our Michael Wing seems to have lived. But all his entries appear to be either abbreviations or in code."

"Yes, we know. That's a bit of a pain, but if we can crack it, we're going to be busy."

"As they say in that Spielberg film, 'you're gonna need a bigger jail'. Itzkowitz laughed at her own joke.

Bee grinned at his colleagues. "Looks like you two have

had a good morning and I don't want to pour cold water on this discovery but don't forget this is essentially only information, it's not evidence. It helps. It helps enormously but on its own it won't convict anyone."

The diary was for the preceding year and Wing had used it to record details of numerous events. Most looked like drug trades or sexual encounters. But it wasn't always clear because he had adopted some form of shorthand or code, presumably to offer some security if the journal should fall into the wrong hands. Additionally, it carried details of what appeared to be phone calls back to his mother and sister in China. There was no mention of a father.

Bee closed the diary and passed it back across the table to McTierney, "Any major revelation so far?"

"Nothing to identify his killer. About the only entries that are not disguised are his conversations with his mother, and they don't make for joyous reading."

Bee raised his eyebrow.

"It appears that he would contact his family in China once a week and throughout last summer it seems his mother was getting progressively worse. It's not clear what she was suffering from, but the notes suggest that she spent more and more time confined to bed."

Bee pursed his lips, "That can't be easy having a sick parent when you're 5,000 miles away on the other side of the planet."

"It reads as if Mickey had a sister still in China taking care of the mother. But it get worse; the notes imply that they're on the run from the Chinese government and having to move location on a regular basis."

"Wonder what happened to create that situation."

"It's not necessarily the government they are running from; it doesn't specifically say the government it could be someone else." Itzkowitz chipped in to the discussion.

Bee stopped to absorb the comment for a moment and then McTierney reclaimed the mic, "The interesting thing for us is that it seems Mickey was regularly sending money back to his sister in China. Whether for medication for the mother or for other purposes it's not clear, but what this starts to tells us is that Mickey was getting into a life of crime over here so he could send money back to his family in China to keep them alive and safe."

"Interesting," said Bee.

"One of the comments from the sister, that Mickey has recorded suggests she thinks she's been followed."

"By whom?"

"It doesn't say, but it's logged after a call between Mickey and his sister alone making us think that the sister didn't want the mother to know." Itzkowitz again.

Bee shook his head, "This could become a bit unwieldy. We need to keep our focus on the UK crimes."

"Oh, we are," said McTierney emphatically. "The issue we might face is that potentially this diary gives us an insight into local crime that could keep us busy for weeks." He picked the journal up and tapped the back of it. "It suddenly opens up a whole new realm of possible murder motives; it's easy to create a scenario in which Mickey is rubbing a few people up the wrong way if he's trying to steal a slice of the action in and around Redhill."

"I knew you'd bring it back to the drug gangs and turf warfare," laughed Bee. "To be honest we can't take that or anything else off the table at the moment."

The three detectives paused, and each began to digest the enormity of what had just been discussed.

Meanwhile Bishop had received some news from the National Archives concerning Wing's passport and thought Bee should know immediately. She walked along to the ops room exactly at the moment that they had broken off the conversation. With the door partially open Bishop could only see Bee who appeared to be deep in thought and staring at the wall. She didn't like to interrupt in case he was about to crack the case, so she stood for a minute, and then another. Eventually Bee grunted and turned slowly to look at her, he smiled in surprise like some sort of animal waking from hibernation and beckoned for her to enter.

"I have some news that you ought to know."

"Come in, grab a seat, tell us all."

Bishop acknowledged McTierney and Itzkowitz as she took a seat around the white table. "I was talking with the National Archive Office trying to get some idea of whether Michael Wing had left the country recently."

"How did you get on?"

"Not well. They couldn't tell me anything. It seems the passport you found is a fake."

Bee gawped at her. "A fake?"

"Yes."

"That's unfortunate, but maybe while the document itself is a fake, perhaps the data being used was correct. It's probably easiest to keep the same date of birth etc to save from having to learn a new one."

"Maybe, but it wouldn't take much effort to learn 1st of April." Itzkowitz shrugged her shoulders as she spoke.

"No maybe not." Bee exhaled deeply. "Where does that

leave us?"

He answered his own question. "This diary, if we can make sense of it appears to give us an interesting insight into the life and times of an upcoming criminal in the Surrey underworld." He paused and rubbed his chin, "While you two are busy reliving the Bletchley Park experience don't forget that the most important skill of a detective is observation. Look for patterns, and or repetitions. Keep your eyes open. I think I'd better go and brief Beck." With that Bee got up from the table and started towards the door.

"There's one more thing," said McTierney.

Bee turned around, "More?"

"The box also has a key, but we don't know what the key unlocks but it's bound to be good on the back of this discovery."

McTierney slid the small metal key across the desk. It was as ordinary as it was possible to be. A small silver blade attached to a dark blue tag with no markings and no indication of what it might open.

TWENTY-FOUR

McTierney and Itzkowitz spent all Monday morning reading through the diary and trying to make sense of the abbreviations, emojis, and sets of initials which they found on every page up to the last entry made on Thursday October 6th. This appeared to be the best clue, yet that Wing had died on that day. They were also able to pinpoint the date of the kidney removal operation as Friday February 11th, 2022. A further note implied that Wing had been paid £8,000 for his kidney and that this sum had been sent to China ten days later. McTierney made a note to follow up on a money transfer office in Redhill to verify if these payments were being made from there.

By early afternoon McTierney needed some fresh air, like a puppy that had been kept inside for too long he needed to be active, hence he decided to make another call on the address where the elusive waiter from the Giggling Squid lived. Each time he'd visited the estate he was struck by the number of parked cars on the roads, even in the middle of the day. The congestion gave him a 100-yard walk back to the property through rows of multi-coloured three storey town houses. As he approached the front door McTierney's heart sank, the house looked deserted, there were no lights on, and a newspaper hung half out of the letterbox. McTierney rang the bell, knocked on the door, tapped on the window and called through the letter box, all to no avail. He looked at the paper that he now held in his hand; it was last Thursday's free advertiser. He turned it over in his hand and ran his eye down the second-hand car sales listed on the back page. He really ought to get on with his own new car purchase, once this case was cracked he'd make it a priority. He shoved the paper back and all the way through the letter box and stomped back to his car and drove into Redhill town centre in search of a Western Union office and their money transfer services.

McTierney ran a quick Google search on his phone and within a couple of minutes he had located 4 alternatives all within easy reach of the centre of Redhill; three of them were in Redhill itself and a fourth was in Reigate. It seemed each was associated with branches of the post office. McTierney popped a pair of Airpods into his ears and added some AC/DC to help him think. It occurred to him that Mickey might value a little privacy for these transactions and therefore he was unlikely to have chosen the nearest outlet to the town centre.

And so it proved, neither of the offices on London Road or Station Road recognised the name but McTierney had more success when he tried the small post office on Hatchlands Road next to the railway bridge. He pushed open the single door and a bell attached to the top rang. He stepped in three paces and went back in time by twenty years, the shelves sagged with the weight of every comestible known to man, a layer of dust acted as an adhesive to keep everything in place. He crept forward to the counter and introduced himself to an elderly Indian lady. He had to slow his speech but once she understood he was from the police she closed the shop for him and then made a cup of tea before fetching the large blue tome that housed all their monetary records. McTierney was surprised that it wasn't all maintained on line, but the woman explained that she didn't trust these fancy computers things and felt much happier with a written record. Tierney considered the recent scandal involving the post office sub-postmasters and thought that all her extra work had been vindicated but decided not to mention it.

The woman flicked back through a few pages and found the transaction to match the notes in Wing's diary. It was all there. A single £8,000 transaction from Wing to a Luqi Wing in Beijing on Monday February 21st. The woman seemed to enjoy her moment in the spotlight and Tierney pushed her to check the account that Wing had opened. Within a few minutes McTierney had a list of several other transactions. There was a clear pattern, more frequently transfers and larger and larger suns involved. Whatever Michael Wing was doing to earn his money he was getting better and better at it, or he was working a lot of overtime. Of course, there was also a simpler explanation. Crime.

McTierney left the post office and turned back towards the centre of Redhill where he'd left his car to begin his daytrip to the money transfer sites of the town. Directly opposite the post office was a chip shop and the smell of fried food drifted across the road to him. His nose twitched but he thought he should get back to the office and update the team with his recent discovery. He walked the first thirty yards, but his stomach took control of his legs, and he scampered back to grab a late afternoon snack. As he reached the door, a thin man was leaving – it was the waiter from the Giggling Squid.

Time stopped for both men as they recognised one another. The waiter dived to McTierney's right, but this time the detective was ready for him and stuck out his boot tripping the waiter and sending his chips sprawling across the pavement. "Not so fast sunshine. You and I are due a long conversation down at the police station." He spun him round and slapped a pair of handcuffs on him. "You won't be running away today."

An hour later the waiter was sitting in interview room 1 at the police station refusing to say anything. Bee had advised leaving him to sweat for a bit and had requested a duty solicitor to represent him. When the solicitor arrived McTierney took the interview himself.

"You're here being interviewed in connection with a bag theft in Reigate High Street on Monday 17th of April, and the subsequent assault of a police officer, me, after I gave pursuit."

The waiter glanced up from looking at his hands, shrugged his shoulders and bowed his head again. McTierney paused. "The Giggling Squid restaurant, where I believe you worked, told me that your name is Carlos Hanbing. Is that correct?"

Carlos gave the same response.

"They also told me that you live at Goldworth Road in Redhill. Number 77. Is that correct?"

Still no response. The pattern continued for five minutes and McTierney found his frustration growing. "You could at least tell us your name; we can't hang you for that!"

The solicitor looked startled, "I think you'll find hanging ended in the last century."

"Turn of phrase," said McTierney.

"Perhaps you could find an alternative."

"You get him to confirm his name and I'll use a different term."

The solicitor offered a weak smile, but cupped his hand and spoke to Carlos, who then nodded and said, "My name is Carlos."

"Thank you," said McTierney with loaded sarcasm. "Now how about you tell us why you were nicking handbags from old ladies last month?"

Carlos reverted to the silent approach.

"Look Carlos, unless you want to spend the night in the cells, you'd better start talking. We've got a murder case to solve out there and I was in the mood to cut you a deal, even though you smashed me in the ribs with an iron bar, but that's a once only deal and it expires in two minutes."

All three parties sat in the room staring in different directions as the 120 seconds ticked by. McTierney closed his notepad, ending the interview and switched off the tape recorder. As he pushed back his chair, he threw one final comment on the table.

"Here's some news for you, unless you start co-operating we'll be visiting that house of yours tomorrow and if nobody opens the door for us, we'll be knocking it down while we try to ascertain who you are and what you're about. Got it?"

McTierney thought a flicker of fear rushed across his face. "Right now, I've got better things to do, so I'll get the custody sergeant to take you back down to the cells."

McTierney slipped down to the canteen hoping to grab something hot to keep him going through what was likely to be a long evening and was relieved to find Juliet still in situ behind the counter. He took the last plate of lasagne and found himself a seat by the window and began scrolling through the messages on his phone. He'd eaten 5 mouthfuls when John James the custody sergeant came to find him, "Your boy wants to talk now, do you want me to put him back in the interview room?"

"Does he?"

"So, it seems. What's going on? Is he playing games?"

"Don't think so, I think the threat of raiding his home has spooked him. Go back and tell him that you can't find me. I need to request a search warrant for the morning. You'll be keeping this one overnight."

McTierney finished his meal, wandered over to flirt with Juliet, the canteen manager as he returned his tray and leisurely climbed the stairs to find Bee. He recounted the story that James had shared and asked him to endorse the search warrant. "There must be something interesting hidden at the house, old Carlos was shitting himself at the prospect of us searching it."

"Don't forget we've got a murder enquiry on our hands, and you've just uncovered the best clue we've had in three weeks. That diary needs a lot of work."

"I know. Itzkowitz is going through it with the fine-tooth comb as we speak. It's a classic case of 'Action: FBI'. You know."

Bee nodded his agreement and signed the form allowing McTierney to return to the interrogation.

"You've decided to speak then Carlos. What changed your mind?"

"The legal man told me I should help you with your enquiry. Help you to find the person who stole the lady's bag."

"I don't need help to find him. I know who it was. It was you."

"No sorry sir, not me. Someone else who maybe who looks a little like me. But not me."

McTierney smiled to himself, he preferred it when a criminal tried to argue their innocence. He decided to give Carlos some rope. "Do you have an alibi for that Monday lunchtime, April 17th."

"I was at home, but on my own. Maybe one of my neighbours heard me through the walls, I don't know, perhaps you could ask."

"Not the strongest alibi I've ever heard. Looks like this could end up your word against that of a police officer. If so I don't fancy your chances." McTierney knew that it wouldn't go to court if he didn't produce some additional evidence, but he guessed that Carlos might not know that and decided to let him sit and sweat for a few minutes. But Carlos had a bit more composure than McTierney had given him credit for, and he sat there enjoying the silence. McTierney was the first to break. "Tell you what I'm going to do. I'll see if I can organise an identity parade for the morning. I'll contact Mrs Kennedy and we'll bring her in to see if she can select you from a line-up."

Carlos shrugged his shoulders. "Okay."

McTierney pursed his lips, time to play his ace. "We'll keep you here overnight while we locate Mrs Kennedy. In the meantime, I think I'll drop back to that house of yours and have a snoop around. See if I can find that bag you stole."

Carlos sat straight up as if a bolt of lightning had struck him. "Don't go to the house, there's nothing there, you'll be wasting your time."

"It's mine to waste."

"Don't go to the house, it's not mine. You'll start a riot. Honest."

"A riot? Really, wow, we've got some officers who enjoy those. I'll let them know."

Carlos became agitated "Look I'll admit to the bag thing if you leave the house alone."

"Why would I want to do that?

"You don't understand. He won't be happy. He'll go mad."

"He. Who's he?"

"The Red King."

"The Red King. Does he have a name?"

"That's all I know. The Red King."

TWENTY-FIVE

McTIERNEY YAWNED AND pushed back his sleeve to look at his watch. Not yet 6:30am, yesterday afternoon it had seemed like a good idea to search the house that Carlos Hanbing was supposed to be living in, but sitting in his car waiting for the dog support team to arrive he was less convinced.

"They'll be here in a minute," said Bee reading the mind of his colleague.

"Better be. I'm already thinking of going home to bed. Was it really necessary to bring the dogs along?"

"If you're right that Hanbing is hiding something major, then the dogs will sniff it out much quicker than either you or I can find it."

"I guess." McTierney took another sip from his takeaway McDonalds coffee and screwed his face up at the taste.

A white van pulled into the road, headlights blazing and stopped behind them. "Here they are," said Bee, replacing the cap on his bottle of carbonated water.

He jumped out of the car to meet the dog team. The team comprised of Monica the handler and Whiskey the German Shepherd, the undisputed star of the pairing. Bee briefed Monica on what they were seeking and made his way to the front door, McTierney trotted off to cover the back door and prevent anyone from escaping. There was no answer at the door and Bee used his shoulder to force entry, he stood in the hallway and shouted "Police. Make yourself known and come slowly to the door." His plea was met with silence. He turned back to Monica, "Looks like the place is yours, you take the upstairs, and we'll begin down here." Then Whiskey began to growl, there was movement in the kitchen at the back of the house. Monica and Bee exchanged nervous glances, then the wooden kitchen door slowly opened.

"Bet that had you scared."

It was McTierney, who had gained access through the back door.

Bee exhaled loudly, "Stop dicking around. Right, this is a three-storey town house, so Monica and Whiskey are going to start upstairs, we'll search here, and meet them on the middle floor. You can have the kitchen."

Bee left his colleague and turned on his torch to help him penetrate the darkest corners. He held his torch between his teeth to keep both hands free to lift and sift. Methodically he searched through the limited and tatty furniture in the extended lounge diner at the front of the building; he started with a pine cabinet which was laden with small boxes and drawers. He lifted the clothes and papers and ran his hand underneath each – nothing. He turned his attention to a small bookcase, pulled out each book in turn, flipped it upside down and flicked through the pages.

But it was a fruitless effort, the only unusual item of interest was a green football scarf from the Legia Warsaw team. Tierney didn't fare any better in the kitchen; the two men met in the hallway and climbed the stairs to the first floor when Monica called out from the top floor. Both she and Whiskey had been successful.

Behind the side panel of the bath the German Shepherd had sniffed out three bags of powder which looked suspiciously like drugs. "I'm guessing that'll be amphetamines in the first bag, and the other two look like white ecstasy pills. Whiskey's especially good at finding them."

"Well done Whiskey," said Bee.

"The front room is interesting, you ought to take a look. It appears to be a sex chamber, there's all manner of sex toys and plenty of alcohol and a box of burner phones for good measure. It looks like it was used as a shag-pad or a brothel. To cap it off I found this stash of photos under the bed in the front room. I've not been through them, but they look like porn images."

McTierney's eyes lit up, "Can this case get any better?"

Monica stared at McTierney for a second, then turned her attention back to Bee. "I'll take Whiskey downstairs and check the rooms down there, but I don't think there's anything else up here to interest us."

Bee nodded his thanks and took the Sainsbury's carrier bag of photos from the dog handler. "There's no food in the fridge and only a giant tin of coffee to drink, apart from the alcohol up here, so it looks like it's uninhabited, at least during the daytime."

"Could be," said Monica heading down the stairs.

Bee turned his attention back to McTierney who was clamouring to get hold of the bag with the photos in it. "Don't judge anyone we discover involved in this case." McTierney pulled a face.

"I think we need the forensic team in here, can you call Kelly and get him here as soon as possible."

McTierney nodded.

"Then we'll need another chat with your waiter friend."

"Looks like he's had more on the menu than prawn balls."

Bee lowered his gaze, "Did you have to?"

"Can't help it."

Bee shook his head, "Did you ever send the forensic team into the garage you discovered?"

"Didn't think it would produce much."

"I think you should, It's not a big area it wouldn't take them long."

"I'll get them to do a double header with this place. Now anything interesting in the bag?"

Bee began to flick through the bag of photos that Monica had found. None of them were portraits but they all included people, people in explicit sexual positions, mostly men. "These have been taken with a hidden camera" said McTierney looking over Bee's shoulder.

Bee stopped to rotate the next shot by ninety degrees trying to make out what was happening. "It's two men," said McTierney, "And I think one of them is Mickey Wing."

Bee turned his attention back to McTierney, "Now if your waiter knows Michael Wing, that would be an interesting development. Can you go back to the station, get him a legal brief, and get him ready to speak. I'll be there as soon as I can. In the meantime, send Bishop back here. I want to interview a few of the neighbours.

"Sure, but he's not my waiter."

★ ★ ★

McTierney headed back to the station and while Bee waited for Bishop to arrive he took the opportunity to speak to Dr Kelly himself and convey a sense of urgency over the examination of number 77. As they finished speaking Bishop appeared and Bee briefed her on their findings in the house and his hopes for finding a neighbour who had witnessed some of the many goings on at the property. The first couple of houses didn't offer much return but the elderly lady at number 5, Mrs Baker, welcomed them inside and insisted on making tea and bringing biscuits to the table. They took seats at the wooden pine table at the rear end of a long lounge diner room. A cheese plant stood in a plastic pot in the corner, the far wall was dominated by a wooden cabinet displaying vintage china dinnerware. Bee thought he'd gone back in time by 40 years. He smiled across the table at Bishop, "McTierney will be outraged to miss out on free tea and biscuits." Then he turned to Mrs Baker and explained why they were making enquiries.

She nodded her understanding, then crossed her arms with her lips pressed together, Bee sensed that she was about to unload. "I must say you took your time to come. I telephoned the police station three times last year to complain about the noise, but nobody did anything." Bee was about to speak, but realised that Mrs Baker hadn't finished, "It was terrible, a party next door almost every night, certainly every weekend and all sorts of people coming and going, heaven knows what was going on next door, but I'm sure it wasn't legal, well it couldn't be." She paused. "It wasn't right. What with my Harry suffering with his cancer, he needed a bit of peace and quiet, and all those yobs did was make noise 'til 3 in the morning. I went to complain and all they did was threaten me, and what did your lot do about it? Nothing."

Bee tiptoed into the conversation, "Do you remember who you spoke to?"

"Yes. It was a detective called Church. I remember the name because it was my maiden name."

Bee grimaced but wrote himself a note. Bishop looked across at her boss and felt the need to speak "On behalf of the Reigate police, please accept my apology."

Mrs Baker smiled gratefully at Bishop, who reached across and touched her sleeve, "Why don't you tell us everything that happened."

Mrs Baker nodded and started to talk, but then her eyes welled with tears as she explained how her husband had passed away three months ago. He'd lost weight and faded away quickly at the end. Mrs Baker was pleased that he'd survived Christmas and been able to see his grandson.

When she finished, Bishop said, "I'm so sorry."

Bee felt grateful for the intervention as he knew from bitter experience that whenever he tried to offer someone sympathy he came across as sarcastic. As they left the house he mustered a clipped "thank you," wanting to get in on the act somehow, but also keen to escape.

Bee and Bishop walked back down the short path and Bee turned to his colleague, "Thank you for stepping in there. Sometimes I have a problem reading people's expressions."

Bishop pulled a face, but said, "No problem."

Then Bee noticed the forensic team had arrived at number 77, he stuck his head around the front door and called out to the nearest forensic officer. "Have you found much?"

A man Bee didn't recognise stood up from where he'd been kneeling on the thick carpet in the corner of the lounge and padded over to Bee. He was wearing a white protective suit, purple latex gloves and disposable shoe covers. He nodded at Bee, "I need a break, so I'll give you a quick summary."

"I don't know how you found this place, but it would make a perfect practice area, there is just about every human bodily fluid known to man somewhere in this place."

Bee smiled at him, "I can imagine."

"It's going to take a while to get it all logged and analysed but there's been a fair few parties here."

"Sure. But if you find any blood, can you let me know immediately. I'll leave my card here for you."

TWENTY-SIX

BACK AT THE station McTierney went down to the cells to have a discreet word with Carlos Hanbing. He marched down the whitewashed corridor a big grin across his face, he was going to enjoy this moment. In his mind he was convinced that Hanbing had been the one to whack him with the iron bar and he still owed Hanbing, and this was the start of a long payback. He banged his fist on the metal door and slide back the peep hole. "Wake up Hanbing, I've got some news for you."

Hanbing was sitting on a wooden bench on the side of his cell, he looked washed out and slowly got to his feet.

"Guess where I've been this morning?"

Hanbing shrugged, he didn't have the energy to play games.

"Don't worry, I'll tell you. I've been to your house at Goldworth Road. Guess what I found?"

Hanbing wasn't playing.

"A bag full of drugs, some nasty drugs, and another bag of naughty photos. Seems you've been a busy boy. One of those snaps includes an image of Mickey Wing, the deceased Mickey Wing who we found in a cave in the middle of Reigate. Linking you with our murder case. I hope you didn't have any plans for the next few days because you're going have to change them. My colleague is sorting out the paperwork as we speak, I think you'll be spending your next few days here. Answering questions. We'll see you upstairs shortly."

This time Bee led the interview, McTierney sat next to him, across the small wooden table sat Hanbing and another solicitor provided by the police. Bee outlined the situation as he saw it which had Hanbing as their only contact to the murder victim, not to mention the only resident at a would-be brothel in the town. But Hanbing had retreated into his shell and wasn't saying anything. Bee turned off the tape recorder and spoke directly to the solicitor who he had met once or twice in previous cases. "We'll give you some time with your client and perhaps you can persuade him that he would better serve his own interests if he would co-operate with us."

The lawyer accepted the offer, and the detectives left the room. When they returned it seemed that Hanbing had recognised the value of the advice and began answering their questions. But his answers didn't take the investigation any further forward. Hanbing insisted that he didn't live at the house in Goldworth Road, although his claim that he lived in a squat in Redhill didn't sound credible.

At this point the solicitor challenged the process, "Do you have any evidence to suggest that my client does own the property?"

Bee grimaced and looked away, "Let's talk about Michael Wing. Do you know him?"

Hanbing shook his head, but Bee thought he detected a slight flinch in the body. He decided to switch his approach and appeal for Hanbing's help rather than throw accusations across the table.

"Was he your friend? We're trying to catch his killer. Can you help us? Some of the photos we found at the house in Goldworth Road seem to include him."

Bee pulled a couple of images out from the folder he had on the desk in front of him. He spun the picture around on the table and pushed it across to Hanbing. "Is this Michael?"

Hanbing kept his eyes on the detective until McTierney picked up the photo and pushed it into his face. "Is this Mickey?" Hanbing jolted back in his chair.

"It is, isn't it?"

Hanbing's lips began to tremble, but no words were formed.

"Look it's obvious that Mickey got himself into some dodgy situations and maybe one of those led to him being killed. Why won't you help us catch his killer?"

Still Hanbing refused to speak. Bee stopped the tape for a second time. "I need to go." He turned to McTierney, "Can you finish up here? Get Beck to approve an extended stay for Mr Hanbing and we'll talk more later."

The solicitor looked startled, "If you're off to do something else, maybe you can consider releasing my client. His been in custody for close on 24 hours already and you've no evidence to connect him to any crime."

Bee and McTierney exchanged looks. "Yes we have," said McTierney, "Our friend Carlos here stole a handbag in Reigate High Street three weeks ago. I've got the lady concerned coming in after lunch to identify him."

The solicitor turned back to Hanbing with a weak shrug of his shoulders. Bee nudged his colleague and the pair stepped outside of the interview room. "Sorry, I have to accompany Bishop to the market, to see if we can find Wing's aunt. I'll leave this with you. Be aware that the mail that I picked up from the hallway at the house was all circulars, there was nothing with a named addressee. Maybe Hanbing is right, perhaps he doesn't live there, but I'm sure he knows more than he's saying. If you can get anything out of him that would be great, and it'll be interesting to see if the old woman picks him out."

★ ★ ★

"I CAN'T BELIEVE it's been nearly a week since we came here last time," said Bishop as she and Bee walked through the Belfry shopping centre on their way to the market.

"I know, I feel we're getting somewhere on this case at last. I only hope the aunt hasn't got disillusioned when we didn't make contact on Friday."

Bishop dipped her chin onto her chest and mumbled, "Sorry."

"Oh, I didn't mean you," said Bee backtracking as he realised he'd inadvertently criticised his colleague, "I mean I think she has a trust issue with the police, and we all need to work hard with these communities. You've done more than anyone to build that with her."

Bishop offered a disbelieving smile and thanked Bee for his words. As they approached the crossroads where the stalls operated, Bee offered one more piece of advice, "If you get the chance take her away from the stall and buy her a coffee. If you're both out of sight, hopefully she can talk freely."

Bishop nodded. It looked like their luck was in, the old lady was on the stall as was another woman that neither of

THE CAVE OF DEATH

them recognised but the large Asian man was nowhere to be seen. Bee walked directly up to the second woman and asked her for a pound of oranges and then began looking through the carrots, leaving Bishop to approach the aunt. Initially the old woman was wary, looking up and down the street as if she was expecting someone to charge out of a doorway and come towards her. Bishop noticed a purple bruise on her cheek which she guessed had been a result of their interference last week. Bishop glanced across the stall and caught Bee's eye urging her to act. "I had some very nice pears from here last week, I wonder if you have any more the same this week?"

The old woman grabbed a paper bag and began to fill it with pears, Bishop reached out and touched her hand as the third pear dropped into the bag. "I'm in need of a coffee, I think I'll go to the Christian coffee shop now I've finished my shopping. I would have liked to have gone there on Sunday, but I was busy."

Bee cringed as he heard the conversation, but it seemed to be doing the trick. He thought he saw the old woman nod and two minutes later she barked some instruction at the other woman and scuttled away in the direction that Bishop had gone.

In the coffee shop Bishop had positioned herself facing the door, as she watched the old woman enter she thought that she had shrunk, clearly she had been emotionally marked by the news of her nephew's demise, maybe she had been physically scarred too, maybe the bruise on her cheek wasn't the only reminder she carried from last week. The woman came straight to Bishop's table and sat down but didn't say anything. Bishop pushed a latte across the table and started to gabble. She spoke for a minute without reply, then realised that she was going too fast. She stopped took a deep breath and started again much slower. She reached out to cup the old woman's hands with her own and said, "I'm so sorry about your nephew, Mickey, please help me find out what happened to him." A tear started to form in the old woman's eyes and Bishop offered her a tissue.

The old woman took it, smiled, wiped her face, and then began to speak, and the words begin to pour out of her like a dam that has been burst. The aunt's English wasn't perfect by any standards, more a collection of three-word phrases, but the message was clear, "Mickey a good boy. Mickey work hard. Mickey send money to his mother. Mickey go to college, get proper job, make good money. Something bad happen to Mickey. You find Mickey. I go now."

★ ★ ★

THERE WAS EXCITEMENT to be had back at the station where McTierney enlisted the help of Itzkowitz to run the identification parade. He gave her the task of getting the five participants lined up in Interview Room 1 and then brought in Carlos Hanbing and offered him the choice of where to stand. He opted for the third position. Once they were assembled Itzkowitz gave each a number to hold and McTierney skurried off to collect Mrs Kennedy from the second interview room and took her into the neighbouring room where she could see all the participants through the one-way mirror.

"What's happening constable? Why am I here?"

McTierney bristled. "We think we have the man who stole your handbag. We want you to identify him if you can."

She leant forward and stared through the window. McTierney was hoping for an instant recognition, but it wasn't forthcoming.

"Do you see him?"

"Don't rush me constable."

"If you want them to speak we can do that," said McTierney biting his tongue.

"He didn't say anything, so no good them speaking, is it constable?"

"Okay, how about an action? And by the way I'm a sergeant."

Mrs Kennedy looked him up and down, "Good Lord they'll promote anyone these days. Was there no one else?"

McTierney smiled while he clenched his fist in his pocket.

"Can you make them reach out with their right hand and then turn away quickly."

McTierney's heart sank, this was turning into a pantomime, "Okay, give me a minute." He left the room and passed on the request to Itzkowitz.

"Are you jive-talking?" She said chomping heavily on some gum.

"Am I what?"

"Jive-talking. Bullshitting."

"No, it's what he did, she wants to see his shape side-on moving away."

Itzkowitz shook her head but went back into the room and conveyed the instruction. McTierney returned to the other side of the mirror to watch, thinking that at least it would be funny. As soon as Carlos performed the snatch and twist, Mrs Kennedy called out, "That's him, number 3, little bastard. Hang him!"

"We let the courts deal with punishment but thank you for your time."

"Did you get my handbag back?"

"Not yet."

"Well keep looking."

TWENTY-SEVEN

McTierney took advantage of Bee's continued absence to begin to level his score with Hanbing. He left him in the interview room and escorted the other participants in the parade out of the station, then returned to taunt his prisoner.

"She picked you out of the line-up. That's you done for. Theft, and assaulting a police officer, you'll be spending the next few years in jail. Once the jury sees a little old granny being attacked by someone like you, they'll convict you as soon as look at you. I reckon ten years minimum."

Hanbing lost the little colour he still had in his cheeks.

"Of course, that's where your problems will really start. Once the word gets round the prison that you're into some of the games we've seen in those photos you'll become the most popular inmate in the block. You'll be taking showers five times a day." McTierney stopped to laugh.

Hanbing sat quietly in the chair and pulled his elbows close into his body, McTierney thought he saw him tremble. Now was the moment.

"Of course, I could help you." Hanbing looked up, his eyes blinking quickly.

"But you need to help me, and it needs to be before the big chief gets back from his trip to the market. Capiche?"

Hanbing nodded a little too eagerly for his own good.

McTierney pulled the chair out and plonked himself down at the table, "Right, let's get to it. Where do you live?"

"Redhill."

"In the house in Goldworth Road?"

Hanbing shook his head, "No, in a flat with many other people, we share it."

"A squat?"

Hanbing looked lost and shrugged his shoulders.

"Doesn't matter. Where is this flat?"

"In the middle of the town. Above a shop. I can show you."

McTierney nodded and leaned closer to Hanbing, "Okay, don't worry, we can do that later. Now do you know Mickey Wing?"

Hanbing hesitated but nodded, "Yes. He was my friend, but I haven't seen him for months and now you say he's dead. Is that right? I hope not."

"Sorry, but it's true. Someone put a bullet in his head last October."

Hanbing slumped back in his chair and fell silent, his head down. McTierney decided to give him a moment. Then bowed his own head to catch Hanbing's eye and spoke more softly than he had previously. "If you help me, we can catch the bastard who killed him. If he was really your friend, then surely you owe him that much."

Hanbing brought his face back up to meet McTierney's, "But I don't know who killed him."

"No problem, that's my job, I just need you to help me understand a few things."

For the next twenty minutes Hanbing explained how he

and Mickey Wing had started to operate a small-time drugs and sex shop in the house in Goldworth Road. Always under the control of the anonymous 'Red King' but growing their network and when necessary fighting their corner to protect their interests. Mickey, according to Hanbing, had been ruthless and often acted without any moral compass. He was only interested in earning as much money as he could as quickly as he could to allow him to send money back to China to help his mother and sister. It was his ambition to get them over to England, but his mother's health appeared to deteriorate faster than Mickey could raise funds to send to her. He was obsessed with his mother and this obsession drove him on. It had been this fixation that had led Mickey to sell a kidney to some shady doctor in the previous year. Although he'd been given some instructions on what to eat and how to take care of himself, the doctor had disowned him after the operation. Mickey had become ill and Hanbing thought he might die, but he hadn't. But the incident had changed Mickey and made him more callous and more desperate. He'd even gone after the doctor, Hanbing thought he'd kill him, but had struggled to find him. It was following this incident that Mickey decided to broaden his outlook.

Hanbing was sketchy on some of the details, but he gave the impression that Mickey was fast with both his fists and a knife and wasn't at all worried about stepping on the toes of other criminal gangs. Hanbing maintained that he hadn't got personally involved in the violence, preferring to leave that to Mickey who seemed to have a talent for it. Hanbing suggested that Mickey was a martial arts wizard. McTierney was doubtful of that part but kept scribbling as Hanbing recounted his tale. He found it easier to believe the idea that

Mickey was the brains of the operation and had been the one planning the deals and takes. And even that since Mickey's demise Hanbing had given up his life of crime and replaced it with a series of part-time jobs in the catering trade. The biggest problem he was going to have was explaining to Bee how he'd got the confession.

McTierney spent all of Tuesday evening with Bee firstly in the kitchen at Bee's house and latterly in the lounge watching some detective programme on Netflix, but he couldn't quite find the right moment to turn the conversation around to Carlos Hanbing's tale. Even when the TV show presented a confessional scene, McTierney squirmed in his chair and said nothing. He took his burden to bed and lay there thinking that it would all disappear in the morning, somehow.

TWENTY-EIGHT

MCTIERNEY HAD WOKEN early and decided to head into the station early to psyche himself up for his confession to Bee. It didn't seem right to do it in Bee's house and anyway he thought Bee might be more subdued at work than he would be at home. He took his usual seat in the CID communal area with a view across the floor so he could see when Bee entered from the opposite side. He would grab the first opportunity that arose, make his confession, and then head downstairs for a full English breakfast. Alcohol always helped him through difficult times and if there was no booze, food was a good substitute.

Bee bounced back into the station and took the stairs two at a time. At last, the case was starting to turn, and he felt they were making some useful progress, maybe they wouldn't be making an arrest in the next 24 hours, but they were starting to understand a lot more about their dead body and Bee believed that it was necessary to understand the victim before you could catch their killer. He went in search of McTierney eager to discover why he had disappeared so early this morning; Bee suspected that McTierney had made a breakthrough with the diary and so he was hopeful that they could soon close the case. He marched across the open plan first floor directly over to the set of desks allocated to the CID team. McTierney saw him coming and appeared to shrivel back into his seat. Unperturbed Bee slid into the seat opposite him, clapped his hands and said "Well?"

McTierney offered a meek "Well, what?"

"How did it go? The parade. Did the witness pick out your assailant? Are the streets a little bit safer?"

"Er, yeah. Be with you in a sec." McTierney fiddled with his keyboard, pretending to type something. Bee ignored the delay and rattled off the headline news from Bishop's chat with Mickey Wing's aunt. Itzkowitz was sitting alongside McTierney and perked up at the story and leaned across to nudge McTierney, "Go on then, tell him your glory story."

McTierney glared at her. Then realising that he had run out of options looked directly at Bee and whispered, "Could we have a quiet word in the ops room?"

Bee looked surprised but accepted the invitation and followed McTierney across the grey carpeted floor to the big room at the end. As he closed the door, he asked "Is everything alright? Not like you to be quiet, especially if there's glory to be taken. What's happened?"

"Mrs Kennedy picked Hanbing out of the line up with no trouble at all. She'll be a solid witness, a touch old-fashioned but she'll do the job."

Bee looked mystified "That's all good isn't it?"

McTierney took a deep breath and unloaded. "Yes that bit is. The next bit, less so. I didn't think that Hanbing was anything significant in this case, so I offered him a deal to get him to talk about the place at Goldworth Road."

"Yes." Bee took a seat at the table and moved subtly away from his partner.

"It turns out, at least he told a story of him and Mickey

Wing being some later day criminal double act, like the Kray Twins of Redhill or something. He alleged that they've been running some major league criminal drug and prostitution ring in the town. He made it sound like Wing was the principal but clearly he would have been involved in the activity."

Bee's eyes bulged, "Go on."

"I mean it's ridiculous to think of Hanbing as some master criminal but that was the line he was selling. He's more like a Nolan sister than a Kray boy."

Bee didn't smile.

McTierney continued to re-count the story of Hanbing's confession, pouring scorn on each element but somehow presenting it as gospel.

Bee lifted his hand, "There's so much here, I think I need to hear the tape."

"Er I didn't have the recorder on, all of this was an 'off the record' chat between friends."

Bee shook his head. "What did you promise him?

"A sort of get out of jail free card."

"What? If even 10% of this is true he's going to be in jail until he's an old man"

"I didn't know what he was going to confess; once he started I couldn't stop him."

"You didn't think! We can drop charges against him for whacking you and maybe even the case with granny's handbag but some of this; drugs, prostitution, Christ it's heavy-duty stuff."

McTierney dropped his eyes to the floor, while Bee stood up and marched around the room casting occasional glances at his colleague. "Hanbing could be making this all up, or at least some of it. Telling you what you want to hear simply to avoid a spell in prison." He paused and looked around the room. "You can't verify any of this!"

"I know. Well not yet, maybe some of his information can help us crack a few cases."

Bee looked at him in disbelief. "I think I'll file this under unbelievable cock-up!"

McTierney shifted in his chair. "He did mention some deal with that Albanian dealer Adil Hoxha we picked up a few months ago. The implication was that he and Wing, maybe more Wing than Hanbing, had turned him over to the authorities to get him out of the way."

Bee frowned, "I don't remember the details of the case, I think it was one of Church's arrests. I guess we can check the details. Although quite frankly the name sounds like a hoax! Are you sure he's not playing you?"

McTierney didn't answer. Bee stopped pacing and stood with his hands on his hips. "Look we'll have to come back to this, for now I want to get the whole team in here and brief them on the recent developments."

Ten minutes later and loaded up with caffeine and mid-morning snacks Bee's team shuffled around the white table to hear an update on the case. Bee took the team through the highlights of the earlier conversations with McTierney and also Bishop's chat with the aunt.

Bee returned to the white board and wrote 'criminal' next to Michael Wing, and then 'blackmail?' in red on the line beneath. He turned back to the group and a sea of shocked faces, "Come on, that's what you're all thinking."

Bishop raised her hand and Bee invited her to speak, "Not disagreeing, but his aunt's perception is totally different.

Her chatter is all positive, about how good Mickey is, about him sending money home to his mother and sister, hard-working and polite. Going to evening classes to get qualifications and a proper job."

Bee smiled, "My take on that is Mickey is telling his aunt, and others near him, one thing while he lives a double life. But can you check with the local colleges and see if he's ever enrolled. It might give us a different perspective."

He then added the name Carlos Hanbing to the board and wrote the same two words against his name, McTierney squirmed in his seat. Next Bee drew a line between the two names and wrote partners in crime along the line. This time nobody queried it. Bee turned back to face his audience, "Perhaps this should be a dotted line, because we don't have much evidence to confirm this." He turned back to the board and rubbed away some of the ink to create a broken line. "That's better. Now McTierney is going to attempt to verify some of the crimes and deals that Hanbing is claiming were carried out by him and Michael Wing." McTierney nodded his agreement.

"Do we think Hanbing is still in the game?" asked Itzkowitz.

"No," said McTierney. "Or at least not to the same extent."

"His bag theft seems a long way short of some of the things he's claiming," said Bee.

"A bit like Andrew Ridgeley after George Michael dumped him and went solo," added McTierney.

Bee shook his head, "Okay, maybe Hanbing is not the head-boy, but when we searched Goldworth Road earlier it didn't look like it had been left untouched for 7 or 8 months.

I could believe that Hanbing is not doing as much as he once was, but it looks like somebody's been busy."

There were nods of agreement around the table.

"I'm going to set up a surveillance team on the property, and also McTierney and I will go back and interview the rest of the neighbours. The place was clearly a den of depravity and in all probability it still is. Bishop can you check out who owns the place, and we'll pay them a visit."

Itzkowitz waved her hand to catch Bee's eye. "I did a lot of stake outs in The Bronx, so I'd like to volunteer for this one."

"Good. You're on it then. I'll find you a partner, but you need to start tonight."

Bee stopped to write himself a note, then rejoined the conversation.

"Now Itzkowitz, you've had your head in that diary for several hours this week, what have you discovered?"

"The easiest stuff to understand is the bits he wrote about his mother. It's sad to read, every time he calls his mum it seems her condition is worsening. She spends most of her days in bed. His sister is worried and there's an urgency in his notes. Not hard to believe the story that Hanbing tells us about Wing being obsessed with money to get his mother out of Shanghai. I wonder if she's still alive."

"I think his mother was in Chengdu, not Shanghai," said Bee.

"Oh, was it? Yes, you're right," said Itzkowitz.

"How do you know that?" Asked McTierney. "You've barely looked at the diary."

Bee looked embarrassed and Itzkowitz rescued him. "Whatever. Wing's sister is worried about being followed by someone, probably a government official or spy or something."

"It all sounds horrific," said Bishop.

"Maybe, but let's focus on our issues. Any dark secrets?" asked Bee.

Itzkowitz tugged on her bottom lip before speaking, "Maybe. There's pots of info in here, but it's all in code. There's a few initials which come up time and again. Dr D is someone Wing doesn't like at all. BSC features a lot and DG seems to be a popular client. He's someone who paid Wing for sex in some shape or form and appears to have paid extra for a 'golden shower', whatever that is."

"If it's what I think it is, then you don't want to know," said McTierney.

Itzkowitz frowned at him, and McTierney shook his head.

"Oh, I hope DG turns out to be Dean from the football club," said McTierney.

Bee glowered at him.

"Not that I would say or do anything with that information outside this room, obviously."

Itzkowitz smiled and flicked over a page on her notebook. "I did pick up a pattern which seemed to refer to a shipment of something, I'm guessing drugs, coming into Redhill aerodrome late at night last April, and again each month across the summer. It seems to follow the pattern of the full moon. Unfortunately, the notes stop with Wing's death. I went to see Phil Church to ask him about the possibility of drugs being shipped into the region by the aerodrome and he dismissed the idea out of hand."

"No surprise there. He wouldn't entertain the idea of

anything bad happening on his patch."

Bishop coughed, "When I worked on the drugs team, the aerodrome was considered a high-risk location. Almost every week we'd send a patrol up there at night. But we didn't have the resources to stake it out continually and there are quite a few unmanned airfields where you can land a small plane at night."

"What do you think boss?"

"Why don't you take me through your findings after this session."

"If there's a strong pattern to these alleged drug shipments, maybe it's still running," said McTierney, "If it was when would the next one be?"

"That's the interesting thing," said Itzkowitz fiddling with her fingers, "It would be next week the 15th."

TWENTY-NINE

IN THE END Bee failed to rustle up a partner for Itzkowitz so she agreed to take the night shift on her own. Bee was still worried that Church might have some involvement somewhere in the case and was reluctant to ask him for support. Additionally, he decided not to ask Beck for additional resources as he felt this would inevitably get back to Church. Bee recognised his own stubbornness and assuaged his guilt by promising Itzkowitz than he would come and find her at 4am and take over the early morning shift. McTierney shook his head at all the misgivings and told them both he was going for a pint.

Itzkowitz left the station earlier than usual and stopped at the BP petrol station on the Brighton Road in Redhill, partly to top up her car but principally to restock her supply of snacks to help her stay awake through her night shift. She waddled out of the retail shop with an armful of chocolate bars and dropped them on the bonnet of her VW Beetle, while she searched her pocket for her car key.

Four hours later and bolstered by the two-hour power nap she had taken at home; Itzkowitz manoeuvred her car onto the end of Goldworth Road. It's part of a newish estate in Redhill where the council has maximised the number of houses that can be arranged across a few acres. Garages and lawns were at a premium as were late night parking spaces and Itzkowitz rolled her car onto a yellow line. The houses on Goldworth Road meander along the edge of the estate but the one that Itzkowitz wanted sat in the middle of a short terrace of six. She stopped at the end of the terrace and pulled in behind a dirty black BMW. She had an excellent view across the street. Number 77 was a three-storey town house, much like all the other houses on the estate. But there was one difference; every other house she could see had a light on somewhere, but 77 stood in total darkness, no surprise there.

Itzkowitz looked across at her carrier bag of goodies, she pulled it open and ran her fingers over the three bags of crisps and four chocolate bars; almost one per hour, if she had one now that would leave one per hour. A Double-Decker bar kicked off the feast. Then Itzkowitz picked up the diary and began reading through the pages. Wing had written the notes about his mother in regular English but encoded all the details about his customers and what she believed to be the drugs supply route through Redhill aerodrome. She put a pencil to her lips as she imagined Wing jotting notes in his book, but her attention was caught when a light popped on in the upstairs room of the neighbouring house, Itzkowitz rolled up her sleeve to look at the time, a shade after 10pm, a bit early for bed she thought. A young woman walked quickly down the road, passing by Itzkowitz's VW but didn't appear to notice the detective. Two minutes later a youth in dark clothes and baseball hat followed the same route on an e-scooter. Itzkowitz had a bad feeling about the scooter. She looked across at the house – it remained shrouded in darkness, and she made a snap decision. She took a stick of gum and jumped out of her car and followed the route of the woman. She found herself almost running to keep up as the scooter turned left and right through the labyrinth of the estate. She saw the woman stop at a door, pluck a key from her bag and open the front door. Meanwhile the scooter turned right and sped away. Itzkowitz found herself looking at child's play area in the centre of courtyard. A tall hedge surrounded the area and a council 'no ball games' sign had been defaced. She spun around not sure of where she was. She flicked on Google Maps and identified a path back. The route took her along a new road, and she found herself approaching number 77 from the rear. She decided to take a closer look and walked along the front of the short terrace, as she passed 77 she looked in at the property, it was cold and lifeless, with paint peeling from the window frames. "There's no one here," she muttered as she got to the end of the terrace and looped back around to her car via another manicured area of grass.

Back in the car and time for another chocolate bar, Twix this time, she screwed the wrapper up and tossed it into the footwell. She reached across to check the digital camera she had was within reach in case anyone appeared and then switched to her binoculars to scan the whole terrace. Still nothing to see at number 77, but two houses along the owners had some scaffolding up, Itzkowitz wasn't sure what they were planning to do, but it covered the entire front of the property. The sight of it took her back to a stake out she'd been on back in New York. She and a partner had been stationed outside the back of a hotel block where a life-long criminal had been reported to be hiding. That too had scaffolding all the way down the back of the building. A little after 2am there had been movement on the scaffold and she and her partner had left their vehicle believing it to be their chance to apprehend the felon. There was a sound, she thought her partner had been shot, but he'd slipped at the wrong time, Itzkowitz returned fire. But it was a car backfiring, and she'd shot an unarmed kid. In all probability the kid was casing the joint, maybe worse, but she'd shot him dead and now nobody would ever know. The backlash had been intense, and she'd been advised to leave the city for her own safety after a gang had issued a kill order on her. She assumed that the Reigate police hadn't bothered to check up on her record.

But nothing untoward would happen tonight, she was only armed with a camera and a pair of binoculars, and neither were getting much use. She ripped open a large sized bag of cheese and onion crisps and picked up the diary for another look. She read the first few weeks of the year so many times so this time she started from the back. Two pages in and it seemed to make more sense, perhaps her brain had switched into a new gear or maybe reading backwards was how Wing had set it up. Perhaps the initials just needed to be turned around. She flicked back to a page she'd read many times; Saturday March 26th, 2022, there'd been a fight in Croydon and AC, or perhaps CA had been taken out of the game. She made a note to check with Bee if they could verify the name or the initials.

She looked at her watch again, it was nearly 2am, she stretched out her arms and legs. She wanted to go for a walk but knew that she'd already broken stakeout protocol once and if she did so again at this time of night the courtesy light in her car would turn on and announce her presence to the world. Not that she believed there was anyone in number 77.

Maybe another chocolate bar would ease her muscles, she rummaged around in her bag and pulled out a Mars bar, that would do.

Suddenly a burst of golden light erupted behind the front door of number 77. "Hello, someone's turned up," muttered Itzkowitz stretching, yawning, and reaching for the camera. "Are we about to have a late-night party?"

But as she pulled the camera to her eye she realised that it wasn't a light that had been turned on. "Shit! Someone's set fire to the place."

She dumped the camera back on the passenger seat and grabbed her phone to dial 999.

"Emergency services. Which service do you require?"

"Fire please."

"Fire?"

"Yes! Quick get a fire truck to Goldworth Road in Redhill now. Someone's started a fire in number 77. The whole row could burn."

"Okay, calm down. An engine's on its way, now can I take your name?"

"I'm DS Itzkowitz from Reigate station, I've been on a stakeout at Goldworth Road, and someone's just torched the place. The fire started downstairs but it's already spreading. The houses here are wood based and packed close together, if it spreads we could have a disaster on our hands. Send every fire truck you can lay your hands on."

"I've placed the call with the Reigate station, they'll be with you in 5 minutes."

"Great. Now I've got to go."

Itzkowitz jumped out of her call and ran across the road and hammered on the door of number 77. She didn't wait for an answer, but stepped across the drive to bang on the door of the house next door and then darted the other side to wake the residents there. As she reached the fourth house, her pounding on the door was drowned out by the siren on the first engine. It screeched into the close and stopped in the middle of the road outside number 77. The property was fully ablaze now with flames engulfing the structure, the windows at the front of the house had blown out. A fireman ran towards her "Is there anyone in there?"

"I don't think so, but I can't be sure."

"What?"

"I'm police. I've had the place under surveillance for the last 4 hours and there's been no movement, but this has all the signs of an arson attack. I'm sure there's people in the neighbouring houses, I've woken them and they're getting out."

"Great. We'll take it from here. Stand well clear."

Three firemen ran past her uncoiling a hose and began spraying the house. Itzkowitz found herself being pulled back away from the fire and standing next to the engine. A man she presumed to be the crew leader came to speak to her.

"Are you the one that called this in?"

"Yes."

"Good work. I gather you're an under-cover officer. Can you hang around, we'll need to talk to you when it's done."

"Yes sure."

The rest of their conversation was lost under a second siren as another fire tender rounded the corner. Another 5 fireman began tackling the blaze and Itzkowitz slunk back to her car. She picked up her phone and called Bee on his mobile. A groggy voice picked up the call.

"Sir, 77 Goldworth Road is on fire. I think it's an arson attack, there's been nobody here all night. The fire trucks are here now, and they seem to have it under control."

"Stay there, I'll come down."

Bee and Itzkowitz stood and watched as the second fire crew pulled their ladders down and rolled up their hoses. The chief walked over to speak to them. "You were lucky, we were just about to change shift when the call came in, so in effect we had two crews on. Also being night time, there was minimal traffic to get in the way. I reckon those two factors allowed us to get enough men here quick enough to stop this becoming a major incident. All these houses have a lot of wood in their construction, and they're all squeezed together. This could have been a major tragedy."

"Have you got everybody out?"

"Yes I believe so. The one in the middle is destroyed but that seems to have been empty, everyone else is out and okay." He turned his attention to Itzkowitz, "You probably saved a life or two tonight. You've done well."

Bee patted her on the back.

"Just doing my job."

The fire chief turned back to Bee, "I know it's early days but there's a strong smell of lighter fluid here, I'd bet my mortgage on this being a deliberate burn. But we'll know for sure in a couple of days."

★ ★ ★

MCTIERNEY STUMBLED INTO the kitchen and switched on the radio more to wake himself up than for the music. On the table Bee had left him a note. McTierney picked it up and rubbed his eyes as he tried to read it.

'Itzkowitz called. Goldworth Road on fire. Gone to help. Call me when you're up.'

McTierney dropped the sheet of paper, "Shit. A bloody fire. Some bastard had burnt the damn place down, all the evidence will be lost, and I forgot to ask Kelly to start the forensics. Bee will go nuts."

THIRTY

MCTIERNEY WAS STILL sitting at the breakfast table contemplating his next move when his phone rang. He looked down at the caller's name and decided to take it on the chin.

"We've had a sobering night down at Goldworth Road, our house has been gutted in the fire. I'm going to give them all a couple of hours to sort themselves out and then we'll start some door-to-door questioning."

"I guess they might be keen to talk if they think one of their ex-neighbours nearly burnt them all to a crisp."

"Precisely."

"Boss, I'm going to be late into the office today, I've got a theory I want to test."

"Don't be too long we're going to need all hands-on deck today, and I've had to send Itzkowitz home to get some sleep."

"I won't be long, and it's work related."

"Really? It's a bit early for this kind of shock. What are you doing?"

"I've got an idea where we might find an extra witness for all the activity at Goldworth Road."

"That would be helpful, who is it?"

"I think I might know who took all those photos for

Mickey and Carlos. I'll check it out and meet you at Goldworth Road to help with the door-to-door interviews."

"Sure, I'll take Bishop down there with me to get it started, always useful to have a second pair of eyes and ears."

McTierney parked his car in the railway station carpark at Redhill and sauntered across to the taxi booking office opposite to McDonalds. He pushed open the long glass door and wiped his feet on the mat inside, his attention was caught by a news report on the small TV perched high up on a black metal frame. Some young reporter was standing on a quayside somewhere in the Caribbean telling the story of a police raid on the hideout of a drug baron. "Good job boys," he muttered to himself. As he had hoped Julie was behind the desk and the office was empty apart from the two of them. She beamed her 'Debbie Harry smile' at Ron and he felt convinced that Mickey Wing had felt the same jolt of sunshine.

"You again Ron, looks like you can't keep away from the place. Are you after a ride?"

McTierney grinned and Julie hooted at her own joke. He walked across the linoleum floor and lent on the counter. "Not today. But maybe you can help me?"

"Sure, anything for you Ron," she picked up a pen and sucked the end of it.

McTierney cleared his throat, "How long have you worked in this office?"

"About three years, something like that. I started before Christmas '20, and the guys kinda like me so I stayed."

"So, you must see a lot of what goes on around the town."

Julie nodded, "I guess."

"Did you see a lot of Mickey Wing?"

Julie blushed. "Yeah. A bit, we hung out together sometimes."

"I found some photos of him and a few friends having a party in a house over the way. You know the one I mean? Were you there?"

"I've been to a few parties with Mickey, but what's this about?"

"As you know I've been investigating the murder of Mickey and I'm working on a theory that he might have stepped on the toes of some nasty people and one of them had him shot, a sort of execution."

Julie looked shocked and put her hand to her mouth.

"It's possible that one of these people attended one of these parties." McTierney let the point register. "So, if you were there and happened to take some of the photos of Mickey and his friends, then I'd like you to tell me everything you can about those nights. Any little detail that seems random to you, might be key for me."

Julie sucked the air in over her teeth, swallowed twice, looked at the clock, the door and back to the clock. "Okay. I don't think I know much but I'll tell you all I can."

THIRTY-ONE

BEE DECIDED THAT he would get to Mr Dickinson before the morning surgeries had a chance to get going and was sitting in the waiting area of Gatwick Park hospital before anyone else. He watched the various members of staff arrive and tried to determine what role they held in the building. He was getting good at dividing the personnel into high-paid consultants, well-paid support staff and well-off clients when he spotted a tall athletic and suntanned man march confidently into the building. He nodded at the receptionist and strode on into the building. *That's him*, thought Bee and he jumped up to intercept him. The man glared at the intrusion and tried to side step Bee but was caught out when Bee used his name, "Mr Dickinson?"

Dickinson hesitated momentarily and knew he was trapped.

"It is. What can I do for you. I believe I'm fully booked this morning; you'll have to see my secretary and make an appointment for next week." The consultant had a voice that immediately defined him, public school thought Bee, then Oxbridge perhaps.

"That won't be necessary, I'm with the police," said Bee flashing his warrant card, "I'll only need a few minutes."

Dickinson, stopped to inspect the card, and grunted his

disapproval, "Very well. Walk this way. I'll introduce you to Caroline Lambert, my secretary at the same time." Dickinson continued at a pace round a few corners, along a corridor and into a plush area where gentle piped classical music soothed the ears of his clients. Or it would have, had there been any this morning, only Caroline was in the room. She greeted Dickinson cordially, but offered a second glance at Bee as he followed close behind. Dickinson stopped to introduce Bee, then scribbled something on Caroline's pad and opened the door to his inner office and invited Bee in. The room looked more like an art gallery that a medical office; two of the three solid walls each held large scale paintings, a mini marble figurine stood on a plinth in one corner. Alongside this was a mahogany bookcase and next to this was the certificate which confirmed Bee's early suspicions, Dickinson had graduated from Cambridge. But maybe now he was practicing in the gutter. Bee didn't mess about. "I believe you performed a kidney transplant operation on a young girl by the name of Penelope Trimble. Is that correct?"

Dickinson looked surprised by the question and hesitated for a moment. "I do a lot of operations, extend the lives of many people, I can't remember the precise details of all my patients but if you give me the name I'll have Caroline check it for you."

Bee gave him a look of disbelief. "We can return to that. I also have reason to believe that you have conducted illegal kidney transplants. Do you have any comment to make?"

Dickinson held up his hands, "Whoa. Slow down. I'm an ethical surgeon, using my skills to improve the lives of my clients. I do a lot of good for this world. I can't have you going around saying things like that. My lawyer will go crazy."

Bee listened to the expected defence and noticed that Dickinson hardly blinked at all. He wondered if he was high on caffeine before he started his days work. Then to partly answer his question Caroline returned with two fresh coffees in art deco mugs and placed them on the desk between the two men. She turned back to the door, then stopped, "Sorry to interrupt, but I've just had your daughter's school on the phone, apparently Abigail has been sick twice since you dropped her off, they've tried to contact your wife but can't locate her. They're saying someone needs to collect your daughter, she can't stay at school if she's unwell."

Dickinson offered the most insincere smile Bee had ever seen, opened his palms and got up from his seat. "Apologies inspector, I have to go. Perhaps you can make an appointment for next week with Caroline and we can continue this interesting discussion at that time." With that he brushed past his secretary and disappeared.

Bee followed Caroline back out of the office and waited patiently for her to find a slot in Dickinson's diary for the following Friday. He was irked to find that the surgeon was completely booked during the preceding days. Caroline excused herself suggesting that she needed to make some calls and Bee sauntered back to the main reception area, but as he arrived he decided that he wasn't prepared to wait another week and skipped back to Dickinson's suite, but when he arrived he found Caroline had gone.

Not only had she gone but she had cleared the desk and taken all her belongings including her laptop and diary. Bee had a bad feeling about the disappearance, he walked around the desk and sat in the seat that she had recently vacated. He glanced down at the waste bin, which had only the pink Post-it note that Dickinson had scribbled something on when Bee first arrived. He retrieved it from the bin and read 'code red'.

"Damn!" This had been a rehearsed scam. He realised there would be no sick child at any school. He searched around the laptop docking station but there was nothing useful to be found. He sat back in the hi-back chair that Caroline had used and scanned the surfaces. There was a purple felt board on the wall next to her desk it offered a few standard notices illustrating the escape routes in case of an emergency, some generic phone numbers for the building and a photo of Caroline with her daughter. He pulled at all of the drawers in hope more than expectation. He wasn't sure what he was looking for, but he didn't want to walk away from here empty handed. But to no avail, she had locked them all. He jumped up and tried the door to Dickinson's office, but that too was locked. "Damn!"

He ran his hand through his hair. He rattled the desks again and darted along to the next office area, where a man in a long white coat was talking to a woman about knees. Bee flashed his warrant card and borrowed a paper knife. He slipped back to Lambert's desk and slide the knife into gap at the top of the set of drawers. He'd seen this done in Tom Cruise movies, a quick flick left or right and everything fell open. Unfortunately, Tom Cruise is never around when you need him, and the lock refused to budge. He shoved the knife into every crack he could find but each time with the same result. He felt the sweat start to build on his collar. Time to change tactics, Bee put the paper knife to one side and reverted to a sharp kick at the mechanism. But with the same result. His discreet attempt to surreptitiously find some information was turning farcical, the pantomime was complete when a caretaker came by and asked what was all the noise. Bee felt embarrassed to explain himself, but showed his overused warrant card to the man and asked him to open the drawers. The man hesitated and Bee saw his opportunity.

"Quickly, this is linked to a murder case. I need access to whatever might be in these drawers."

Under pressure the caretaker fumbled in his brown coat pocket and produced a giant key ring with dozens of small keys. He knelt down to read a number on the lock, then spun a few identical looking keys around in his hand, found the correct key and ten seconds later stood up to display his handiwork.

"Excellent work," said Bee. "Now could I ask you to get a map of the layout of this hospital."

The man looked a little perplexed, "I'm sure that won't be too challenging for a man of your talents."

The caretaker grumbled but turned and wandered off. Bee didn't want a map, but he didn't want an audience for what might happen next.

He pulled out each drawer in turn; the top was a narrow stationery drawer containing a few pens, the second carried some glossy brochures detailing the services to be provided by The Dickinson Clinic. Bee flicked through the 4-page leaflet; it heralded the potential of a new life for would be kidney recipients if they chose the Dickinson way, illustrated by sportsmen and women each with a bright beaming smile. Bee felt a wave of revulsion ripple through his stomach. But it was evidence, first rate evidence. He continued his search and the bottom drawer revealed what he had hoped for; it was the personal folders of many, perhaps all of Dickinson's past clients. Bingo.

Bee bundled up the khaki personal folders and a few of the brochures and pushed the drawers back to leave the place tidy. He got up to leave but lent back across the desk and plucked the photo of Caroline Lambert and her daughter from the pin board. He presumed it was her daughter but cautioned himself against believing anything. He took the photo and returned to the main reception area, where he introduced himself to the hospital chief administrator and asked for their contact information on the lady in the photo. It took him a few minutes, but Bee left with a piece of paper giving the home address of Caroline Lambert, conveniently it was in Tadworth, a few miles north of Reigate.

★ ★ ★

BEE CHECKED HIS watch as he approached the back door of the station and guessed that his colleagues would be in the canteen; eager to find some positive news to compensate for his own disappointment, he elected to join them. He picked up his usual cappuccino and made his way over to a long table against the far wall, from where he could hear McTierney regaling the team with some outlandish story. Bee mumbled a general good morning and slid in next to his colleagues. As the laughter from McTierney's anecdote died away, Itzkowitz looked across at Bee "Is that a new scarf you're wearing?" It's rather smart, a little too smart for your taste if I may say so."

McTierney slapped his hand over his mouth to stop him from spraying the table with coffee, as he chortled at the comment. "What she means is, that scarf is too smart for you to have bought yourself, so who did?"

"Yes come on, who's the secret admirer?"

Bee opened his mouth, but his throat dried on him, while Bishop blushed and knocked a teaspoon on the floor. Itzkowitz's eyes burst out of their sockets, while McTierney nudged her in the ribs. "Come on detective, we've got work to do."

McTierney and Itzkowitz were still sniggering ten minutes later when Bee and Bishop walked up the stairs and crossed the long open plan area to join them in the CID area. As they arrived both McTierney and Itzkowitz buried their heads in their laptops and pretended to be engrossed in the most captivating reports ever written.

"Okay you two quit the charade, it's a very thoughtful, belated birthday gift. We've got a few items to catch up on, so let's have 15 minutes in the ops room."

The four of them congregated in the white plastic room and Bee began the meeting by recounting the highlights of his trip to the hospital and his attempt to interview Mr Dickinson.

"I don't know where it leaves us, but Dickinson is a rogue who we need to apprehend. As yet I'm not sure if he's connected to the demise of Michael Wing, but I'll pursue his secretary today or tomorrow and hopefully McTierney and I can talk to him early next week."

He shot a glance at McTierney who seemed to be pondering whether he could make a comment about Dickinson's fancy escape but decided against it. Bee then passed the meeting baton to Bishop who told the group that she'd had difficulty tracking down the owner of Goldworth Road. Evidently the property was owned by a company which in turn was owned by another offshore business and so on. It was clear that the real owner had gone to a lot of trouble to remain anonymous. She had been no more successful tracking down Mickey Wing's alleged college course. None of the colleges in the area had any record of a Michael or Mickey Wing or any another M Wing. Bee let the points settle in the room.

"Perhaps no surprise that Michael Wing wasn't an evening college student, probably too busy with his other nocturnal pastimes, but easy to see how this double life he invented gave him a good cover for his aunt and other family members."

"If she is his aunt," challenged McTierney.

"That wouldn't surprise me either, but it probably doesn't matter for now."

"Someone has gone to a lot of trouble to disguise a cheap property." This time it was Itzkowitz. "It's probably costs them as much in fences as it did to buy the place."

"Yes, absolutely. I think it just underlines our belief that it's not your regular three-bedroom home. We should have the forensic reports back this afternoon, I asked them to prioritise it."

There was a murmur of agreement around the table, then McTierney spoke, "So we'd better all be here after lunch."

Bee nodded, "Two other minor things; Beck is away for a week's holiday next week, so I'm deputising for him."

"Going anywhere nice?"

"The Algarve I believe, but don't quote me. But it will make it easier for me to sign off any major surveillance plan you come up with for the 15th," He looked across the table at Itzkowitz. "Cool. I'm on it."

"Finally, I've been told there's an infestation of honey bees up on the top floor. Someone from a pest control company is coming out today to tell me what we should do about it. So best keep off the top floor for a while."

"Has anyone seen any of these bees?" asked McTierney.

Nobody had.

"Only room for one bee in this station hey?"

THIRTY-TWO

Bee's phoned beeped with a message from Maria to come to reception to meet Joe Higgs from the Bee Patrol company. Bee wondered for a moment if Maria was taking the mickey with the name but then dismissed the idea; the P.A. for the chief superintendent didn't make jokes in the office. Bee had expected Higgs to be wearing overalls, but instead he met a middle-aged man wearing a blue suit that wouldn't have looked out of place in Canary Wharf. A second surprise hit him when Church joined the meeting.

"What are you doing here?" Bee demanded.

Maria intercepted the hostility, "I invited Phil Church as the pair of you are both direct reportees to the chief and in case anything major is needed to be done to his office I thought it better to have two opinions."

"Huh, you'll never get agreement."

"Let's see if we can work together and help Maria," oozed Church and Bee scowled at him.

Maria led the three men up to the top floor and showed them the area that Beck had earlier identified as a possible bee's nest, even now there were half a dozen lively bees around a small hole in the corner of Beck's office.

No sooner had Mr Higgs seen the first few bees than he clicked into salesman mode; he sucked the air in over his teeth and said "You'd better get this sorted straight away, looks like them bees are looking for a new nest. Once they get established and bring their queen over they'll be harder to shift."

Bee looked a bit doubtfully and Higgs played the health and safety card to full effect. "You do know that bee stings are always unpleasant and can be life threatening. Although they're not naturally aggressive, but they will become defensive if they feel threatened, that's especially likely when they are building a nest and establishing a colony in a new area."

He pointed up at the ceiling to emphasise his point. "I'm sure you want a safe environment for the police, any visitors, and of course the prisoners in the cells. Plus, the weather can have an adverse effect on their temperament, when the weather gets warmer they get active, that's when they're more dangerous, and it looks like we're in for a hot weekend."

"Doesn't sound like we have much choice," said Church.

"Yes, okay, you've got the job. I don't want the chief super coming back from holiday and getting stung. How soon can you start?"

"I'll be back first thing Monday, should only need a day, most colonies can be collected and moved in that time. But can you move everything away from that corner and also have a look around any dark corners, drawers, and cupboards for other possible nests and hidey-holes. They tend to like dormer windows or cavity walls or flat roofs, so the top floor of a house or building is always their first choice. Might as well get them all at the same time."

"Can we make it Sunday? Get it all done when there's no one around? I'll come in and clear the area as you've just described but I'd like to minimise the disruption to the office and there's fewer people here on a Sunday."

"Sure thing, but it'll cost you double."

Bee made a mental note to cancel any plans for Sunday morning.

★ ★ ★

IT WAS MID-AFTERNOON when the team gathered in the ops room to hear Dr Kelly present his findings from his recent forensic investigations. McTierney was still feeling guilty about forgetting to call Kelly on the Wednesday morning and kept his head bowed as he led the team into the room.

Kelly seemed to sense his reticence and slapped him on the back, "You're quiet today, are you feeling okay?"

McTierney offered a weak smile, "Look it's my favourite West Indian pathologist. I hoped it was going to be you."

Kelly looked over his glasses at McTierney, "As a matter of interest how many West Indian pathologists do you know?"

"Only one, but you've misunderstood me."

"Have I?"

"I meant favourite pathologist who just happens to be West Indian."

Kelly offered a rueful smile, as he withdrew his papers from his brown briefcase, "Thanks for the clarification and the compliment." He chose to stand at the end of the table and deliver a presentation using the screen behind him.

"Now if we're all here, I'll share with you what my team has uncovered from each of these locations. You all know how much I enjoy cricket, so I thought I'd treat them as if it's a first and a second innings."

"Second innings? I thought you'd only been to the garage at Baxter Avenue."

Kelly grinned across at Bee and the two men started laughing.

"What?" demanded McTierney.

"Lucky for you, your detective inspector is not as forgetful as you. He called me himself on Wednesday morning and stressed the importance of searching Goldworth Road, so I got my team in there just after lunch." Kelly allowed the point to settle. "Before the fire."

McTierney smiled and muttered, "Bastards."

"It's been so good having you on best behaviour for the last 48 hours, even though I knew it would have to end." Bee had a smile a mile wide, and Itzkowitz and Bishop joined the party.

"I'm glad you've all been enjoying yourselves. But in case anyone has forgotten we've still got a case to solve."

Bee brought the room to order, "Before Dr Kelly gives us his findings, I think there is a serious point here, which I want to highlight."

Everyone turned to face Bee. "I made that call to Kelly on Tuesday, not because I had no faith in our DS here, but because I had a bad feeling about the place and burning it to the ground was the sort of thing I would have done, had I been involved in this. I'm guessing that the sight of the police dogs turning upon Tuesday morning was the trigger point." He paused to see that the team were following his every word.

"It shows that we're onto the gang behind this."

"But who knew the dogs were there," asked Itzkowitz.

"The whole street. Every resident."

"Are you saying you think there's a spy in the street?"

"It wouldn't surprise me."

"But who?"

"That's the $64,000 question, that and can we find them?"

"Well, we know someone who it wasn't," said McTierney. "It wasn't Hanbing, he's been downstairs in the cells for the last few days."

With a brief pause in the conversation Dr Kelly seized the initiative and began his presentation. "As it's been a while since we were altogether let me take a moment to remind you of the work we do. It's a four-pronged attack, like the great West Indian team of the 1980's."

"Is that the last time, you had a decent cricket team?" Asked McTierney.

Kelly shot him a look of daggers, "I see we have the old McTierney back already!"

"The four elements are visual inspection, chemical analysis, a microscopic examination and rounded off with a spot of analysis with specialised instruments where applicable."

"We know all this," moaned McTierney.

Kelly shook his head, "What a impatient child you must have been." He duly clicked his presentation along a couple of slides, "Very well, we'll jump to the results page. I appreciate that not everyone has the attention span of others." He smiled to himself.

"In the garage, we found blood soaked into the concrete floor, not large quantities, so I doubt anyone died there, but obviously blood finds capture the headlines and even the imagination." He threw a glance at McTierney, who smiled his appreciation. "This was blood type O positive so not that same as the deceased, and also the most commonly found type in the country."

"We should get a sample of Hanbing's blood to see if it matches," said Bee.

Itzkowitz nodded, "Sure, I'll set it up when we're finished.

"Fair enough, but be aware that as blood samples go, this one is a bit dull. Indeed, the entire garage is a bit dull. No drugs, no alcohol, no bodily fluids, my guess would be that someone cut themselves or bashed their hand on someone hard or metallic in the garage and that's why we have the sample."

"Thanks for the advice, doc, but even so, we'd better check it," said Bee, looking at Itzkowitz as much as Dr Kelly.

"You may have more work as a result of our search of the rooms at Goldworth Road." Kelly took a deep breathe, as if preparing to dive into a pool. "There's blood here. Blood in the carpet of the back bedroom and here's your headline; it's a rare blood type, AB negative. As you probably know that's more or less the rarest blood type in the country. Roughly 1% of the nation has that running through their veins. Those of you with a good memory will recall that our cave victim had the same blood type. So, if he did sell one of his kidneys, he should've got a premium price for it."

"Don't suppose he knew," said McTierney.

"No, but I bet the doctor who removed it knew," added Bee.

The room paused for a moment while the occupants each made a mental calculation of the potential value of one of Michael Wing's kidneys. Kelly brought the process to a close.

"About three times the normal market rate, so something

around £10-£12k. Although since it's illegal there's not a published price list to use."

"I'm glad you recognise it as against the law," said Bee with a stern face.

"Moving on," said Kelly. "The more significant point is that it's possible this is where our victim was shot. There's not a lot of blood here, but it could have been cleaned. My instinct is to suggest that Goldworth Road is a more likely murder scene than the Barons' Cave."

"Now you're talking," said McTierney.

"We used an ultra violet lamp to scan the room and in addition to the blood on the carpet, there are a few splashes on the bed linen which were missed by whoever did the clean-up."

"That's excellent work," said Bee. "It'll be a great help to definitively identify the murder scene and maybe someone burning it to the ground adds weight to that argument." He paused to consider his next statement. "It's a smart move on behalf of whoever is behind all this to set up a den of iniquity and then hide everything in plain view. Goldworth Road is a pleasant newish neighbourhood hiding one bad apple. It's not your obvious crime scene."

Kelly held up his hand. "Yes no doubt finding the murder scene is positive, but here's the downside. There are so many different fingerprints all over the place, it's a hellish job to narrow down the visitors. It's like there's been a party in every room."

Bee clicked his tongue disapprovingly. "Yes I was afraid of that."

"Our UV scan produced a cocktail of bodily fluids. It shows blood, sperm, saliva, and urine. None of them are fresh, a week or three old at least, some older."

McTierney pursed his lips, "Sounds like whoever ran these 'parties', had got wind of our investigation and decided to close the place down."

"Or they wanted to cover up the murder," added Itzkowitz.

"Most likely it's the same person responsible for both. Taking care of their loose ends all in one go," said Bee.

"I did get the impression that no one lived there; there's no evidence of any kind of cleaning regime. That helps us track prints of one sort or another but is also a hindrance as many are superimposed over another. We collected 7 distinct different prints that we can use from more than a hundred smudged or damaged images."

"The idea of a few parties would certainly fit with the witness statement from Mrs Baker, said Bee, "Anything else?"

"Oh yes. This house is a modern-day Aladdin's Cave." Kelly moved his presentation on. "Two more big hitters. First, We found six playing cards but all the same card, the king of diamonds." He plucked a plastic bag from his case which contained the cards and placed it on the table.

"The red king," said McTierney, "Hanbing talked about the red king, maybe someone used it as a calling card."

"6 times over," said Kelly as he pushed the bag across the table.

"The question is, did Hanbing hand out the cards or did he receive them?" asked Itzkowitz.

"Hanbing has suggested quite strongly that he wasn't the red king. He gave me the impression that this red king person was the head of the tree. Someone he feared and hadn't met."

Bee reached across and took the package. "We need to re-

THE CAVE OF DEATH

interview Hanbing. He could be inventing this person to distract us. He told you the story about Wing and him creating a new criminal gang, perhaps the red king was their way of marking their territory."

McTierney shrugged his shoulders, "I guess it wouldn't be the first time someone has tried to downplay their criminal lifestyle to avoid a long sentence."

"Second big play is drugs. We didn't find a large stash, but I gather the dog team did that, but we did find plenty of scrapes and residues suggesting use, even excessive use of cocaine and amphetamines. No great surprise given the description of the place that you gave us. In fact, the site would have made a perfect training ground for an apprentice forensic officer, there was so much to find there."

"Excellent summary, Kelly, thank you." Bee turned his focus to his team, "Looks like Goldworth Road is going to be making an appearance on our whiteboard. For now, let's treat it as the probable murder scene. We'll pick this up on Monday, before then McTierney and I will try to pick up this doctor character and his secretary."

McTierney did a double take at the use of his name. Bee caught his eye and smiled, "And before that McTierney and I are going to have another word with Hanbing." Bee pointed across the room to his colleague, "Can you get him into the interview room."

The team pushed their chairs back and started to move, but before they left McTierney chipped in, "If anyone has any energy left after all that's going on, come on down to Meadowbank tomorrow, the home ground of Dorking Wanderers and watch the Surrey Police team featuring your two favourite detectives win the Surrey Intermediate Cup. Kick-off is 3pm."

THIRTY-THREE

AS THE TEAM dispersed from the ops room, Bee grabbed the sleeve of McTierney and pulled him back into the ops room. "Before you go to find our suspect, we need to be clear about your earlier indiscretion."

McTierney looked abashed.

"I know there's been a few but I'm talking about your comments to Hanbing suggesting he could avoid a prison sentence if he shared some information with us."

McTierney remained silent.

"In the light of what we've discovered lately and the potential for more revelations, we can't make that kind of deal."

McTierney kept his eyes focused on his shoes.

"But if I'm right, there were no witnesses and there's no evidence of the deal."

"No sir."

"Much as I hate to be dishonest, this time we may have no choice. If we later discover that Hanbing hasn't been heavily involved, then maybe we can look at a lighter option, but for now all bets are off. So don't mention it again, and if Hanbing brings it up, you'll have to deny it."

"Yes, boss."

"Good, now if you can retrieve him from the cells, I'll

meet you in interview room 1."

HANBING APPEARED SURPRISED to be back in an interview room but didn't speak. Bee pulled out a chair, took his seat and started the tape recorder. "Carlos Hanbing, you are under caution for this interview, because we are investigating the death of your associate Michael Wing, and you are a suspect in his murder. Do you understand?"

Hanbing jolted forward as if hit by an electric charge, "But you said no prison, if I talk." He looked directly at McTierney, but Bee fielded the challenge. "There are no deals on a potential murder charge. Now would you like a solicitor to be present. You're not being charged with anything at this stage, but you are entitled to have someone with you."

Hanbing scowled at Bee. "Yes I want my lawyer."

Bee stopped the tape and turned to McTierney. "Can you get him back to the cells and then get a solicitor down here, I'm going to check out some old cases to see if there has been an upturn in martial arts type injuries. Give me a call when the brief arrives."

Bee walked back up the stairs but as he passed the CID area his eye was taken by a light on in the ops room. He stopped in his tracks; he thought he'd turned off the lights. He took a step up the stairs to his room, but a doubt brought him back, he tiptoed across the main floor and stepped into the ops room, standing in front of the white board reading the notes was Phil Church.

"What the hell do you think you're doing?"

"Keeping abreast of the investigation."

"You've no right. This is private. Get out you scumbag."

Church swung around, "I have every right. Beck asked me to keep an eye on your progress. He's worried that you've lost the plot. He's thinking of taking you off the case."

The accusation hit harder than any punch could have, and Bee grabbed the desk for support. Church continued his assault. "Yep the old man is starting to doubt you. Thinks you've lost your touch. I reckon by the time he gets back from holiday; your goose is cooked. Admin duties for you."

Bee steeled himself, "No. No way. Beck would have told me himself. He doesn't need you to deliver his messages. Not that you're worth much more than that." He strode across to face Church, "Now get out of my ops room, before I throw you out."

Church held his hands up in mock surrender, "Only trying to help. You've got to admit it's not going well."

"It's going fine, just fine," said Bee as he held out his arm indicating that Church should leave. Church walked towards the door but stopped at the entrance. "A diary, full of code words, I bet you're loving that. But none of it will be admissible in court. All open to interpretation. Have a good night."

Bee clenched his fist and slammed it down on the desk. He was mostly cross with himself for not locking the ops room door when the earlier meeting finished. But Church had wound him up and touched a nerve. No, the case wasn't going well. Beck had kept his distance lately which wasn't at all like the chief. But the thought that wouldn't dissipate was the one about Church. What was he up to? Did he have a role in this murder? Bee struggled to believe that another police officer could commit murder, but he kept turning up in the wrong place. Before he could give this thought any proper consideration, McTierney called him to say they were ready to continue the interview with Hanbing.

Bee stomped into the room and allowed the door to slam behind him. McTierney looked shocked. "You alright boss?"

"Of course," snapped Bee.

"Good, well this is Mr Lawrence, he's here to represent Carlos Hanbing."

The introduction seemed to break Bee out of his disposition, and he meekly offered his hand to the solicitor. "Shall we start, I'm sure none of us want to be here any longer than necessary."

"Amen to that," said McTierney.

Bee took the initiative, set the tape going and spoke to Hanbing. "Silence won't work this time. Not with a potential murder charge hanging over you."

Hanbing shifted in his chair and looked to his solicitor for support, but none was forthcoming. Then he lent forward and spoke quietly. "I didn't kill Mickey; he was my friend. Why would I kill him? I already told your friend all that I know about Mickey."

"Who do you think killed Wing?"

"I don't know probably some weirdo."

"Probably not. Statistically most murder victims know their killer, so it's likely that Wing knew his killer, – probably a friend. And since you've spent a lot of time telling us how you and Wing were best friends, you probably know him as well."

Hanbing frowned and his face contorted as if he'd been asked to eat something foul tasting.

Bee allowed the point to register. "So, I'll ask you again and this time give it some thought. Who do you think killed

Wing?"

Wing took a moment to think, then shrugged his shoulders rather than speak. Bee allowed him to ponder the thought then decided to change his approach. He reached for a khaki folder on the table and pulled a photograph from it. It showed the front cover of Wing's diary. He pushed it across the desk. "Do you recognise this diary?"

Hanbing pulled it closer to him for a brief second, and pushed it back, "No."

"It belonged to your good friend, Wing. It contains coded details of some of his contacts and crimes that you say you've been party to. If you knew him as well as you say you do, then surely you'd know about this diary. He seems to have written in it every day."

Hanbing shrugged, "I don't know it."

Bee paused, "Hmm. Let's see if you know some of the contents. Did Mickey ever talk to you about his mother?"

Hanbing perked up, "Yes. I know his mother was ill, very ill. She was back home in China and Mickey wanted to get her out and bring her to England. He was worried that the authorities might put her in jail."

"Why would the Chinese police want to put her in jail? What had she done?"

Hanbing shrugged. "I don't know. All I know is that Mickey was worried about her and sent lots of money to her and his sister. He sent almost every penny he had."

"Did you think he was wasting all the money you and he stole? Was that a motive for you to kill him and keep more of the money for yourself?"

Hanbing's eyes flashed. "No. Look I told your friend, Mickey had the ideas, he was the brains of the operation.

Once he'd gone, everything stopped. I didn't know how to get the stuff; I couldn't sell it. That's why I had to get a job as a waiter."

Bee sighed. "So, if you didn't kill Michael Wing, who did?"

"I don't know. If I knew I'd tell you."

"Who were the enemies of Mickey? Who wanted him dead?"

Hanbing stopped and seemed to think about his answer. "I guess some of the drug gang from Croydon would want Mickey out of the way. He'd upset them when he stole one of their big deliveries."

"And how did he do that exactly?"

"He found out that there was a shipment coming in overnight. A small plane came into the airfield at Redhill, this gang was due to meet it. But Mickey took them by surprise. He was a martial arts specialist. I've never seen him lose a fight."

"A modern-day Bruce Lee."

"Sorry, I don't know that person."

Bee shook his head. "Can you give me a name of the gang leader from Croydon?"

"I'm not sure, Mickey talked about a John. I think his name was John Mace or John Mast, something like that."

"So, you didn't go and help your mate when he attacked this Croydon gang?"

"No, well yes. I drove the car and I waited out of sight for him, but there was only two or maybe three men. Mickey laughed at their incompetence. Three men wouldn't be a problem for him."

Bee stopped and looked at McTierney, "If Wing is this

supreme fighting machine, it re-enforces the idea that he must have known and not felt threatened by whoever got close enough to him to kill him."

"It also explains why they used a gun," said McTierney.

"We ought to check with our Croydon team if anyone knows a John Mace or John Mast."

McTierney jotted down a note and wrote 'Action FBI' beside it.

Bee turned back to Hanbing. "When did this happen?"

Hanbing pursed his lips, "About May time. The nights were light, so the planes didn't come in until after midnight."

"Not August or September."

"No, it was early summer. I remember because we had a lot more money over the summer. It was good."

Bee frowned, and Hanbing brought his expression back under control.

"Did you know that Wing sold his kidney to make some money?"

"I did yes. Mickey was angry with the doctor. He felt abandoned by him, after the operation he was ill, but they didn't care, they threw him out of the hospital. For a while he was so weak, he could barely move. They gave him a leaflet and told him to eat some special foods, but they didn't help him. Mickey nearly died."

"But he did recover."

"Yes he did."

"Given Wing's taste for challenging situations he didn't like, did he have words with the doctor?"

Hanbing smiled. "Yes he did. I think the doctor took a few weeks off to recover after Mickey spoke to him."

"When was this 'discussion'?"

"Sometime in September, I think the children had gone back to school and it was starting to get colder."

"Not long before Wing disappeared."

"No. That's right."

Bee paused, as if unsure of which direction to take the conversation. McTierney caught his eye, and Bee remembered himself.

"In case you don't know someone burnt down the house in Goldworth Road on Wednesday night."

Hanbing didn't react.

"Who might have done that?"

Hanbing shrugged, "I don't know. It wasn't me."

"No, we know that. You were here."

The solicitor grabbed his moment, "Since you've shown no evidence to link my client to any of the crimes you've discussed I think you should release him. You've had long enough to charge him, but we all know you don't have the evidence."

"He will be charged with several counts of drug dealing and prostitution, but in light of his helpful contribution tonight, I'm prepared to release him on bail on the condition that he surrenders his passport and contacts this office each day to notify us of his whereabouts."

McTierney ushered Hanbing and the solicitor out of the building and hurried back to meet Bee. "Come on, I've got work to do in the pub."

"It's pushing 9pm, you must be dying of thirst."

"I am."

"I don't think Hanbing killed Wing, he hasn't got it in him. His life has collapsed since Wing died. He was living the life of Riley, riding on Wing's coat tails and now he's lost.

Finally resorting to stealing the handbags of old ladies. He's even a bit thinner now than he was when some of the photos were taken at Goldworth Road."

"I agree he's lost since the death of Wing, but maybe he killed him in some drunken or stoned moment of rage. A mistake."

"Hmm." Bee stopped to ponder the thought.

"Look I hate to rush you, Sherlock, but could we have this conversation with a pint in my hand?"

Bee ignored the request. "No. Wing's murder was planned, not a random act. I think it's telling that he's not pushed to leave the cells. He's got nothing to escape to. We could have left the cells unlocked and I don't think he would have walked out. Such a shame to be so young and have no desire for life."

"Yeah. Such a shame to see Friday night disappearing before my eyes and I do have a desire. A big desire for a pint. You know it doesn't matter how many pints you have, there's always the opportunity for one more."

"Well don't overdo it, don't forget it's the final tomorrow."

"Aren't you coming? I'll get the first round. I've got work to do and I'm behind."

"I'll try to make the last round in The Bell, tell Tom to keep one for me and I'll be there by 11pm. But before that I want to check out these martials arts claims; see if we've had any reported injuries that fit this claim. Plus, I'll put a call into Croydon about this John Mast guy."

THIRTY-FOUR

"WHY DO WE have to do this on a Saturday morning? And not any Saturday, the Saturday of a cup final. Our cup final."

"It's our job."

"Yes, but we do our job every day of the week. We get to play in a cup final once in a lifetime. When I was a kid I used to love Cup Final Day, if United were playing I'd plonk myself on the sofa before lunchtime watch all the build-up and then the whole match. I don't think I even left the room to go to the loo."

"What a delightful image you're painting."

Bee and McTierney were driving through Reigate and on their way to Tadworth to the address they had for Mrs Caroline Lambert. Bee had insisted that his DS accompany him due to his previous experience with Lambert and her boss the consultant surgeon Dickinson. Bee was expecting something to go awry and wouldn't be at all surprised to find that the address didn't exist.

McTierney grinned. "Are you excited?"

"Not really, a bit nervous maybe but not excited. More worried that she's going to do another runner, or more likely she's already done one!"

McTierney screwed his face up. "I'm not talking about

the arrest, that's just work. I'm talking about the football!"

Bee turned his face to look at his partner. "What is wrong with you?"

"More to the point, what is wrong with you?"

Bee looked offended but quickly turned his eyes back to the road.

"Come on, this should be a great day. You're a half-decent footballer, although don't quote me on that, you'll be playing at the ground of your favourite local team in a cup-final, and you might even score the winning goal and you look like Church has just crapped on your cornflakes. I don't get it."

Bee quickly scowled at his partner but kept his focus on the road. They were driving along the A217 heading north from Reigate on a dual carriageway, but one that was limited to 40mph. A restriction that was enforced by average speed cameras.

"It's not as simple as that."

"Why not?"

"It just isn't."

Bee hoped to let the moment pass but McTierney held his silence.

"I know something will go wrong and that it will be my fault."

McTierney still wasn't biting.

"You're right about what you say and when it's all over I will be delighted to have walked out on the pitch at Meadowbank, but at this moment I'd be happy not to play. If there was a subsidence on the pitch and the match was called off and we shared the trophy, that would be perfect."

"You can't be serious."

"Oh yes I can. Life is one long series of cockups and setbacks. As soon as I have two good days I know there will be a problem with day 3; that's how my world works. And quite frankly I should be pleased to enjoy two good days because half the world doesn't even get them; I, or we have it easy."

McTierney shook his head. "No, play the hand you've been dealt. You can't solve the problems of the world on your own. It's not your fault that half the world is hungry, and half the world is corrupt. Focus on your little bit and let someone else worry about the rest."

"An appalling attitude. What would the world be like if everyone thought like you!"

"Everyone does think like me. It's called getting by."

"Well thank you Dr Freud. Have you been reading again? I thought we agreed that you'd give it up."

"That's more like it show a bit of fight. Someone's got to win today, why not us. We deserve it as much as they do."

"Don't get me started on just deserts."

"No okay, but one final thought on the football. If it comes to penalties, don't volunteer."

The conversation had taken them to the Lamberts' house, although it was closer to Walton on the Hill than Tadworth, Bee was delighted it did exist.

"Wow! Who says crime doesn't pay?" asked McTierney.

"We do."

"Okay, but it's a beautiful property."

They were looking at a modern two-storey detached house with an imposing double-aspect, brick façade, manicured gardens, and a gated drive. A Porsche stood on the drive. Even the sun glinted gently on the front windows.

"Perhaps her husband has a well-paid job in the city."

"Perhaps they won the lottery six months ago."

"It's all possible."

McTierney rolled his eyes, "Come on let's get this over with, I've got medal to win."

Bee's expectation of a difficult morning didn't come to fruition, Caroline Lambert appeared ready to accept her fate. She opened the front door and welcomed the two detectives into her kitchen, a room so large that Bee felt he would need a map to find his way around.

"Can I make you a coffee gentlemen? I would appreciate you waiting a few minutes for my husband to return from his parkrun. Then he'll be able to look after our daughter and I'll be happy to answer all the questions you have."

Bee looked across at McTierney who made a face, but Bee struggled to interpret it and readily agreed to the request. Their reward was a piping hot mug of filter coffee, and once Lambert lifted a biscuit tin down from the shelf Bee felt McTierney would be back on side with his decision.

A young girl came walking into the kitchen, a miniature version of Caroline Lambert and her mother introduced her as Abigail. Bee smiled in recognition of the name that Dickinson had used at the hospital the day before. McTierney had munched his way through three chocolate biscuits by the time the front door opened and a burly man who looked more accustomed to the rugby pitch than an athletics track entered. He removed his shoes and walked through the long hallway and into the kitchen. He addressed his comments directly at his wife.

"Are these the police officers you were expecting?"

"Yes. I need to accompany them to Reigate station, so if

you can take care of Abi, that would be great. I'll call you when I'm done."

He opened his arms to his daughter and whisked her up into a big hug, she giggled, "Come on sweetie, let's go play in your room, Mummy's got some work to do with these men." He turned away and didn't look back.

"He's not happy," added Lambert as an explanation.

Thirty minutes later the venue for their conversation had moved 15 miles south to Reigate police station. Bee and McTierney escorted Lambert in to see the desk sergeant then McTierney's mobile rang. Bee scowled at the sound.

"It's Itzkowitz. She's in the canteen. Wants to know if you want a coffee."

"What's she doing here?"

"She's stepping in to take over from me. Cost me a fortune in promises."

Bee dipped his eyes at McTierney.

"Hey Scott, come on, we need to get moving or we're going to be late for the football."

"You go ahead, and I'll be there as soon as."

"Don't be crazy, this is a once in a lifetime opportunity. Let Church take the statement and process Mrs Fancy Pants. He rarely lifts a finger around the place, it won't hurt him to do some work. Itzkowitz will keep an eye on things for us and make sure he doesn't do anything stupid."

Bee pursed his lips. "I can't. I don't trust him an inch. You go ahead and I'll be there before kick-off."

McTierney threw his hands up in the air. "Do yourself a favour. Just don't be late." He turned and headed out of the station.

THIRTY-FIVE

AN HOUR PASSED before Bee and Itzkowitz took their seats in interview room 1 opposite Caroline Lambert and her impeccably attired solicitor. Bee took them through the preliminaries and set the tape recorder playing.

"Mrs Lambert, you are here in connection with our enquires into a case of suspected unlawful removal of an organ, specifically a kidney removed from Michael Wing, although there are other instances which interest us. You're not under arrest at the present time, and you are free to leave whenever you wish, but we would appreciate your assistance in this case. Do you understand?"

Lambert smiled at Bee, "May I talk to my solicitor."

Bee raised his hands in resignation but stood up and he and Itzkowitz left the room.

"What does she need to talk about? She's not under arrest?" asked Itzkowitz as soon as the door closed behind them. "I think she will plead innocent to any potential indiscretion and seek to make a deal to avoid going to jail."

Itzkowitz turned her nose up, but Bee ignored it. "I imagine her solicitor is explaining to her the finer points of the Human Tissue Act of 2004 and her risk of imprisonment if she is found to have been complicit in a series of unlawful kidney transplants."

"Is that what's going on here? I thought we were on a murder case."

"We are."

Itzkowitz looked confused. "So, what's with the organ theft?"

Bee led her away from the corridor and stepped into an empty interview room. "I think the consultant surgeon who performed the transplants, conducted one on Michael Wing. I'm sure of that. We know from Wing's associate Carlos Hanbing that the operation didn't go well, at least not for Wing. I think it's possible that Wing confronted the surgeon over his perceived mishandling of the operation and that may have created a problem for the surgeon." Bee paused thinking that Itzkowitz would complete the theory, but she didn't. "He may have solved that little problem by either killing Wing or having him killed by someone else."

Itzkowitz's eyes widened. "No way."

Bee nodded, "This surgeon, Mr Dickinson, has proved hard to track down, and when I finally caught up with him on Friday he then escaped with a well-rehearsed routine. I'm hoping to use Lambert to locate him again. If she plays ball, then I'm comfortable with offering her a degree of leniency."

"You think that's what they are discussing right now."

"I imagine so."

"So how do you want to play it?"

"Given that they called for this recess, I think the emphasis is on them to take the initiative, so let's see what they say."

Itzkowitz didn't have to wait long to discover what Lambert was going to say. No sooner had she and Bee stepped out of their interview room, than Lambert's solicitor opened the door to room 1 and indicated that his client was ready to speak.

Bee's fingers slipped off the record button on the tape player and Caroline Lambert launched into her speech.

"Inspector, I'd like to apologise for my behaviour when you came to the hospital on Friday. It was unprofessional of me and totally out of character."

Bee thought about challenging her description, but Lambert was like a river in full flow. She brushed her long brown hair back behind her right ear and lent in to the table. "I didn't know who you were or what you were doing. Derek had given me a series of protocols to follow, and I just did what he said, I was on autopilot."

She finished on an ice-cream smile, but Bee didn't melt. "Can I assume that you are now prepared to tell us everything you know."

"Absolutely inspector, I've always believed that the police do an important job, Darren and I have brought Abigail up to respect law and order."

Bee allowed himself a half-smile, "Very well. We'll need you to make a full statement on the exploits of Mr Dickinson and his transplants and I'd like to know his whereabouts."

"Of course. I'm sorry but I don't know where he lives, I think it's somewhere in Richmond, but I can tell you that he has a 10am appointment on Monday morning with a Mr and Mrs Lynch and their son Joshua."

"Where will that take place?"

"He has an office in the Regus building in Reigate, up by the station. That's where he meets his Surrey clients."

Bee nodded, he could imagine the scene when he and McTierney arrived and dragged Dickinson away in handcuffs. "Good start, now can you tell us what you know about these unofficial organ transplants that Dickinson has been conducting."

Lambert squirmed on her chair but steeled herself for her confession. "I've worked with him for 15 months and I'm aware of 12 cases where payment has been made to facilitate a fast transplant."

She paused, as if waiting for absolution, but none was forthcoming. "I want to say that I didn't know it was illegal when I started. I thought that if the donor was willing and was paid for his kidney, then it was okay. A bit like going private rather than using the NHS."

Bee frowned, "I'm afraid it's not like that."

Lambert swallowed, "So I've discovered."

Lambert's solicitor joined the conversation, "As you will be aware inspector, section 1 of Human Tissue Act 2004 does allow for the consultant surgeon to receive expenses for the operation, so it's easy to see how a lay person such as Mrs Lambert might find the legislation difficult to follow."

Itzkowitz coughed and Bee smiled, "That's a decision for a court to make."

He pulled a sheet of paper from a manilla folder. "But while we are talking money, perhaps you could explain to us, how the finances of organ transplants work. Who was paid what money, by whom and into what accounts?"

Lambert stiffened herself, "In simple terms, people requiring an urgent transplant, mostly parents would pay Dickinson for the organ, a deposit of 50% when the booking was taken and the remainder 48 hours before the operation."

Bee grunted, "And the donors?"

"They would be offered a donation to a cause of their choice."

"A cause of their choice?"

"That was his phrase. But I think everyone chose their own personal cause."

Bee shook his head, "A donation is still a payment. Do you have details of the names and the sums paid?"

"Not to hand. I issued invoices to people who received a transplant, and I arranged bank transfers to the people who'd donated a kidney, and from time to time I would check that the correct sums had gone in and out of the bank account. But I couldn't give you all the details this minute."

"But you could get them."

"I believe so."

"We would want them as early as possible on Monday morning."

Lambert nodded her understanding.

"Out of interest, what did Dickinson charge for a kidney transplant?"

"It varied, depending on the complexity of the operation, but usually something around the £15,000 mark. I think the biggest invoice I ever issued was for £18,500."

Itzkowitz whistled.

Lambert smiled at her, "There are a lot of desperate and rich people in this area. I know I would do anything to save my daughter."

At the mentioning of saving daughters Bee turned wistfully towards the wall and let his mind wander. There were times when he wondered why he was doing this job. It had been 21 months since he'd lost his own daughter, but it still felt like yesterday.

Itzkowitz prompted him, "Sir?"

He turned back to the group with an apology and then

focussed on Lambert. "Now perhaps we could focus on the case of Michael Wing. I believe he was a kidney donor for Mr Dickinson, back in February of 2022. His case is of particular importance for me."

Lambert tilted her head and thought for a moment. "Oh yes, Mickey. A Chinese lad. We were lucky to find him because he has a rare blood group. We paired him up with a young girl from Reigate, I think her name was Penny, but I'd need to check to be sure."

"Can you talk us through the process?"

"I'm not involved in the details, but Mr Dickinson would meet both parties several times and make a number of tests to ensure the kidney would be compatible. Once that had been done, then both parties would be brought into Gatwick Park hospital and Mr Dickinson would perform the surgery."

"Who would help him?"

"He has a small team of specialists who he always works with."

"We would need those contact names as well."

Lambert nodded, and Bee had the feeling that she was only starting to realise the scale of the case.

"What happened to Wing after the transplant?"

"We would have kept him under observation for a day or so and once he had recovered, he would be free to leave. We would provide him with some pain relief and with some general advice for the immediate period after the operation; what to eat and drink, that sort of thing."

"What would happen if he fell ill after the operation?"

"I don't know. I don't recall anyone ever getting ill."

"Are you aware of Wing and Dickinson meeting up again

after the transplant."

"No. Mr Dickinson didn't have follow up meetings with donors after the transplants."

"Left them to suffer quietly." This was Itzkowitz.

Lambert looked affronted "I don't think any of our donors suffered. Mr Dickinson is a good surgeon, whatever you many think of him."

"Do you handle all of Mr Dickinson's appointments?"

"Only the days when he is in the Reigate area. He also works in London at the Royal Free Hospital."

"So, it's possible that Wing could have arranged to meet Dickinson without your knowledge."

Lambert shrugged her shoulders, "Yes. I guess it's possible. But generally, Derek would tell me what he was doing if it was with a donor, or a client."

"How would you describe Derek Dickinson?"

"He's an intelligent, ambitious man and a first-class surgeon."

"Likes to get his own way?"

"Yes. But don't we all."

Bee smiled. "Some more than others. Do you think Dickinson is capable of murder?"

Lambert looked shocked by the question. "No. He's spent his life trying to help people and save lives. I don't think he could kill anyone."

"What about if his livelihood was threatened?"

Lambert screwed up her face. "No, I don't think so."

"Thank you Mrs Lambert, I think we'll leave it there for today, but I would be grateful if you could make a full and signed statement with my colleague DS Itzkowitz. I'd like as much detail as you can remember about the names of donors and patients, and we'll want those missing names and bank details first thing on Monday."

"Of course."

"Your co-operation is duly noted, Mrs Lambert."

Her solicitor took his opportunity, "I trust that the police will look favourably on my client's position should any of this come to court, given the considerable help she has provided. In the circumstances any custodial sentence would seem," he paused searching for the right word, "improper."

Bee looked at the solicitor but addressed his comments to Lambert. "At this stage, I can't say what will happen with the investigation; it's still early days. But don't leave the country."

Lambert offered a weak smile.

"And you'll be needing another job," added Itzkowitz.

Bee decided it would be a good moment for a break and led the foursome into the station canteen and bought everyone a coffee, but then they split into two groups at separate tables.

"If you can take her statement that would be very helpful, I need to be elsewhere now and I think we've wrapped up most of the important details."

"Sure."

"Thank you, I think we can file this morning under successful perseverance."

"Good luck with the game."

"Thanks, but I'm dreading it. I'm sure I'll give away a goal or something equally catastrophic."

"That's the spirit, boss."

THIRTY-SIX

THE FINAL OF the Surrey Intermediate cup was scheduled to be played at the home ground of Dorking Wanderers Football Club, otherwise known as Meadowbank, and also the home of the Surrey County Football Association, meaning that the chairman wouldn't have far to travel. The ground was situated in the centre of Dorking, but only a short walk from the shops and the main area and overlooked by the spire of St Martin's church. St Martin, a humble servant of God, best known for helping others was a good choice since the stadium was regularly in need of a rebuild or a fresh coat of paint, despite rarely pushing the boundaries of the 3,000 capacity.

This afternoon the sun was an interested spectator, and the ground was bathed in bright sunshine. In addition, there was close to a thousand paying spectators spread around the three covered standing areas. Fans of Cranleigh Wanderers had occupied the east stand known locally as 'The Bank', not that this game required any segregation of the fans. The supporters of the police team had spread themselves between the West End and the Main Stand, perhaps the location of the in-house supporters bar in the Main Stand had influenced that choice. As the clock ticked round to the 3pm kick off the hum of chatter and singing began to grow, expectations were rising.

The Surrey Police team had arrived at 2pm, in a collection of private cars; Ron had picked up two team mates on his way and together the three walked from the car park and followed the concourse round to the players' entrance.

"This is a bit different," said Jem the goalkeeper, "Normally we walk from the car park directly into the changing rooms, dodging any stray dogs on the way."

"We've made the big time," said midfield dynamo Dean, who had forgotten his threat to stand down if Scott made the team.

"For one day," added Ron.

An official entrance was the first of several basic amenities which appeared like stardust to the Police team who never before had played in a real stadium. Floodlights, covered stands, paying customers, individual changing pegs for each player, even independent linesmen, and referee. It was a world away from their regular football.

"I bet the pies still taste of cardboard," said Dean, as the team congregated in the Home changing room. The banter continued to flow.

"Hey this'll be the first time we've ever played with straight lines around the edge of the pitch."

"The grass looks a bit sparse,"

"Makes a change not to have to put the nets up before we start."

"Where's old Sting, putting the nets up is his job."

"He's just wrapping up an interview," said Ron.

The team manager Gary clapped his hands together. "Apparently Dorking have agreed to let us have the stadium announcer, so he's going to read out the teams. You'll hear your name. Don't let this go to your heads lads. It's just another football game, and we're going out there to win."

The banter continued for thirty minutes, and Ron noticed Gary checking his watch every couple of minutes, Ron tried to avoid catching Gary's eye, but he knew what was coming. At the half hour, Gary couldn't hold it back any longer. "Ron, where the hell is Scott?"

Ron shrugged his shoulders.

"Come on he's your mate. Is he coming?"

"I think so."

Gary pulled out his mobile and dialled Scott's number. He shoved the phone back in his pocket in disgust. "Okay, looks like our lanky centre-forward isn't going to make it. Harry, you'd better start up front in his place. Put yourself about as much as you can. The rest of you, remember Harry doesn't have the height of Scott, so keep the ball on the ground."

A turgid first half of football saw the police team under the cosh for the majority of the time, and unable to create a single meaningful attack. Cranleigh dominated possession and created chance after chance but couldn't score. The Police goal lived a charmed life as the ball pinged around the Police penalty area as if the game was being played on a giant green pinball machine. It seemed that if Cranleigh could score now, they would score again and probably again, and the match would be gone. Although Cranleigh hit both posts and the crossbar, they didn't score. The most significant incident was an injury to Harry Cane, the police substitute who had replaced Scott, this depleted their team down to ten players. As they trudged off at half time the mood was subdued but that changed when Scott pushed open the changing room door and stepped inside. A chorus of abuse was thrown at Scott who looked stunned and unable to respond. A tube of Deep Heat was flung across the room and hit him on the chest.

"Good of you to turn up," said Jem the police goalkeeper. "Where the hell have you been? This is a bloody cup final. What's more important?"

"Sorry I had to interview an important witness."

"Is there nobody else in your grubby little station able to ask a few questions?"

"There was nobody else I could trust."

"Jesus. Get a grip man. If we lose this match, it'll be your fault."

"You better bloody score a goal, you lanky git or you'll be buying all the beer after the game."

"Huh, he's doing that anyway."

The abuse was flying in from all directions.

"The manager clapped his hands together, "Okay lads, come on. We're all one team, let's behave like it and pull together."

"Don't tell me, tell him. He's the ponce who's been missing."

"Yeah, you've had your say, now listen up. It's still goalless, we're still in this. So, it's back to plan A. We'll play the ball up to Scott, you hold it up and bring our wide men into play." Gary started pointing at the players. "Dean, you use the opportunity to break into the box and get onto the crosses." He turned to find Ron.

"Now Ron, they got a fast winger on the right, and I think it's fair to say he's got the beating of you for pace, so hold off, give him 5 yards. You're on a yellow card, I don't want you getting sent off."

Dean started to remonstrate, "If you do that, it's going to cost us our most creative outlet, letting Ron push down the wing gives us a chance."

Gary put up his hand as if on point duty, "We need a firm defence, that's my decision, now go play."

As the players stood up, Dean nudged Ron; "If you want my advice the way you slow down your winger is next time he's close to you, you accidentally run into him, don't hack him down, but slyly squeeze his nuts. That'll take the colour out of his cheeks."

But Gary was still in earshot, "Don't listen to him, you'll get sent off."

A disgruntled Dean stomped out of the room, shoving Scott down the steps as he left, "I've been running my nuts off so far, trying to fill the gap you've left, so you better bloody perform this half."

The atmosphere in the stadium changed after the break; with the police team back to full strength both teams engaged in a fiercely competitive battle with tackles flying in from all parts. The tension on the pitch transferred to the stands, but despite the effort of both teams the scoreboard remained barren. Cranleigh still held the balance of play but as more chances went astray the pressure began to grow in their game; patience evaporated, and tempers flared with each mistimed pass. Then the police scored; Dean Grant collected the ball in the centre circle and ran forward thirty yards before letting fly with a shot from the edge of the box; the Cranleigh goalkeeper raised his arms signifying his belief that the ball was sailing wide, but it deflected off the shoulder of Scott and trickled into the opposite corner. A total fluke.

Despite a frantic final ten minutes the police held on to win the Intermediate Cup; the first win in their history. Ian Bryant, the Football Development Officer of the Surrey Football Association presented the trophy to their captain Dean Grant, who lifted it towards their fans in the West End who erupted into a deafening roar belying their small number and pandemonium ensued. The team set off in a lap of honour tossing the cup between them as they went. Ron found himself passing the trophy to Scott and as he did, he caught his eye. "Told you it could be our day. Aren't you glad you came now?"

Scott beamed back at him, "Yes, you were right. This time. But there will be something equally ghastly happening somewhere else very soon."

Ron shook his head and ran after Jem to launch himself onto his back. The celebrations continued in the changing room and afterwards in the bar area of the stadium. Scott was the last to leave the changing room, as he closed the door he took a long look around, had he really been part of a successful, happy team. It didn't feel right, it was a strange feeling for him. He walked up the stairs to the lounge, he could hear the party before he got to the door, Dean was conducting the team in a chorus of 'We are the Champions.' Scott put his hand on the door handle but stopped. This wasn't his scene. He sent a short text to Ron and disappeared back to his sanctuary in Outwood.

It was nearing 10pm when Ron arrived back at Scott's house. He'd left his car in Dorking and taken a taxi. The journey had given him the opportunity to reflect on what had occurred that afternoon. He was still flying high after the victory but as the car drew nearer to his destination he began to think about how he would handle Scott. Despite the success of the team, the other players had united against Scott; they wanted a team player; someone to score goals and drink beer after the game. Ron had been given the task of explaining the situation to his friend.

Ron was hoping that Scott might have opted for an early night, but he was sitting in the lounge in the dark, Springsteen blasting out of the stereo. He pushed the door open and tip-toed into the room.

"You didn't fancy rejoicing in our moment of triumph?"

"Not much. Not my scene." Scott used his remote to temper the volume of Springsteen.

Ron nodded in agreement.

"Was it a good night?"

"Yes, not bad. The boys got smashed; then we had a meal in the town, took the cup with us. It was fun. Shame you didn't make it."

Scott shrugged his shoulders "Good. I hope my absence didn't upset anyone."

"No, not really. There was some laughter, some happiness, and a few ugly bad words."

Scott frowned, "Bad words?"

"They were the ones used to describe you."

Scott grunted. "Hmm."

"But mostly it was a night of excess. Beer, fizz, wine, shots, everything. Jem set off the fire extinguisher in the restaurant and I'm sure Dean slipped out to the washroom for a tactical chunder on at least one occasion."

This time Scott laughed.

"See you would have enjoyed it. You should have come."

"Maybe."

"What's that Latin phrase of yours? Carne something?"

"Carpe diem."

"Yes that one. Seize the moment. It might be your last." A thought flashed across Ron's mind about telling Scott that in fact he had played his last game, but decided to ignore it, "I could bust my knee chasing some two-bit handbag thief down Reigate Hight Street and never play football again. I want to make sure I enjoy every moment of this football stardom."

"Stardom? It was me that scored the winning goal! By the sound of it, you were lucky to be on the pitch."

"That's more like it show a bit of fight."

Scott shook his head at his friend.

"So, what have you done with your evening?"

"Bruce and I have been working on the case."

Ron gave him a funny look, but Scott ignored him.

"I grilled a steak, opened a bottle of Malbec and then Bruce and I took a trip down to 'The River' for some brain food."

"And has Bruce cracked the case?" Ron reached out for the sofa to steady himself.

"I know you're taking the piss, but I think he has."

Ron looked bemused, but Scott stood his ground. "Okay, show me."

"We've been looking at this all wrong. We've invested hours and hours in trying to decipher some complicated code; making an A, a B, or changing a T to an S; moving letters forward or back by three spaces in the alphabet and what have we got to show for it?"

"Nothing?"

"Nothing. That's because we're not thinking in the same

way as the man who wrote it." Scott paused thinking Ron would speak but he didn't.

"What do we know about Michael Wing?"

"He's dead."

"Yes, apart from that. Give me 3 facts about Wing."

"Er, he's a criminal, he loves his mother and, er oh yes, he's Chinese."

"Exactly, he's Chinese."

Ron jolted in surprise at getting the right answer but still wasn't on board.

"How do Chinese people write?"

"With pen and paper."

"No. Come on. Think."

"I can't, I've a dozen pints or more." He looked around the room for inspiration, but the alcohol was numbing his brain. "In Chinese, no Mandarin."

"That's better."

"What do you know about Mandarin?"

"Spoken by millions. An ancient language. That's about it."

"It doesn't use letters, like we do. It's a character-based language."

"You mean like Egyptian hieroglyphs."

"Exactly."

"What does that mean?"

"It means that Wing wouldn't create a code like we would. He wouldn't think of spelling words backwards, or missing every second letter, he would think in terms of pictures or images."

Ron stared across the room for a moment, as if trying to decipher the words Scott had spoken but came up blank.

"You'll have to tell me."

"It means we can ignore all the narrative in Wing's diary, that's a smokescreen. All we need are the occasional single characters and phrases, they mean a lot more than they suggest."

"Ah. Interesting. Let me get us both a whiskey and you can show me what you've discovered."

THIRTY-SEVEN

Early Sunday morning and Scott was in the bathroom; he reached across for his toothbrush and stared at his reflection in the mirror. He remembered the conversation from last night; to him it had been as clear as his own face in the mirror, but Ron had refused to accept it. Maybe that was because Ron was too drunk to see anything that didn't come in a bottle. But to Scott it was incontrovertible, the character that Wing had drawn in his diary was a church, and that meant Phil Church, his colleague at Reigate station was implicated in shady goings-on at Goldworth Road and possibly in the murder of Wing. Bee rinsed his mouth and spat out the last residue of the toothpaste; the action irritated his tooth, and he yelped in discomfort. He would have to get it sorted once this case was over. He stopped to stare at himself; was he really accusing a colleague of murder? Either way he knew that a sketch in a dairy was not evidence. He would need to find something that could be presented to a court.

As he walked down the stairs and into the kitchen, he stopped at the door of Ron's bedroom and shuddered, Ron was snoring loud enough to wake the dead. Scott turned the radio on but couldn't completely lose the rhythmic thunder from the neighbouring room. He traded his usual bowl of cereal and coffee for a swig of orange juice from the bottle, picked up his backpack and headed off to the station. This morning, he needed to replace his detective disposition with a managerial approach as he supervised the extermination of the bee colony from Beck's office, but he couldn't quell his detective insights; his mind was racing with the idea that Church was the killer.

A mainstream police station must operate on a 24/7 basis and Reigate was no different. Crime, like rust never sleeps. But the people who man the station are also no different to regular people and as such they enjoy their Sunday morning lie-ins. Hence the station that Bee walked into on Sunday was quiet, not quite dormant but much removed from the hustle of a Monday. He stopped to inform the desk sergeant that Mr Higgs would be arriving at 11am and took a lift to the top floor. He fished a key from his pocket and let himself into Beck's office. The room had a stuffy atmosphere and he moved to block the door open before remembering the threat of the bees.

Although Bee had spent many hours in Beck's office he hadn't quite appreciated how much furniture the man had accumulated; aside from an overlarge mahogany desk, a filing cabinet, a separate table and chair set, and a tall bookcase, but thankfully that was on the opposite side of the room to the bees and wouldn't require moving. It didn't take long to manoeuvre the desk a couple of yards away from the designated corner. He pulled a note from his pocket and read back through the instructions; 'check all the dark, hidden areas, cupboards, drawers, corners.'

He walked around the room looked around the corners, couldn't seen any sign of bees, then he checked the cupboards, still no sign. He sat down at Beck's desk, he reached down to open the drawer, but hesitated, it didn't feel right to open the private drawer of his superior. But the instructions were clear. He took a deep breath and pulled open the right-hand drawer, a couple of khaki folders but no bees. He switched to the left; lots of paper, he lifted the sheets out of the way and there at the bottom of the drawer was a pack of playing cards. Bee was startled. He dropped the sheaf of papers on the carpet and picked up the cards, but it wasn't a pack. It was a small wad of sixteen cards, before he turned them over he knew they would all be the red king of diamonds. In exactly the same style as the ones found at Goldworth Road.

AFTER HIGGS HAD removed the honey bees from the building, Bee escorted him back down to the door. He stopped at the desk on his way out and asked if Hanbing had dropped into to register with the police over the weekend as had been agreed on Friday evening. He was disappointed to learn that although Hanbing had appeared early on Saturday morning to present his passport, he hadn't been seen since.

THIRTY-EIGHT

BEE JOINED HIS team in the open plan area of the first floor early on Monday morning. Itzkowitz looked up from her notes and smiled at his arrival "My sources tell me that you were responsible for the champagne moment in the final on Saturday, scoring the winning goal. Congratulations sir."

Bee smiled, "You're correct with your facts, although rather than a champagne moment, I think I'd describe it as a lemonade moment. It was a bit lucky if the truth be told."

Itzkowitz looked across at McTierney, "That's not what we were told. Wall to wall football brilliance was the version I heard."

McTierney shrugged his shoulders, "You Americans don't understand the game."

Maria popped up to interrupt the chatter. "Morning all, Bee I wanted to check that yesterday's pest control clearance was successful."

"Yes, no problem," he replied, "Here, let me return Beck's office key to you, I don't want to hang on to it."

"No, I'd hate to lose it, I lost one a few months ago and Mr Beck was not best pleased."

McTierney watched Maria walk away across the floor and turned back to the team, "So we're back to having only one

Bee in the building again. That's enough for everyone."

Bee eyed him suspiciously. "Right gang, we have a busy couple of days coming up; let's meet in the ops room in 5 minutes and Itzkowitz will take us through her drug bust plan for tomorrow night at Redhill aerodrome. Then McTierney and I have to apprehend Mr Dickinson, later this morning."

There was a general rumble of disagreement, but everybody moved. "I'll get the team coffees," said McTierney, "Come on Itzkowitz you can give me a hand to carry everything, we'll bring them back up here."

"Good. Before we start I just want to check that Hanbing called in yesterday."

Bee disappeared down to the front desk but didn't get the answer he wanted.

"Are you sure Hanbing didn't drop in yesterday? He's not the type to go awol. He follows instructions." The desk sergeant checked the log book and opened his palms, "Sorry, Bee. There's no record of him turning up."

Bee sauntered upstairs and slipped into the ops room to listen to Itzkowitz set out her plan for that evening's operation at Redhill aerodrome, but his mind was elsewhere. He had a bad feeling about the apparent disappearance of Hanbing and was relieved when his mobile rang, and he had the perfect excuse to leave the briefing. The call was from Caroline Lambert making good on her promise to provide the police with a full breakdown of the financial records of Mr Dickinson and his clientele. When he rejoined the team he shared the details with Itzkowitz and asked her to begin collecting statements from the local clients who had all paid Dickinson large sums of money for organ transplants over the last two years. Then he and McTierney set off to apprehend the avaricious surgeon.

Once again Lambert had been spot on with her information; Bee and McTierney waited until 10 minutes after the scheduled time for Dickinson's meeting to begin before appearing at the door of his meeting room in the Regus building in Reigate. This time Dickinson was short of options; the room was on the first floor, had one single door, and he was entertaining prospective clients. Although the door was wooden, the walls were glass and Dickinson seemed to understand the game was up as soon as he spotted Bee. He strode purposefully to the door greeted the detectives like old friends, asked them to wait a couple of minutes while he concluded his conversation and then walked compliantly with them back down the stairs and out to Bee's car.

But the mood changed once they arrived at interview room 1 at the station. Bee showed him into the room and left to fetch coffee, while they awaited the arrival of his solicitor. McTierney slipped into the neighbouring room to watch him through the one-way mirror. Derek Dickinson exuded an aura of opulence and arrogance as he strode around the room, his tailored suit accentuating his towering stature. With a disdainful smirk he surveyed the room and drew back the wooden chair in disgust, pitying the impoverished public facilities. His demeanour dripped with entitlement; each movement calculated to assert his superiority. In his world, money was not just a means to an end, but the ultimate measure of one's worth. McTierney intercepted Bee on his return; "Give me that coffee, I want to spit in it now; this guy is a toad. I don't care what we have to do; he's going down!"

Bee jerked the coffee cup holder away from McTierney. "What we're going to do is avoid giving him or his brief any reason to challenge our case and get the judge to throw it out. You play this one by the book."

"Hmm." McTierney looked downcast, but he knew Bee was right.

"But before you lose all your drive, I'd guess he took home north of £400k last year."

"I hate the bastard."

The three men sat in the interview room waiting for Dickinson's solicitor to arrive, no words were spoken but the tension began to grow.

Then Clarence Beaumont entered the room; he arrived with a flourish, full of insincere apology for his lateness and theatrically presented a business card to each detective. Bee caught sight of a diamond stud in his left ear and thought McTierney might explode if he saw it.

Bee cautioned Dickinson, set the tape running and opened the interview, "Let me explain why you are here, because it may not be obvious."

Dickinson glared across the table but didn't challenge Bee.

"Two reasons; firstly, we believe you to be in breach of the 2004 Human Tissue Act; specifically, you have been engaged in a black-market trade for human organs; buying and selling kidneys." Dickinson dismissed the charge with a wave of his hand.

"Secondly; you are under suspicion of being involved in the murder of Michael Wing, one of your kidney donors, who died in October of last year. At this point you are not facing a charge of murder, but that may change."

"Ridiculous!" Dickinson dismissed the charge.

"As you will." Bee shuffled the papers on the desk in

front of him. "For the benefit of the tape could you state your name, address, and occupation. Dickinson obliged while maintaining his air of contempt for everything that was going on around him.

Bee acknowledged Dickinson's response and pulled out a sheet with the names of the donors and recipients that Maria had typed up based on the information Caroline Lambert had provided that morning. "This is a list of people who we believe you have operated on. Each operation would constitute a contravention of the Act."

Dickinson frowned at the accusation but bided his time.

Bee continued, "The act provides a legal framework for the lawful donation of living organs in this country. If the conditions are not met, then a transplant operation may constitute a crime. The key is evidence of voluntary consent being given by both parties. Therefore, I would expect to see documentation to that effect. We haven't been able to find any. In addition, it is an offence to be involved in the buying and selling of organs. Ordinarily this should be supported with a signed declaration confirming that there is no reward associated with the organ donation, but this sheet details significant sums of money either paid to donors by you or paid to you by organ recipients. As it stands you appear to be in breach of the regulations, do you have anything to say in your defence."

Dickinson looked at his solicitor who raised an eyebrow, which was the trigger for Dickinson to unleash.

"Inspector, do you have any idea what's involved in a kidney transplant?"

Bee inhaled ready to speak, but Dickinson had asked a rhetorical question. He raised his palm.

"No, you don't. Let me tell you. It's a complex operation conducted in a tight time frame where you have responsibility for the lives of two patients. It requires specialist medical training, a cool hand, a clear head, and a delicate touch. One careless slip," he paused to illustrate this with a flick of his wrist. "And two lives can be lost. When you are lying on that bed in a hospital theatre you do not want some amateur hack holding your life in their hands. You want a professional. An expert. You want the best and I am the best."

His voice reverberated around the small room as he defended his actions with unwavering conviction, refusing to back down in the face of Bee's accusation. Dickinson's piercing eyes locked on to his adversary daring him to challenge his approach. "I have given life to people. What is the price of life? You don't know, nobody knows." Dickinson puffed out his chest as his tirade built to a crescendo. "But I will tell you this, none of my clients, not one, regrets what they have done. Not one wishes to turn the clock back and keep their money. Not one wishes to be on the exhausting NHS list of desperation. You could ask every single parent if they would be happy to pay more than they did to have the life of their child extended by my work and every single one of them will say yes. And you know that." Dickinson slammed his hand down on the table, but he wasn't finished yet.

"Not enough organs are freely available. The public might not like the private market trade but if more people were willing to donate their organs after say a car crash, then we wouldn't have the same situation. In fact, you could argue that this is a question of economics, not law. I have done nothing but good in this world. I've saved lives and I will go on saving lives. Now you drag me away from a desperate family hoping to save their daughter and for what? To come here, to your tawdry little room, where you can throw your weight around and accuse me of goodness knows what and yet what have you done in this world. Nothing I'll bet. What right do you have to judge me. You're nothing." Dickinson rocked back in his chair.

"Have you finished?"

Dickinson flicked his hand at Bee.

"The law. The law gives me the right to question you. The law gives me the right to take you off the street and it will be the law that will see you punished if you're found guilty."

"The law. Huh. What is the law today will be different tomorrow. It's a question of timing. I will be remembered for saving lives, giving new life. How will society remember you inspector? Will it even remember you?"

"I'd like to be remembered for making our towns and villages safer for the families that live in them."

"And for taking scum off the streets," added McTierney.

Dickinson shot an angry look across the table.

A momentarily lapse in hostilities allowed Dickinson's solicitor to intervene. "Inspector, as I presume you will be aware, section 1 of the Human Tissue Act 2004 does allow for the consultant surgeon to receive expenses for the operations that you've been describing. If this is the focus of your investigation it appears to me that all we are discussing is the appropriate level of compensation for a world class surgeon."

Bee looked at the solicitor but addressed his question to Dickinson. "Are you familiar with the recent case of Ike

Ekweremadu?"

Dickinson shrugged his shoulders.

"No? I'm sure your solicitor will be. For now, allow me to give you a brief summary. He was making illegal organ transplants, and he was sentenced to 9 years by the court. Found guilty under the Modern Slavery Act. Holding his victims against their will. Did you do that with Michael Wing?"

"I can't disclose any details about any of my clients. The medical profession abides by a principle of patient confidentiality. I'm sure you've heard of it."

His solicitor smirked.

"Are you familiar with Goldworth Road in Redhill?"

"No. I live in Richmond. I can't think of anything Goldworth Road could offer me."

"How would you know? If you've never been there?"

Dickinson looked dismissively across the table. "Look. I don't have time for busy bodies. I need to get back to work. Your questions are becoming tiresome. I want to leave?"

"You'll stay here until I say you can leave." Bee paused and waited for Dickinson to meet his eyes and suggest he understood the rules of the game. It took a minute for Dickinson to comply and then Bee changed tack. "Let's talk about the hospitals at which you have been conducting these transplants."

Dickinson rolled his eyes. "As you wish."

"I hope you know that the Human Tissue Authority regulates organisations that remove, store, and use human tissue for research and medical treatment. We contacted the HTA, and they have no record of you as a licensed operator, nor the Gatwick Park Hospital. Have you any comment to make?"

Dickinson shrugged his shoulders.

"They've granted over 800 licenses but not one for you."

Dickinson wrinkled his nose and shifted in his seat. "It's all just paperwork."

"No, it's more than that. The HTA was created by Parliament to be the sole public body to give approval for organ donations, so if they don't have a record of granting permission, then you don't have permission. If you don't have permission, you're breaking the law. Simple as that."

Dickinson went quiet and looked away from the inspector.

"Therefore, we have reason to believe that on at least twelve occasions the transplants conducted by you would be classified as illegal."

Dickinson looked to his solicitor for inspiration, but none was forthcoming. Instead, Bee lent across the table, "Would you consent to allowing us to take a swab test to collect your DNA?"

This time the solicitor spoke, "What are you hoping to establish inspector?"

"It's a standard procedure. It will help rule Mr Dickinson out of certain elements of this case."

"Or place him at the centre," added McTierney.

"I don't like your sergeant's attitude inspector."

"Apologies, you'll have to cut him some slack, he's in training. This might be a good point to take a short break, I'll show you to the canteen and McTierney can organise the swab test. Let's resume in 15 minutes."

As soon as Bee and McTierney were alone, McTierney turned to his partner. "In training, seriously?"

Bee dipped his head towards him. "Lesson one; go ask Juliet for a coffee for the boss."

McTierney hurried back with two cups and thrust one towards Bee. "It's a close contest but I was wrong, Dickinson isn't the most loathsome individual, it's his legal brief."

"I'd say they make a good pair."

"I'll say this for Dickinson he doesn't lack self-confidence; he's not going to enter a plea of guilty."

"Maybe not but hopefully his solicitor will brief him on the finer points of the Ekweremadu case and that might weaken his resolve."

"Perhaps, but I prefer it when they get cocksure. It makes the come down all the more amusing."

Bee shook his head, "Ready for round two?"

With the four men all back in their familiar seats Bee set the tape player rolling and began the second half.

"Did you and Michael Wing row?"

"No."

"Did you know he left a diary? It's full of enlightening details."

Dickinson shrugged.

"It tells us that you met Wing on October 4th."

"Did you and Wing fight?"

"That's between me and him." Dickinson's mojo was back. "Is this the best you've got inspector?"

Bee opened the diary and positioned it to show Dickinson an icon of a doctor with a sword next to it. "I'd say that suggests he wanted to kill you. He wasn't happy with the kidney extraction; perhaps he'd discovered that you ripped him off with the price of a rare blood group. You bought it for £6,000 and sold it for £18,000 three hours later."

Dickinson spun the diary around, casually glanced at the book, sniffed, and pushed it back. "I'm not a doctor, I'm a consultant. If Wing wanted to kill a doctor, so be it. It's not me."

"Doctors, consultants, it's easy to confuse the titles. I know I've done it myself. I think it's reasonable to assume that a non-native English speaker would confuse the two. I think Wing meant to kill you, but you got to him first."

"Nonsense."

"You've told us you're the best. I think the phrase 'world-class' was used. I think you messed up with the kidney extraction from Wing. Something went wrong and he nearly died. As a result, he came back to challenge you. He was going to tarnish your perfect record and you couldn't deal with that and that's why you killed him. He was going to haunt you because you got his treatment wrong."

"This is fantasy."

"He didn't come back for money, but he came back to threaten your work and your reputation and that was too much for you."

Dickinson looked to his solicitor who took the cue, "Inspector, this is speculation, unless you can produce some evidence for this outrageous accusation, I suggest you desist and allow my client to leave."

"Your client will be charged under the Human Tissue Act in the morning. Until then he'll be enjoying the limited facilities of our cells."

THIRTY-NINE

BEE ASSEMBLED HIS team in the ops room for a last-minute review of the plan; he had recruited two traffic cops Stevens and Holmes to bolster the numbers.

"Are we expecting any aggro? Asked McTierney.

"If Wing's notes are correct, we have to assume that the Croydon gang will be armed."

"Are we taking weapons?" McTierney asked.

Bee hesitated; the last time he used a police issue gun it had ended in a fatality.

It seemed McTierney was reading his mind. "It won't change the past, but it may give us a future, we have to be armed, boss."

"You're right. As I'm acting chief in the absence of Beck, I've assigned weapons for everyone here, and also arranged for some back up."

"And Church is blissfully unaware that you're stamping on his toes with this covert operation."

"It's still part of a murder enquiry in my mind. He doesn't need to know."

"That's fine, I made sure he doesn't owe me any beer at the weekend."

On their way down to the car park, Bee stopped by the front desk. He was keen to understand if Carlos Hanbing had checked in under the terms of his bail, but the desk sergeant shook his head. There had been no sign of Hanbing since he dropped into the station on Saturday morning. Bee turned to McTierney, "I'm starting to get a bad feeling about our friend Hanbing."

"No friend of mine, he's the one who whacked me with an iron bar."

"Doesn't seem to have done you much damage though."

★ ★ ★

IN 1933 THE then Minister of Health gave permission for the development of Hamme Farm into what would become Redhill Aerodrome. During the Second World War it became a fighter base with Spitfires stationed there. It was also home to both the Canadian and the Polish squadrons and acted as an advanced airfield for the attack on Dieppe in 1942, housing some 800 odd personnel at the time. Ninety years later there are few signs of the airfield's history, these days the 600-acre site has switched to commercial aviation with a range of helicopter services, training activities and a focus on aircraft maintenance. The aerodrome also provides a home for the Air Ambulance covering Kent, Surrey, and Sussex. Most regular business at the airfield is governed by the hours of daylight, but it was during the hours of darkness that some of the most lucrative trades passed through the site. If Wing's diary was correct then the full moon on the night of May 15th would be witness to another occasion when a secret delivery of drugs would land at the airfield and be silently swept away onto the streets of South London. With the mysterious bread and cross logos being heavily involved.

Bee wanted his team to congregate in daylight so they could get a feel for the scale of the aerodrome. Although the airfield is bordered by country roads on all sides it took the team more than 10 minutes to circumnavigate the site. They reconvened on the western side where converted hangers now accommodated the half-dozen or so new businesses.

"There's grass and trees in every direction. It's enormous," said Itzkowitz, "and I say this as a girl from the wild plains of America."

"It's a good job we've got radios," said McTierney, "we can't see from one side to the other. Without them, we'd have no chance of staying in contact with one another."

"We have Bishop to thank for that touch," said Bee, "She's worked here before. Now let's split into our teams; Stevens and Holmes you cover the eastern gate, McTierney and Itzkowitz head up to the end of the buildings roughly in line with the runway. Bishop and I will stay here on the western entrance."

"The runway? You mean that long strip of grass."

"Yes, that."

Bee ignored the interruption and set out the plan. "It's likely that we'll get little notice of the plane's arrival and I suspect it will be on the ground for only a few minutes. Keep your windows open to listen for the engine, I suspect you'll hear it before you see it. Now don't forget, our mission is to stop the plane, apprehend the pilot and those meeting the plane. Preferably with a minimum of force."

There were nods all around and the three teams headed back to the cars, but as they walked away a familiar vehicle pulled onto the site.

"Shit!" Bee banged his fist on his dashboard.

Phil Church pulled up alongside Bee's old Mercedes and lowered his window. "Hope you weren't going to start the party without me. This is my field of expertise."

"This is an undercover operation linked to a murder enquiry. We've got it covered; we don't need you here. Turn around and return to the station."

"That's not very friendly, when I've made the effort to come all the way out here to save yourself from making a prize idiot of yourself."

"I won't tell you again. Go." Bee began to get flustered.

Church inhaled deeply and looked around the small car park where the briefing had taken place. "Your happy band of 6 goofs looks a bit under resourced to cover an airfield of this size. I think you could do with an extra pair of ears and eyes."

"I'm ordering you. Go back to the station." Bee's voice was getting louder.

"Don't think you can order me about. With Beck away from the station, I believe he leaves us jointly in charge. Bit of a mistake by the old boy if you ask me, but that's what he does. You have no jurisdiction over me." Church dropped his smiley face. "Whatever you're calling it, this looks like a drugs bust, which is my domain, so climb down from your high horse and be grateful I've not reported this."

The threat took the wind out of Bee's sails and Church seized the initiative. "Look you can keep the glory, I'll remain in the background, and only step in if you get out of your depth. I'm only here to ensure you don't make a huge mess in my playground."

Bee bit his lip; he didn't want Church on the scene, but he knew he was on thin ice and if anything went wrong with the operation Beck would ask questions that Bee would struggle to answer. He was also nervous about having issued firearms to the team and knew they would all benefit from having an experienced officer present. "Okay. You can stay, but only in the background, I'll call for your help if we need it."

As the night wore on, a blanket of clouds drifted lazily across the sky obscuring the luminous orb of the moon. McTierney turned to Itzkowitz; "Looks like the weather is going to ruin Bee's big plan."

"You just want an early night."

"You're not wrong there. What did you bring to eat?"

Itzkowitz stretched into the back seat and pulled a canvas bag towards her. "There's a bag of Twiglets in here somewhere and a couple of Hershey bars."

McTierney screwed his face up, "Is that it? That's not food."

But as he spoke the clouds parted to reveal the radiant face of the moon in all its splendour and a determined glow pierced the darkness. Itzkowitz took the bag back, "Game on, I'd say."

McTierney grunted a reply while the silvery brilliance of the moon cast a mesmerising glow painting the airfield below in a soft, enchanting hue.

"That's beautiful," whispered Itzkowitz.

"Beautiful, but I suspect deadly."

McTierney lifted a pair of binoculars to his eyes and scanned the skyline. "Can't see anything, but if it's going to happen it'll be soon." He lowered his car window and pushed his head outside. "I think I can hear an engine."

From the far side of the airfield the sound grew stronger. When it happened, the descent was direct and quick, it was evident that the pilot wouldn't be hanging around. The engine hummed steadily as the wheels gently kissed the grass with a soft thud. The plane had landed three hundred yards from where McTierney had stationed his Jaguar. The small plane quickly spun around and began taxiing across the airfield heading towards the eastern gate where Stevens and Holmes were stationed, kicking up a small dust cloud in its wake.

"Come on, let's get after it."

McTierney started the engine and raced across the grass in pursuit of the plane.

At that moment Stevens and Holmes reported a black Lexus SUV had arrived at the eastern gate. Bee was quickly on the radio. "Observe for now, we don't want anyone warning the plane to take off. But once McTierney's blocked the plane, then move in. First step is to block their exit."

The plane was a single propellor Cessna 172 capable of a 60mph across the grass and highly manoeuvrable, but it would be no match for McTierney's Jaguar in a straight race. But this wasn't a straight race, McTierney had given the plane a 300-yard head start and without his lights he was hitting all the bumps on the grassland.

"Shit! I thought this was a runway!" he yelled as his car struck a rabbit hole and his head crashed into the roof of the car.

"Put the lights on."

"I can't. If I do the pilot will take to the skies again and we'll be left with nothing."

But the engine in McTierney's Jaguar was twice the size of the light aircraft and the difference quickly began to tell.

"We're closing."

But as McTierney cut the difference to 100 yards the pilot suddenly twigged what was happening. He spun round in the cockpit and squinted back towards McTierney's Jaguar, as he did the Cessna started to swerve.

"He's spotted us."

"Damn."

"You might as well put your lights on, then you'll be able to see better."

Itzkowitz grabbed the radio. "We've been spotted. Let's go. Take 'em all down. We've got the plane."

McTierney looked at her. "We've got the plane?"

But as he took his eyes off the grass, he hit another rabbit hole and they both lurched forward. "There's more damn holes here than in a Swiss cheese."

The plane had slowed to a normal taxing pace but now changed tack. It abandoned the planned meeting and turned back towards the runway strip and revved hard while the pilot prepared to take off.

"Get your foot down, you've got to stop him."

McTierney was almost alongside the plane now."

"Get in front of him."

"How's that going to help?"

By now both the plane and McTierney were doing 70mph across the grass and the fence on the opposite side came into view.

"Quick, he'll soon have enough speed to take off and then he's gone."

McTierney was now level with the cockpit, the pilot looked over his left shoulder and swore at the car.

"Oh shit." McTierney swung the car to his right and smashed into the side of the plane tipping it over onto the

THE CAVE OF DEATH

high wing. The Jaguar raced ahead of the plane and in his rearview mirror McTierney saw the small plane explode into a fireball. He swung the car round. "Get on the radio for an ambulance, this isn't going to end pretty."

McTierney pulled up alongside the plane, but Church was already there. He leapt from his car and ran towards the plane. The plane had landed on his right wing, and he pulled the left side door open but quickly fell back from the plane.

McTierney ran across to help him, but Church grabbed him before he could get to the plane.

"It's too late the pilot's dead. We're better off staying back in case the whole thing blows."

McTierney stood mesmerised by the burning plane and Church dragged him away. Seconds later Bee's car arrived, and the three men cowered as a final explosion destroyed what was left of the small plane.

Itzkowitz joined them, "I've called the ambulance and a fire tender. Ten minutes."

"Don't think they'll be able to do much for this guy," said Church.

Stevens came over the radio, "We've apprehended the Lexus. What do you want me to do now boss?"

"Take them back to the station. I'll be there shortly."

Bee turned his attention to his colleagues. "We need to secure this site and get the forensics team to go over the scene. Can I leave it with you?"

Church nodded. "Yeah, we've got it covered." Then he looked over at McTierney's Jaguar.

"You're gonna need a new paint job."

"New paint job. Huh. Bee can buy me a new car."

FORTY

BEE ARRIVED BACK at the station early the next morning to face the aftermath of the disastrous midnight sting operation; one dead body, any drugs that were being imported illegally had been destroyed in the fire, no evidence to detain the suspicious Lexus, and the airfield closed for the foreseeable future which was disrupting the Air Ambulance operation. He had secured the crime scene at the airfield and sent McTierney back there with the pathologist Dr Kelly. Whenever a civilian died in a police operation there was always an enquiry, and he knew this would be no different. He slipped quietly up the back stairs and into his office, he opened his laptop and began to type his letter of resignation. He felt it was the only thing he could do. He'd reached the second line when Maria, tapped on his door.

"Assistant Chief Constable Raven will be coming into the office tomorrow; he would like to discuss last night's operation with you and has asked that you don't speak to the press before you've spoken to him. He'll be here at 11am."

"Yes of course."

Maria left and Bee slumped back into his well of self-pity. Where had it all gone wrong? He felt as if he'd arrived at the end of the tunnel and there was no light. When had he stopped being a good detective? He looked back at his screen, he wouldn't need to write the letter anymore, Raven would surely relieve him of his duty and that would be that. Suddenly he was aware that his mobile was ringing, and he broke out of his reverie but not in time to catch the call. He looked at the screen it was McTierney, he wasn't sure he could face McTierney's relentless chatter, at least not without another shot of caffeine.

On his way back from the canteen, he took a detour across the CID section of the first floor. Bishop saw him coming and walked over to greet him. Three minutes idle chit-chat with her and he felt sufficiently revived to face McTierney.

"I missed your call."

"No worries. Thought you'd want to know. Kelly's taking the body back to the lab to conduct the postmortem. We think he's a Dutchman. I've made a few preliminary enquiries, and we should have the full picture this afternoon. Guess what, the gun that the pilot had was a Glock. Small world hey."

Bee put the phone down and deleted his half-written letter.

Despite the late start Bee had taken his morning dragged by. Three times he walked down to the forensics lab in the basement to see if Kelly had finished and three times he trooped slowly back upstairs empty-handed. But as with any watched kettle they do eventually all boil, and this pot was no different. Kelly & McTierney joined forces and walked together up to Bee's office.

"Not often I see you two working closely together."

The two men looked at each and shuffled a few centimetres further apart, but it didn't detract from their message. Dr

Kelly began. "I've made a discovery that might help you crack this case. Although I must say it does surprise me."

"This case is full of strange events, what can you add to the pile?"

Kelly took a seat opposite Bee and laid his papers on the desk. "It's the gun."

"The Glock?"

Kelly nodded. "The gun that killed Michael Wing, we recovered it from the debris of the small plane at Redhill aerodrome."

Bee's jaw dropped. "The same Glock?"

Kelly nodded. "The same."

"Are you sure? How can it be?"

"I don't know. I was surprised but I've checked it three times. It's definitely the weapon that fired the bullet that killed Wing."

Bee shook his head. "But how?"

Kelly shrugged his shoulders. "I can't imagine, but you're the detective. All I can tell you is that we have the weapon that killed Wing."

McTierney joined the debate. "What are the chances?"

Bee turned his attention to his colleague. "Have you identified the pilot?"

"Our preliminary work suggests he is Aart van Ghent. A Dutchman, known to the authorities in Holland, two convictions and suspecting of illegal drug trades. But with no obvious connection to Wing or this country."

"Could he be our regular drug delivery man?"

"Easily. On this occasion he'd rented the plane from a small airfield close to Rotterdam, as he had done before. He hadn't registered any flight plans with the Dutch authorities, or at least none that have come to light so far. It looks like a regular pattern. He's a qualified pilot, rents the occasional plane for a couple of days at a time. Always pays cash. Makes a small inland daytime flight, probably to justify the hire and then makes a special late-night trip across the Channel when the moon is full."

"But this time, things go wrong, the plane crashes, bursts into flames and he perishes."

McTierney nodded his head.

"That's all well and good, but why does he have the pistol that shot Wing? That bit doesn't make any sense."

"I can understand him bringing a gun for his own protection."

"Yes. I'll buy that. But why shoot Wing?"

"Maybe one of the drops van Ghent had set up went awry, he had an altercation with Wing and shot him."

"In the back of the head? If you're making a fast drop of illegal drugs, you don't hang around and get involved. You're in, make the trade and out again as fast as you can. If there's any shooting to be done, it's from a distance. Probably from the plane if you're van Ghent."

Neither McTierney nor Kelly had any riposte, but Bee wasn't finished.

"And just suppose van Ghent does shoot Wing. Why on earth would he take him to a cave in Reigate. That's crazy. I can't believe he'd know about the place, and he's got no ground transport to get there. No, he'd leave the body, get back in his plane and fly back to Holland as quick as he could."

McTierney tilted his head, "Perhaps." Bee watched as the cogs in McTierney's brain began to whir. "Our flying

Dutchman kills him but one of his accomplices on the ground takes the body and dumps it in the cave."

"This would be one of your Croydon gang members would it."

"It's a possibility."

"That's about all it is. Why wouldn't they simply leave the body on the airfield?"

"They might feel that the drug import business was so good that they didn't want to ruin it with a murder on the scene." This time it was Kelly offering his thoughts.

"Come on doc, you deal with facts and precision. Not wild theories. You can't seriously believe that our Dutch drug smuggler killed Wing."

Kelly raised his palms. "I'm happy to leave the detective work to you two. All I'm saying is that we found the gun that shot Wing in the cockpit of the plane next to the body of van Ghent."

A silence engulfed the room.

"I can give you another fact, and you won't like this one either. Van Ghent has size 10 feet. – the same size as the unaccounted-for footprints in the cave."

"You're right. I don't like it." Bee turned away from the conversation and looked out of the window and blew out his cheeks. "But a fact is a fact. Let's say you're right and it was van Ghent. Can we check the records to see if he had rented a plane in early October last year?"

"Already done that," said McTierney. "There's no record of van Ghent renting a plane at any time in October."

Bee shook his head. But before he could say anything McTierney jumped in.

"But we only discovered last night's plane was rented

because we could trace the plane back by its number and hence we found the owner who is now down by a plane and wondering about an insurance claim." McTierney stopped to laugh. "It's possible van Ghent hired a plane from someone else last year and paid cash again on that occasion."

"I don't like it. None of this feels right."

A lull developed in the conversation which was broken by Kelly. "I've said what I came to say. I'll get back to the postmortem and see if there's anything unusual about the body; a couple of incisions for a kidney removal or the such like."

"Presumably it was the fire that killed the pilot."

"Looks that way, although the pm will most likely record smoke inhalation."

McTierney nodded his understanding, and the pathologist took his leave. Silence once again enveloped the pair until McTierney could stand it no longer. "Come on boss. This is a good result. The old man will be delighted when he gets back from holiday; he might even give us the day off."

Bee looked up and eyed him suspiciously.

"With the help of Mickey Wing's diary, you've broken up three major crime rings in as many days."

Bee raised an eyebrow but said nothing.

McTierney lent into the table. "You've taken a rogue doctor off the streets, – he'll get a few years. You've broken up an international drug circus, closed down a brothel and now you've solved the murder of Mickey Wing. So actually, that's four. You'll be a hero. Beck won't know where to pin the medals."

Bee smiled weakly. "I for one don't think we've apprehended the killer of Michael Wing. I think we've been sold a pup."

McTierney shrugged his shoulders. "If we didn't catch the killer of Mickey Wing, then so be it. We're not going to catch every criminal. We've cleaned up the streets and Reigate will be a safer place tonight. I, for one, will be able to sleep easily in my bed tonight."

"Do you really think it's safer?"

"Why wouldn't it be?"

Bee leant across to the side drawer of his desk, pulled it open, reached inside and pulled out an envelope. He passed it across the table to McTierney. "Take a look inside."

McTierney flipped it open and a red king playing card fell into his hand. He turned it over and saw that it carried the exact same pattern as the ones they had found at the house in Goldworth Road. McTierney's eyes bulged. "Where did you find this?

"You wouldn't believe me if I told you."

"Try me."

"I'm not sure it's fair to tell you."

"What?! I don't need a big brother!"

"Okay. But before I do, I should tell you that I think everyone who's got close to uncovering this person has died. I think it's why Michael Wing died."

"Because he threatened to expose the Red King."

Bee nodded. "It's a definite possibility and I think it's more likely than not."

"So come on then, where did you find it, and who's this Red King?"

"I found it in this station."

"A copper? Wow. They do say."

"In Beck's office, when I was searching around for bee

nests."

McTierney's eyes burst out of their sockets. "No. Old man Beck. Really?"

Bee nodded. "There's half a pack of them hidden away in one of his locked drawers."

★ ★ ★

BEE DIDN'T ACHIEVE much during the early afternoon; he was perturbed by the implication that Beck might be involved in Goldworth Road conspiracy. Beck had been his mentor through his time as an inspector and he couldn't contemplate the chief superintendent as anything else. He completed the report on the botched operation at Redhill aerodrome and submitted it to ACC Raven and stood staring out of his office window when McTierney tapped on his half-open door.

"Got something you need to see boss."

Bee turned his head but didn't speak.

"I know you were troubled this morning with the idea that our flying Dutchman could really be Wing's killer, so I went back to our Dutch colleagues and got them to do some digging."

Bee sauntered back to his desk, but his mind didn't follow him.

"Dutch records show that van Ghent was in hospital during the first week of October; he had his appendix removed. He was confined to bed and couldn't possibly be in this country, shooting Wing. No matter whether Wing died on the 6th, 7th, or 8th of October."

Bee's eyes leapt out of their sockets.

"Say that again."

"Van Ghent can't be the killer. He has the perfect alibi."

"Someone is trying to frame him."

"Looks that way."

Bee reached for his phone. "Dr Kelly, my office please as quick as you can."

Kelly arrived a little out of breath, but regained his composure as McTierney repeated his story.

Bee led the discussion, "Only one person ever frames another, and that's the guilty person. Now McTierney tell us everything about the plane crash and Church's part in it."

McTierney began to recount the story of the previous evening. "Church did as you asked and kept out of sight all night, right up to the point where the plane came into land. Itzkowitz and I went to intercept it after the pilot spotted us."

"Or was tipped off." Interjected Bee.

"Yes maybe. Either way he stopped taxing and started to speed up, I was close to him but couldn't get in front, so I swerved my car into the side of the plane to stop it. It spun round, tipped over and caught fire. We ran on for a few yards and the airbags went off. It took a few minutes to sort out, when I got back to the plane Church was standing on the side of the plane, he had the door open and said the pilot was dead."

"But you didn't see the pilot as this stage."

"No, as I ran towards the plane. Church said it was going to blow, so he jumped clear, ran over to me and we watched it blow up. I guess his car was close behind me when I was chasing after the plane, we both had our lights off. I was concentrating on the plane."

"That's fine. But it's possible that Church opened the door to the plane and dropped the Glock inside without you seeing."

McTierney shrugged. "Yes it's possible. Risky, but possible."

"Risky yes, but I think Church has been getting worried that we're close to solving this case, so he felt he had to do something radical to save his skin."

"That's certainly radical."

"All along I've said the key to this case is why would someone hide a dead body somewhere they know it will be found. I think I have the answer. I think Church is our Red King, the controller of this drugs and porn ring we've uncovered. But Michael Wing wanted a piece of the action and started rocking the boat. Rocking it so much that Church had to take some action. So, he kills Wing. With the murder he wants to send a message but obviously not get caught. So, he sets up a murder that will get lots of headlines, make the national news, make all of his enemies sit up and take notice, but be impossible for us to solve."

"Nearly impossible," corrected McTierney.

"Nearly," smiled Bee.

"You know I like a theory, and this is a corker. But Phil Church really?"

Bee grimaced, "I know he's guilty, he's been playing us all along, but here's where we catch him. He didn't know van Ghent was in hospital in October. He was trying to be too clever, and he's made a mistake, and this is where we're going to catch him."

"It's one thing having a splendid theory, but we need evidence," said Kelly.

"We do, and you two brilliant gentlemen have got about 20 hours to find me something. The airfield is still a secure crime scene, get back there and see what you can find."

"But it's a burned-out shell," said Kelly.

"Surely that won't be a problem for a pathologist with your unique skills."

"Come on," said McTierney, grabbing the shoulder of Dr Kelly. "If he blows any more smoke in your direction, he'll pass out."

FORTY-ONE

"ACC Raven has stationed himself in Beck's office. He's got a meeting with Inspector Church, just before you. Can I suggest you loiter outside Beck's office I know the ACC doesn't like to be kept waiting."

It was Maria giving some last-minute advice to Bee. He nodded his understanding and stood up to leave his office. After Maria left he opened his drawer and slipped a playing card into his back pocket.

The top floor of Reigate police station is a cold and quiet place. Few officers venture up to the top floor and many of the rooms are unused. But at one end the décor changes and the lifeless grey laminate flooring is replaced with plush dark blue carpeting. The walls are adorned by paintings and the lighting is transformed from fluorescent ceiling fixtures to soft individual wall-lights. Bee stood admiring a painting of H C Hastings, the first chief constable of the county who had served for 48 years with a force of only 70 officers. Bee stood wondering how anyone could maintain law and order with such a small team, when the door of Beck's office opened behind him. He turned to see Church and ACC Raven standing joking together, the ACC had his arm around Church's shoulder. All at once the two men seemed to spot Bee and the frivolity stopped as if a school teacher had broken up an illicit playground game.

Raven spoke first. "I guess this must be our new hero Inspector Bee."

"Yes it is," said Church. "Not only does he solve crime, but he was also in here working at the weekend to clear the bee infestation that had nested in Beck's office."

Raven turned to Bee. "Well done inspector. I'm sure your chief will be grateful when he returns. It seems there's no end to your talents."

Bee offered a weak smile, unsure of where the conversation was heading.

Church picked up on his hesitation. "Absolutely. I think we can all agree that the best bee is a dead one. One that's lost its sting. Now I should leave you two to talk." Church twisted his fingers into the shape of a gun, pointed it at Bee and mocked pulling the trigger as he stepped away.

ACC Raven laughed, "Stay lucky Phil and don't forget it's my charity golf day at Bramley on the 25th? Make sure you are there I want you on my team."

He turned back to face Bee. "Beck tells me good things about you, inspector. It's high time I got to know you. Don't suppose you play golf do you?"

Bee shook his head.

"Pity. Well, come in and tell me what's going on with this Wing case. I gather you had an action-packed time on Monday night."

ACC Raven was tall, heavy boned and three quarters bald. He had a reputation for not tolerating fools and wanting to see progress. Bee had spent the morning reviewing his own report on the incident at Redhill aerodrome and was expecting to be rebuked for the operation and asked to explain how a foreign national had lost his life. But Raven didn't seem to be too worried about the details.

"I must say that I'm disappointed that you decided to tackle the situation with so few resources. I think it would have smarter to have involved Church and members of his team. But it would be churlish not to recognise the results you've achieved. It's been a good few days for policing in Surrey."

"With respect sir, I don't think we should be celebrating. I'm not convinced that van Ghent, the Dutch pilot could be guilty of the Barons' Cave murder."

Raven inhaled deeply and leant across the desk. "Are you telling me that we haven't had the best day of police work this county has seen in many a year?"

"Yes. I think I am. I don't think van Ghent did it."

"I see." Raven inhaled again. "Let me tell you how this is going to be reported this afternoon. I will be telling the press that we've broken up a major drug supply route from Europe. In addition, we've smashed a local porn business, brought to justice a rogue doctor conducting illegal transplants, and solved a complex murder case."

Bee shifted uneasily in his seat.

"You will be receiving a commendation for your work. Is that clear inspector?"

Bee mumbled a reply.

"I asked if it was clear?"

"Yes sir."

"Good. Make sure all your reports tally. That will be all."

As Bee walked down the stairs from the top floor he felt a wave of disappointment wash over him. A commendation for keeping quiet about a dubious conviction was how he classified it in his own mind. But as he reached his office he was greeted by two beaming faces.

"Have you found something?"

"Have we ever," said McTierney.

"Something to knock you out of the ground, like a flimsy English spinner," said Kelly.

"That good hey."

"Do you remember me saying that it was bumpy on the grass adjacent to the actual airstrip."

"Like it was only yesterday."

"That was because it was soft grass."

Bee switched his gaze to Kelly, who thrust two sheets of A4 paper into his hands.

"On the left is an imprint from the boot that jumped down from the plane of van Ghent."

Bee looked at the image, a large footprint with a gap in the tread at the heel. "Okay."

"We know this boot print must have come from Phil Church. No one else jumped off the plane." This time it was McTierney getting in on the act.

"On the right is an imprint from the boot that carried the body into the tunnel of the Barons' Cave." Dr. Kelly took over again.

Bee switched his focus to the sheet in his right hand. "They're identical."

"Indeed, they are."

"We've got him. Let's inform the ACC, he's going to need a new partner for his golf match."

FORTY-TWO

FOUR DAYS LATER and Reigate was still reeling from the events of the previous week. Inspector Church was behind bars, as was Dickinson, whereas Inspector Bee had graced both the front pages and the back pages of the local newspapers. He was embarrassed in equal measure by the stories of his apparent heroics. Beck had returned suntanned from his holiday in Portugal and as McTierney had predicted, he had pinned a medal on the self-conscious chest of his favourite detective. Perhaps the most surprising event of all was that McTierney had accepted an invite to the chief superintendent's May barbeque. But not without twice checking that there would be free beer all day.

Chief Superintendent Beck owned a large house in the southern side of the town with a sprawling garden, a sanctuary of verdant tranquillity. Towering trees cast dappled shadows over lush flower beds bursting with vibrant colours. Meandering pathways weaved through the landscape inviting his guests to explore. Somewhere in the distance stood a marble statuette of Venus.

But the real excitement was to be found by a small table next to the carp pond where a small group of people were discussing the events of the last few days. All the principal actors were present; Inspector Bee sporting his medal, DS

McTierney in jeans with a beer can in his hand, DS Itzkowitz in pumps and a grey pencil skirt and DC Bishop in a dark blue dress, and conducting the discussion was Chief Superintendent Beck in his new burgundy Polo shirt.

"It's good to have the whole heroic team here. Now I can thank you all personally for the wonderful work you've been doing."

"All in the line of duty sir," said Bee.

"Nonsense." Beck dismissed the claim with a wave of his hand. "You've all done way more than could be expected."

Bishop and Bee both lowered their eyes, but the more brash pair of Itzkowitz and McTierney allowed the praise to wash over them. Beck continued his admiration.

"Have we concluded the case against our nefarious surgeon?"

McTierney took the question. "By and large. His secretary Caroline Lambert has swamped us with evidence. I think she was so keen to help her defence that she's completely sold Dickinson down the river."

Beck tilted his head to listen.

"It turns out Dickinson has a connection with someone in China who does lot of preliminary work, blood checks and the like to assess kidney well-being all under the guise of a general health check to secure a UK visa. Then he passes the details on to Dickinson who taps them up when they arrive."

"A nasty business. Hopefully Mr Dickinson will be off the scene for a long time."

Beck was enjoying entertaining his troops and switched his attention to Fran Itzkowitz. "Look, our new American colleague has a commendation from the Fire Department. You should be proud."

Itzkowitz blushed. "Just doing my job sir."

"You probably saved two or three lives."

Beck turned back to Bee. "Did Church confess to starting the fire."

"He did. But once we started searching his flat his involvement was beyond doubt."

"So, he was the Red King."

"Without doubt." This time it was McTierney.

One of Beck's Mexican caterers brought a tray of drinks over to the party and the conversation stopped for a moment as each took a glass from the tray.

"Tell me about this diary, have you cracked the code?"

Bee took a sip of his wine, replaced his glass, and started the story. "Most of it I think. Wing created his own code of characters to replace key names or incidents. For example, he drew a church to signify Phil Church, a stethoscope to signify Mr Dickinson, a boat for John Mast, and what we thought was a ball, is probably a stone and code for Billy Mason the well-known fence in Croydon."

"Clever."

"Yes. Wing was a sharp operator. Unfortunately, he applied his skills to crime."

Beck took a sip from his wine glass. "Reverting to our former colleague Church, is that all sorted now?"

"More or less. We found a huge stash of drugs and photos, details of his criminal partners from Croydon, including that John Mast guy and more of those playing cards."

"You think he planted the cards in my desk?"

"He confessed to it, once we showed him the evidence." Bee had taken back control of the conversation leaving McTierney to sample Beck's wine.

"We found the missing key to your office. Church had pinched it from Maria and then used it to plant the playing cards in your desk, knowing that I would find them when I prepared your office for the pest control man."

"Of course," nodded Beck. "How long do you think Church had been running this syndicate?"

Bee sucked the air in over his teeth, "It looks like it's been a few years. The disruption caused by the Covid outbreak probably gave him the opportunity to step into the market. He would've known many of the players from his days in the police force. He was in a great position to establish a new order."

"Until Mickey Wing came along, demanding a piece of the action." McTierney had rejoined the conversation. "That quickly led to a confrontation, and we know what happened there."

"Indeed, we do." Beck looked around himself to check that no one could overhear him, then bent his head into the group. "I have some news of my own for you."

Each of the group closed ranks to hear the chief speak.

"I have decided to take early retirement. I will be leaving the service at the end of next month."

"We'll all miss you sir."

Beck smiled. "Thanks Bee. You've been a great support to me. But there is a second chapter to this story. Reigate station will be closing temporarily while we sort out this concrete issue that has plagues some public buildings. For the interim and perhaps beyond, Chief Superintendent Lisa Singfield will assume responsibility for this area."

There was a sharp intake of breath around the group.

Beck smiled, "She's a good leader, young, ambitious, but

fair. You'll all do well with her."

Beck's news punctured the atmosphere among the group, heads dropped, and they returned to the plates of food. Bee took a bite from his burger and yelled. He tilted his head to one side and pulled the half-chewed burger from his mouth, as he did his troublesome tooth came with it.

"I think we'll file that under providence" laughed Beck.

THE END

If you've enjoyed reading this story,
then sign up for more stories by Phil Hall.

ALSO in the series

PLUS

Inspector Scott Bee will return in …A Vote for Murder

VISIT

www.philhallauthor.com

ACKNOWLEDGEMENTS

Thank you for reading this story, I enjoyed writing it and I hope you enjoyed it too.

If you did I can think of two things you should do.

1. Tell someone about the book. Word of mouth recommendations are pixie dust to an author.
2. Read another book in the series. 'Game, Set and Death' is a good place to start and available from Amazon.

No writer can succeed without a small army of beta readers willing to plough through early copies of their work. My battalion of unpaid warriors are Andy G, Andy L, Britt D, Dave H, Eleni C, Roger C, Debbie P, Ian R, Julia R, Pat B, Stuart M, Suzi J and all at The Wealden Cave and Mine Society. All were generous beyond what I had any right to expect. Especially those blessed with reading the first draft, a tortuous process at any time.

I can't ignore the one professional involved in this process, especially as he kindly returned to fight again after the first book – and he really should've known better. Patrick Knowles – a first rate cover designer and great sounding board.

My eternal thanks to you, one and all. It's been a slice.

As regular readers will know I like to weave my own stories around real-life events and The Cave was no different. The inspiration for this story was the case of Ike Ekweremadu, the imprisoned Nigerian politician, who Bee quotes in the book.

Beyond that I try to use real locations in and around Reigate and the Surrey Hills, but with a key difference; I modify the address of any property that is going to 'suffer'. In this case there is no 77 Goldworth Road, I wouldn't want anyone to feel that their house had burnt down.

Printed in Great Britain
by Amazon